There was a shout, in ⟨...⟩
and a blow. And then ⟨...⟩ ⟨...⟩oud it felt more
like being hit than anything that came through the ears,
and a horrible, horrible, long, choking, strangled cry, and
the noise again, the noises. Again and again. And I realised
it was gunfire, saw Jill, insanely, running towards Saul's
door, and threw myself at her, dragging her down, covering
her, as the three of them came out, swinging squat, ugly,
black metal boxy objects, throwing their briefcases at
people's heads to force them down. One of the young ones
swung on us and pulled on his box. There was a spit of
flame, the stench of cordite, the tops of two desks flying
everywhere, splinters ripped out of their surfaces. Someone
was screaming, face lacerated by flying fragments. The other
young one turned, squeezed his trigger, spraying bursts of
three, shredding partitions, ripping bits of masonry out of
walls. The sprinkler system went haywire. And then they
were gone.

ZERO YIELD

John Ford

CORGI BOOKS

ZERO YIELD

A CORGI BOOK   0 552 13275 6

First publication in Great Britain

PRINTING HISTORY
Corgi edition published 1990

This book is set in 10/11pt Plantin
by Busby Typesetting, Exeter.

Corgi Books are published by Transworld Publishers Ltd.,
61–63 Uxbridge Road, Ealing, London W5 5SA, in Australia by
Transworld Publishers (Australia) Pty. Ltd., 15–23 Helles
Avenue, Moorebank, NSW 2170, and in New Zealand by Transworld
Publishers (N.Z.) Ltd., Cnr. Moselle and Waipareira Avenues,
Henderson, Auckland.

Reproduced, printed and bound in Great Britain by
BPCC Hazell Books
Aylesbury, Bucks, England
Member of BPCC Ltd

for
Colin Murray
safe hands

and
Max Eilenberg and Caroline Royds
safe house

Prologue:

Before the Beginning

There wasn't any sign that day I'd end up stealing fifteen million dollars.

It was the day Willy Loman went apeshit on the trading floor of Jokanaan Frères, dancing around bollock-naked except for the Y-fronts on his head till the guards could grab him by anything that came to hand and hustle him out of the door. It was the day I went to lunch with a bunch of equity-broking friends and, by the time I got to Le Gamin in Old Bailey, a few minutes late, just gone 12.30, they were all already pissed as rats having been at it since 10.30. 'Market was off another hundred then, old boy. What's the point of trying?' It was the day most everyone I knew began razoring their excess credit cards, and putting flats on the market and dreaming dreadful nightmares of a City filled with piles of gently rusting new red Porsches. It was the day the new boys in the trading rooms of the City, the ones who'd only ever seen the brash few years of the bull market, broke and ran like puking cowards, while a few of the old lags tried to hold the line. It was the day the market finally began to hold and turn and every smart-arse analyst both sides of the Water tried to come up with a reason or, better still, a conspiracy, when anyone with a brain knew that it happened just at the point where Blue Chip British equities started yielding 4½ per cent again, their historic long-term return, after being out far too long on price/earning ratios of eighty and a hundred and returns of 1 to 2 per cent.

It was, in short, Tuesday, October the 20th, 1987. The day after Black Monday on the Stock Exchanges of the world. The day I finally saw reason.

What made it worse, in London, was that we'd been able to see it coming. Everyone was jittery, waiting for the market to turn down, looking to be first into the lifeboat unlading from the sinking ship. The previous Friday it began. Wall Street began to fall apart – its morning, afternoon London time. Began to fall apart on a scale no one could pretend was just another temporary correction. And when Wall Street farts, London shits its way into the Guinness Book of Records. Only, this time, there was nothing anyone could do about it. No way the boys could all join in the headlong rush, lemmings looking for the safety of numbers.

They couldn't because Thursday night had seen the worst storm in the country's collective memory. Hurricane force winds. Public transport completely stuffed. Half the trees in England down. And almost no one able to make it to their desks in the City. The ones who could could barely trade. All the other players in the game were still at home. There was no volume to the market. And half the electronic communications in the country were shafted, too.

So the equity boys just had to sit and watch it on their tellies, their Reuters screens and Telerate links and read about it in their weekend newspapers.

And when they all finally got into work together on the Monday morning, having seen the greatest market of the Western world sell itself down into oblivion, they all sold like there was no tomorrow. Sold in blind panic, hopelessness and rage. And sold and sold and sold till we had ourselves a good old-fashioned Stock Market Crash.

The funny thing was, no one cared.

They had been the lucky ones, the ones who rolled the giant salaries when deregulation came into the market and the big American and Japanese players and the London clearers rolled into the market looking for any itty-bit of talent they could find at whatever salary it chose to command.

Those were the days when you could find yourself telephoning someone's salary by mistake. In New York.

So no one wept when their world fell open, least of all me. My kind of banking was something altogether different, and nothing like as well paid. Not that that stopped people hating my guts on principle, and who can blame them once you'd seen the pigs at the trough?

Trouble was, I could see the writing on the wall, as they had never been able to, and I knew what the Crash would mean, in the long-term.

It would mean a shake-out in all the City. Jobs cut. Salaries slashed. Anywhere they could be. Anything to staunch the bleeding losses.

That made everyone vulnerable, including me, and I hadn't even made my pile.

Which is, I guess, when I first made the decision to do something about it. Not the detailed, specific decision, not just yet. But that would come.

For now, leaning against the window watching the stillness in the City's streets as people huddled indoors around green computer screens, struck silent and immobile with panic, all I knew was that I had to do something about it.

Which led to everything else. To all the other things.

Which is what you want to know about.

You want to know how I stole that fifteen million dollars.

Part One:

The Beginning

CHAPTER ONE

It all began one overcast winter morning, end of '87, standing around outside the Greenhouse, the champagne bar round the back of the Royal Exchange in the City of London, drinking with O'Malley. (Pommery, it was. Very particular about his Poo is O'Malley. Pommery & Greno till noon. Moët or the Widow from noon till four. Bollinger from four till eight. And Krug from then till passing-out time.) I'd been whining on about almost everything, including this one really big inactive account, when the old sod leant forward and said, 'Well, why don't you just steal the money?'

It was all O'Malley's fault.

I'd better tell you about O'Malley. I'd better tell you all about me.

Ford's the name. John Ford. It isn't my real name, of course. All the names are changed, for reasons you'll come to understand soon enough, but all the rest is real. You could say this book is an insurance policy. But more of that in its proper place.

North Londoner, I am. Highbury way. Banker. And bloody good at what I do. But I was twenty-nine back then, and still not a millionaire.

I know what you're thinking. What's a North London wide boy like me doing working in the City of London? Well, it isn't so very rare. Back where I come from, blokes have three options, after school: they can go into the print trade (thousands of them do – the whole London commercial print industry's run by North London lads, including all the boys in the big money firms – the security printers who do the documents for banks and stockbrokers. Well, think about it, something like the Telecom flotation, millions of prospectuses had to be printed, and someone had to do it. It beats a smack in the teeth. Working in one of the hot security printers is the next best thing to having the print contract for the London phone book); they can go into villainy; or they can go on the dole. Going on the dole has a special meaning where I come from, though. It doesn't mean you aren't working, it just means you don't bother the tax man all that much. The Black Economy. Cash up front, no questions asked, squire. Plumbers, builders, drivers and, best of all, market traders. Get big in the markets, of course, and you have to get serious. Accountants, lawyers, limited liability companies, all that stuff. But it's the market trader end of my bit of London that got me where I am today.

About a third of the blokes who grew up with me are villains. Didn't fancy that. Didn't have the bottle for it, I suppose. Didn't fancy all those holidays at Her Majesty's expense (which are part of the deal; every professional expects to serve his porridge, and we don't breed amateurs round our parts; 'If you can't do the time, don't do the crime,' as they say.) Seems a bit odd, now, being a really serious villain. (Well, fifteen mill is hardly petty cash, is it?) But if you ask me, I was only being smart. If you're going to do a crime, then make sure it's one you get to do in a suit and tie by shuffling papers about. A good brief and a good jury and you can walk away from court, while you'd get seven years in stir for stealing motors, which takes real skill if you're going to do it as a full-time job. The other great thing about the white collar stuff is that, unless you're greedy, like Ivan Boesky, want to be a billionaire and sit on the board of the Metropolitan Museum of Art, it isn't a career. You don't have to do it year in year out. You don't have to go out in all weathers, casing cars, houses, banks, never seeing your wife and kids, never having time to enjoy the money. No, white collar crime, one big job will set you up for a lifetime. Then it's off into the sunshine with the cocktails and the señoritas.

I didn't fancy the print trade either. They really do work, that lot. No, I don't mean the idle bastards who gave Fleet Street such a bad name all those years, I mean the boys in the commercial sector. I know the money's good. I know it means you're a somebody. Get out on the road and it's all flash whistles, expense accounts, and company motors, but if you are on the road, you give up half your life to Yah-Yah turds in banks and brokerage houses, taking them out on the raz, giving them days at Lord's, or playing golf, or buying them the tarts they're too stupid, too idle or too mean to call up for themselves. And if you're on the inside, as a technician, then there's no way round it when you're young and fit, the money's all in night work.

But there again, I didn't fancy the dole, the markets, the little bits of business. (While we're on the subject, for those of you who've always wondered how exactly things fall off the back of a lorry, it's simple: you slip the driver a little present, he stops the engine, gets out the cab, hands you the keys and goes for a little stroll while the doors on his cargo mysteriously open. Depending on how big the job is, you might have to rough him up a bit, to make it look right. That can make it more expensive, but I've never known it cost more than an Archer – two thousand quid to you – and that was for a lorry load of VCRs.)

That only left two ways out: sport, and the serious markets. I wasn't quite good enough with my hands or my feet. Came close to an apprenticeship with the Gunners, but not quite close enough, and though I play a lot of snooker I was never going to give Interesting Davis a serious run for his money, and I was never going to let myself get fat enough to be a major darts contender. Darts players have to be the best deal in the world for their sponsors. They're forever drinking or smoking the product right there on the television, and they're so bloody fat you can get the product name up really big on their tee-shirts. And it's all in close-up. A much better deal than all those little logos on the strips of football players.

17

Anyway, sport was out. That only left the serious markets.

It's a funny thing about the City of London. Everyone always imagines it's full of cretins straight out of Eton who wouldn't know their arses from their elbows if they didn't have their daddies round to point them at the toilet. That's always been partly true, and it's still true that the big jobs and the big money do tend, still, to be in the hands of the crustier type of person. Even now, Eton, Oxford and the Brigade of Guards isn't going to do you any harm, but it isn't going to do you as much good as an accountancy qualification through Price Waterhouse, a decent law degree and the Middle Temple, and an MBA from Harvard, either. At the end of the day, the City's just a square mile full of marketplaces, and what really matters is how good you are at working in those markets. What counts is if you can come away holding a profit more days than not. Which means there's always been a fair number of people working in it who don't come from the Green Wellie Guards at all. Any rush hour morning, you just go stand outside Liverpool Street or Fenchurch Street stations. Those kids streaming in from Essex and North London have quite as much chance as the foggies (thick, wet and up from the country) barking into Waterloo and Paddington, if they've got good nerves, steady hands, and know the difference between a plus and minus sign. I fancied that myself, a whole lot more than juggling dinner services down the Petticoat or over the water in Deptford Market.

Trouble was, my family were all print. They weren't too happy. I might as well have said I wanted to be a policeman. Well, nearly. My cousin Eric did say that once. Got told to let other people volunteer to get themselves killed. What would have suited me down to the ground was commodities trading. I could see myself, Nerves of Steel in the Metals Ring. But commodities are still in the hands of Flash Harries from the minor public schools, and I had no access there, or the Golders Green Mafia, and my family had never got itself organised to get alongside a friendly Jewish family. (Well, why do you think North Londoners

18

have tailors?) The boys in the print put out the word with stockbrokers, but there wasn't a likely vacancy on hand, and all the time my old Ma was getting worried and wanting me to do something respectable, like breaking and entering. So finally I thought, it has to be the money markets, and compromised: I got a job in banking.

It was just about the worst mistake of my life, especially those first few years. I mean, I knew nothing about it. I was sixteen, I had a few O Levels, a Building Society Account. What did I know? Bugger all. I just went down the High Street, went into each of the clearing bank branches and picked up the application forms for clerk-trainee.

Well, I got a job, and it was respectable. Whistle, tie, clean shirt every morning. But I have never been as bored as I was in those first three, three and a half years. I'd thought, give it a year, show a bit of spunk and enthusiasm, and then it's the swift transfer to head office, the trial in Merchant Banking subsidiary or Treasury Department, and that's it. I'm away. Running an investment portfolio, or playing the international currency markets. How was I to know the clearing banks still worked on the principle that, if you were very good, and very boring, and very safe, and very very lucky, you might just work your way up to assistant manager by the time you were thirty-five? You might just get a branch of your own to play with, by their rules, by the time you were fifty. How was I to know that it was going to get even worse because, very soon, the whole banking industry, including the High Street clearers, was about to be revolutionised by the invention of graduate entry? That, suddenly, all the paths to promotion were going to be blocked by people with bad second class degrees from places like Aston and East Anglia in subjects like Comparative Shopping, and Applied Lipsticks? The only good thing about that whole period was that I got myself some A levels in night school and (anything to staunch the boredom of smiling at old biddies across the counter) crashed my way through the Banking Exams on Day Release.

It was the third time my application for a transfer to Head Office was turned down that I finally had enough. I started looking through the trade press seriously, for another appointment, in the City. Looking back on it, I wasn't a bad prospect. I'd worked my nuts off. I knew the bread and butter of the business. (You would be amazed at how many people at the top end of the business have never processed a credit-rating, wouldn't know how to clear a car-loan). And I had my basic qualifications. I wasn't even twenty. And looking back, I got luckier than I ever deserved. I got hired by Myles O'Malley at IIIB.

O'Malley is a legend. O'Malley may be the last of the real legends. Irish. (Don't tell me; you guessed.) In his late forties by now. Not that tall – about five ten – but broad with it. Whenever I see him, the phrase 'brick shit-house' leaps to mind. They say he made a useful wing three-quarters in his day, and I can see him showing the pack a clean pair of heels – good turn of speed and turn on a sixpence and hand off anything short of a charging bull in its prime. He looks good – silver hair, square man's face with a boxer's nose and a scar on his chin, but it isn't his looks anyone's interested in. It's his brain.

He comes from the lost bowels of Kerry, and the Irish tell the same jokes about Kerrymen the rest of the world tells about the Irish, but O'Malley's no bog-artist. He emerged from nowhere when he was fourteen, working as a bookie's runner. By the time he was fifteen he was running a street book of his own. At seventeen he had an on-course book. Within six months he'd sold out to one of the biggest Turf Accountants in the Emerald Isle: cash-payment, a percentage of the profits, and a straight three year contract to run the book and set the odds. It paid his way through Trinity College, Dublin. He was a local hero by then and they didn't ask for anything stupid like paper qualifications. He lived in style. He always has done, but two thoroughbreds of his own, one a racer, the other he rode himself to hounds, more birds than he knew what to do with and enough champagne to fill a medium-sized canal must have seemed a bit toppy for a student, even at TCD. None of it stopped him getting a double first in mathematics and economics. Somewhere along the line he also picked up his wife, Lady Pamela – Polly to all their friends.

That came as a bit of a shock. Myles is a good Catholic lad. Polly's about as high as you can get in the Protestant Ascendancy. One of those really rich, really hot, ash-blondes who swear like troopers, run dazzling houses, and have had a horse between their legs since they were three, and a man since they were thirteen. I don't suppose there's a man who's ever met her who hasn't wondered what a bout would be like and, having thought about it, hasn't decided he doesn't have what it takes. In Dublin, the Protestant gentry say that when you're as grand as Polly you can marry who you like, and just by wedding them, raise them to your level. The left-footers say their marriage is the very emblem of an undivided, class-free Ireland. Myself, I reckon it's just that she'd never had rumpy-pumpy like it and couldn't imagine life without him. (I've seen him in the showers, after a game of squash, remember. The last time I saw equipment like that, the Air Force was using it for in flight refuelling.) And she would have lost it if they hadn't married, because after TCD he took himself off to the London School of Economics where he did an MSc on the impact of exchange-control regulations on the foreign exchange markets which is still the classic in its field. What did they live on in those days? What paid for the flat in Eaton Square, and the house he bought Polly outside Aylesbury? O'Malley went on gambling, didn't he? And he played the foreign exchange markets. Where else were the research figures for his thesis to come from? To this day, he is a great mathematician and a great gambler. He is the only person I've met who can express the odds on anything in any of three major systems, swinging from one to the other without even thinking: from 4 to 1 to 20 per cent. and from 100 to 8 to .074 recurring. And he has the greatest gift of all, from his days as a bookie (I think he still owns a slug of a couple of outfits): he knows when he's

21

over-exposed. He knows when he's taken his book too far out of whack on any one position. He knows when to lay-off his book. He taught me everything I know about the money markets, and he taught me the Golden Rule, the only rule which always works, the Absolute Law in any market. He taught me the line which was the final fruit of the great Nathan Rothschild's experience, maybe the greatest trader of the nineteenth century, maybe the greatest trader ever: Always Sell Too Soon.

That's all there is to it. Don't be greedy. Take your profits. If you end up thinking the currency or stock you sold is going to go on rising, set your profits aside, and buy back in. And then sell too soon. Take your profits in incremental stages if you have to, but never hold on hoping that there'll be one last spurt of growth you can take advantage of and get out at the top of the market. You might get away with it once, or twice, or a dozen times, but in the end, you will lose your shirt, and your backers' too.

And how did I get to work with this genius? Luck.

Straight after he finished at the LSE, Irish International Investment Bank, IIIB, had the best idea of a long and not inglorious history. They hired O'Malley to run their Foreign Exchange book and their Money Market operations, the stuff that nowadays gets called the Treasury Department. (Contrary to what you might expect, the Irish make perfectly good bankers. Perhaps because, again contrary to myth, most kinds of banking don't take a lot of brains. The basic principles are so simple a six year old could understand them. It's the legal and accountancy aspects which are complicated, and those take more application than brains. I mean, have you talked to an accountant recently? Even the market side of banking takes a very special kind of brain. OK, so O'Malley's thick with good degrees. Nathan Rothschild never went to college.)

Hiring O'Malley was a good idea for IIIB for two reasons. The first was simply that he was very good. He made them a lot of money on their cash book, and still does. In fact, he is so good that there are some very big names in international banking who simply hire IIIB to run their Treasury Department for them on a mixed fee-and-commission basis. The second reason was Lady Pamela. There have always been a lot of Irish men and women who don't really see why Dublin should trouble itself too closely with their assets and investments and who have therefore chosen to hold a portion of them across the water, but in a bank they know and love. When the word got out that Pamela O'Malley's husband over in London could get a gentleperson a great deal more in interest on their cash reserve than any Local Authority Bond or Building Society, the money started flooding in. And went on doing so. A great deal of it what were laughably called farm subsidies from the EEC. (The Irish have been brilliant at taking money off foreign banks and institutions. It's true that in absolute terms the Irish owe the rest of the world less than the Brazilians, the Mexicans, the Poles – but there are a lot of Brazilians, Mexicans and Poles. There are barely enough citizens of Eire to fill one respectable medium-sized city. Expressed as a function of population, no country on earth, not even the USA after a deficit-spending mad old Irish president, owes the rest of the world as much as the Irish do.)

Anyway, over the years IIIB's Treasury Department grew and grew. So did the part of it devoted to managing private customers' short-term money. O'Malley hired himself good money-market operators. He also hired civil men and women to glad-hand his rich customers. But after twelve years he began wondering why he was the only person in the Department who could do both jobs, and he decided he was going to try to find and train someone else who could. Which was why he put the ad in the trade press. Which is why I got lucky.

He had a real bias towards a clearing banker. It didn't show in the interviews, which were brutal. (Can you say what the square root of two hundred is, cold? Or compute two to the sixteenth power? Or express the difference between this year and the year the Bank of England was chartered as a power of ten?) Nonetheless, he was keen on the idea of someone who knew the bread and butter of customer management, but with a bit of gumption. He had enough languid aristos who couldn't add two and two together without getting twenty-two, and he had quite enough mathematicians who wore their ball-points in their breast-pockets, had inky fingers, chewed their nails, and when they could be prevailed on to speak up for themselves couldn't be made out beneath the distant bubbling of snot. A long time afterwards he told me he'd been looking for a human being. I think what swung it for me was the third interview, conducted over one of the snooker tables at the old City Golf Club off Fleet Street. I took two frames off him. He doesn't trust well-spent youths. I got the job.

I have to tell you they were, till now, the best years of my life. IIIB's in a little eighteenth-century house in one of the tiny alleys off St Mary Axe, a bit of the old City, of lanes and courts, not freeways and plazas and pedestrian walkways. There are tower-blocks about, but you don't have to notice them. There were old wine bars (they've all gone trendy now, but in those days it was still men, spit and sawdust), shell-fish restaurants and proper pubs. We were a good operation run by a genius verging on lunacy, and I've never met anyone so generous with what he knew and what he'd learnt. There were times I thought I ought to hang a shingle by the front door reading 'IIIB: Private Club. Members Only.' We were good. And we became friends. More often than I care to remember, I've come round with the mother of hangovers in the Eaton Square flat at five on a Saturday morning to the sound of Polly, who'd driven up from Aylesbury before dawn, cooking a full breakfast before dragging a sheepish Myles back down to the country to be there before the children woke. Whatever he got up to, whatever bollockings she gave him, she made sure he was home all weekend for the children. She is a hell of a woman.

It didn't last, of course. My time at IIIB, that is, not the O'Malleys' marriage. It would take Trident to tear those

24

two apart. There was a limit to how big IIIB was going to, or wanted to, grow, and Myles would always have the pole-position. After three and a half years I allowed myself to be head-hunted. It didn't change things between Myles and me. He's still the Old Man. Still the Guvnor. He's still the man I go to for advice and support. But the move was a mistake. I should have been looking to create a position like Myles's in a merchant bank. Instead, I allowed myself to be wooed away by a small clearing bank. I'd better not tell you which one, but it has the Royal Family's personal accounts and makes all its male staff wander around in frock coats all day long. Pompous twits. They wanted to create an operation like O'Malley's for their customers. Said they did. Thought they did. But when it came to it, they couldn't quite deal with the freewheeling nature of anyone trained by Myles. My positions frightened them. Not their customers, I think, to do them justice. Even the English can't manage to be snobs where a profit is possible. Not that either the customers or I ever got to find out, because the directors ended up doing their damnedest to keep me from the punters. I don't think they fancied my table manners, or my accent. I fought them. Making it work mattered to me. Mattered too much. I fought too long. I stuck it out for three years. Three years out of the City proper, out of a real active, trading Treasury Depart-ment. In the end it meant I missed out on Big Bang, the deregulation of the City. I wasn't around, I wasn't in contention, I wasn't on the shortlists when the big six and seven figure salaries were being handed out. I went back to the City all right, and I benefited from the general inflation in City salaries. I made a bloody good screw. But it wasn't enough. I kept feeling like Brando in On The Waterfront. I could have been a contender.

O'Malley got me the job, doing pretty much what I'd done for him, but for a lot more money, with an outfit called Banque de Haifa et Marseilles. As you might guess, with a name like that, it had been set up in the nineteenth century to finance trade between France and what was then

Palestine. Nowadays it's officially entirely Israeli. I say officially because the last French shareholders baled out when the Mitterand government came in and started nationalising private banks. They sold out to what is supposed to be an Israeli-owned Swiss holding company, but I've always suspected that some of the French stayed in, concealed behind nominee shareholdings in the Swiss company. It's as good a way as any of hiding assets and income from the tax-man.

The London Branch was new, set up quite specifically to have a presence in the deregulated City, to provide a presence for Israeli and other customers. It is, I have to say, a damn good outfit. Small but well-managed and intelligently run, and it would have been as good a springboard as any back into the City scene after a few years out. Three years, say, doing the business, being good, I could have moved on and up. That's very nearly what I did. I stayed three years. I was good. Then I stole fifteen million dollars.

It was an inactive account. Every bank has them, even the High Street clearers. Accounts with no movement. Sometimes the customer's dead, but the bank doesn't know it. Sometimes they've moved away and just forgotten about it. Constantly it's old biddies being too careful by half. When I was in the High Street I had an old woman customer whose current account balance never fell below £40,000. I kept trying to persuade her to put £35,000, say, into a term deposit account, to earn some interest for her. She kept whining about needing it where she could get her hands on it at once. She didn't want it locked away in an account where she'd have to give notice to get it out. I tried to tell her she could have the money at once. She was an old and valued customer. All we'd do was cut the outstanding interest by the amount earned in the notice period she hadn't given, but she wouldn't buy it. I had one old fellow who had two accounts, his own which he used all the time, and what had been his joint account with his dead wife. He hadn't touched that one since the day she'd died (he'd paid her death duties from his account) despite the fact it had £17,000 in it doing absolutely nothing. He always told me she would have wanted him to keep it available against emergencies.

So you give up in the end. Inactive accounts are just a fact of life. But this one, this one was rather different.

It was sixteen million dollars altogether. It had been wired to us from a Venezuelan bank a few months after I joined Banque de Haifa et Marseilles (I'm going to call it BHM from now on – everyone does) with instructions to open a call account. That's an account where the customer can have the money at call, immediately, but which is nonetheless a deposit account. There's no cheque-book. Even so, with that amount of money we do pay pretty good rates of interest, though not as much as we would if the money were placed for a fixed term or in an account where the customer had to give us a fixed period of notice before withdrawal.

Like I said, the Venezuelan bank wired us the money, opened the account, gave it a name and gave us a code number which had to be quoted by anyone giving us instructions on the account to make them binding on us. That's standing operating procedure in international banking. It means instructions can be telexed quoting the account name and number and the secret identification code and business can be done without customers having to present themselves in person.

We had our instructions. We carried them out. And then, nothing. For two and a half years. Nothing. Not a whisper. Not a murmur.

Have you any idea how much temptation that amount of money can be to an unhappy man? Unhappy with his work and, increasingly, with his boss, a prim and proper little man called Steinitz who always played safe and made me yearn for Myles.

All of which was why, after two and a half years of silence, I was standing outside the Greenhouse with O'Malley, and complaining.

He doesn't believe in whining. He doesn't believe in just sitting there and taking it. Maybe that's what made him say it. Maybe he just said it to shock me into doing something positive. Maybe. But there was a devilish gleam in his eyes. He has always loved the mad, the extravagant, the wild and the foolish. Maybe it just appealed to the Irishman behind the banker.

I don't suppose I'll ever really know. But whatever it was, he just looked me in the eyes and said, 'Well, why don't you just steal the money?'

I know that in some strange way the suggestion wasn't unexpected or unwelcome. I know I'd been thinking about it. I know I'd been thinking about what would be needed, about how it could be done. I knew there was one previous theft which set down the guidelines about how to do it. I also knew there was one area of expertise needed I simply didn't have. I needed a computer specialist, and I told O'Malley so, trying to make it sound like a joke. 'Oh come off it, Myles,' I said, 'I'd need a hacker. Where do I get a hacker from?'

He was smiling, the small fey smile he used to have before a really big trade. 'I can get you a hacker,' he said.

It suddenly felt hot, sticky, humid. Breath turning from frost to steam. I didn't know how far I wanted to take this. 'Oh come on, Myles,' I told him, 'you and I know some fair villains between us, but a serious hacker? Fifteen mill's worth of hacker?'

He stopped me right there. He ditched the dead champagne bottle in the nearest bin. I waited for the impact. I waited for it to break, but it did not. It rattled. It clanged. But there was no fracture. Myles leaned towards me, still smiling, and tapped me in the middle of the chest with his forefinger and said, 'You think about it. Think about it hard. And if you really want him – Tuesday. One o'clock. The Rat and Rizla. You be there.'

CHAPTER TWO

You bet I thought about it, all that weekend. I did the usual things as well: played squash on Saturday morning, did some shopping, paid the woman who comes in a couple of times a week to reduce the flat to order, went to Steve Curtin's party. Steve's an American show-biz lawyer based in London and one of the few people in the world I wouldn't care to take on in a contract negotiation. (The line at Pinewood is that he was the inspiration of *Jaws* and *Alien*.) His parties are always wall-to-wall with good-looking slags: models and would-be starlets mainly. He's a kind of public service lawyer. All a great deal easier than having to cruise the nightclubs for some trollop. I got off with a little dark-haired piece. Anna? Hannah? Vanna? I can't honestly remember. All I can remember is her plastering herself to me and wriggling, with a chain of little sighs. She was one of those women who have a string of tiny orgasms, like firecrackers rather than a Roman Candle. Normally I like that. Like it a lot. Somehow the longer it goes on, the more I get outside myself, and any market-maker needs that kind of escape.

That night it didn't work, though. I'd done four lines of coke at the party, which wasn't very smart. The Marching Powder stops you coming, which is usually good news, but what I really wanted was to be done with it. She didn't help, just rippling on and on. She drifted off to sleep eventually, and I ended up sitting over my diary thinking through all the daydreams I'd had about pulling off the Big Job. It's the kind of night which makes me understand why so many other people in the business either only screw each other (a woman in the trade will book you into her Filofax; she won't give you any hassle – she has all the same pressures as you) or just whistle up a call-girl on the Gold Card. No muss no fuss. Get it done and go out to dinner with your mates.

I kicked her out on Sunday morning. She wasn't too happy about that, but Sundays are sacred. They have to be. A game of squash, an early lunch, and then down to all the literature: Analysts' Reports, Economists' Reports, Newsletters, Private Research Reports, and all the usual press – the Sunday papers, *Financial Times*, *Economist*, *Euromoney*, *Institutional Investor International*, *International Insider*, *Business Week*, *Fortune*, *Forbes*, the *Harvard Business Review*, the specialist surveys in the *Echo de la Bourse*, *Wall Street Journal*, *Frankfurter Allgemeine Zeitung*, and the best but most boring newspaper in the world, the *Neue Zürcher Zeitung*. I let other people keep an eye on the Middle and Far East. There's a limit, even on a Sunday.

I'm not telling you this to make you think I'm some kind of genius. Some kind of brilliant economist. I'm not, and I don't need to be. That's one of the things O'Malley taught me. All kinds of people think the money markets, the foreign currency markets, are rational; that they analyse the economic results and projections and take a view on the basis of that analysis. Lots of people in the business think that, too. They think a money-market operator's like a really good race-track gambler: knows all the previous form, current progress in training, background on the jockey, the current going conditions, makes a value judgement and puts his money on it.

Like I said, lots of people in the business think that way. O'Malley taught me they were wrong. What really moves the markets is the sum total of all those people's views, analyses and prejudices, so a really good money market operator is more like a bookie than a gambler. He's sniffing out the sum totals of all the punters' individual decisions and constructing his odds accordingly, making sure he won't get burned over favourites, fine-tuning the odds on the other runners. All that reading isn't about economics at all. It's about trying to sniff which way the market's prejudices are moving, scenting all the shifting smelly little orthodoxies which will decide what dealers are pleased to call their minds. Dealers copy each other, which is why the markets move so fast. No one wants to be stuck with currencies or currency instruments everyone else is baling out of, or be left without stuff everyone else is buying. Dealers are sheep really, and a good operator isn't interested in weather conditions, in wool and meat yields per pound of forage. He's interested in which way the flock is moving. Rumours can be, and often are, more important than facts.

It wasn't a good Sunday for me, though. I kept thinking over what Myles had said. I couldn't concentrate on anything else, couldn't get my eye in. I wondered why he'd said it. I knew the man had an eye for a bargain. I don't suppose he's ever paid retail in his life. (New York Jewish joke: 'Why did God create Gentiles? Well, someone has to buy retail.') There's always been a whiff of minor villainy about the man. He was a bookmaker in the old days after all. But I'd never seen him do anything funny at IIIB. Not against the interests of the bank or its customers, that is. He'd rig his competitors as soon as look at them, but that was within the rules of the game. He'd never insider-trade against the interests of people who'd put their trust in him and their money in his hands. Recommending theft was a bit out of the ordinary for him, but he had clearly meant it. I knew the look in his eyes. I'd seen it before. He got it whenever something seriously tickled his sense of humour. I got the impression he was feeling bored and was looking to me for a bit of fun.

In the end, I thought, it couldn't do any harm to meet his hacker. I was intrigued, anyway. You hear a lot about computer hackers, about kids tapping their way into the defence controls systems, that kind of stuff, but meeting one's another matter altogether. I went to the Rat and Rizla that Tuesday lunchtime.

The R&R's just off Bishopsgate, just outside the City,

and no, that isn't its real name. Like every other name in this book it's a snow-job, and if you've got any sense, you'll leave it at that. For the record, it's just beyond the bridge over the train-lines running north out of what used to be the old Broad Street station. Chances are, it won't last very long, because British Rail are redeveloping the land round there, and the development'll stretch, but if you go looking for it while it still survives, frankly sunshine, you deserve everything you get. Don't say I didn't warn you.

The R&R's a special kind of clearing-house. I told you that people like me go into the print, into villainy, or on the dole, the markets or into the City. I also told you there's a close, necessary link between City operators and their security printers. There is a kind of world all that lot make up, where little things like the law are an embarrassment. The R&R's one of the places we can all get together without forever looking over our shoulders. Of course the Met and the City Police and the Fraud Squad all know we all use it. They also know that asking any of its regulars about any of its other regulars is a dead loss. If one of ours gets out of order, we sort it out. In the meantime, the R&R's a place we can go and deal with stuff we don't want to discuss in front of strangers. There's times when a banker wants to pick up his commission from his printer; when a broker's got a problem with his coke supplies and needs someone to consult; and there are always times when people you've been dealing with have been silly – they haven't paid their bills, their credit's gone sour, they're thinking of doing a runner. You can sort it out at the R&R. In fact you can get anything there, so long as you're one of the lads, so long as one of the lads has vouched for you: most drugs, office furniture, computer equipment, porn videos, VCRs . . . Video-machines have become the apprenticeship for serious villainy in the eighties. Everyone's keeping an eye on a bright bunch of kids who specialised in them. From Tottenham way, they are. The eldest was sixteen. They'd do a whole street at a time, every house that was empty on a Saturday night. Bag the videos up in polythene and stuff

32

them under the front hedges. No rozzer ever looked there. They came back a few nights later, after all the hue and cry had settled down, with a van, picked up all the videos. There were nine of these kids altogether. By the time they got picked up and the eldest one had been sent to a detention centre, they'd turned over more than £20,000 apiece. It's still the best apprenticeship for kids, burglary, breaking and entering. They're small enough to get through the little windows people always forget to close. It's good for their confidence, it's better money than any other blag kids can get up to, and it gets them used to working in teams. Everyone's got high hopes for this bunch. All they need now is some time in an adult prison to finish off their further education and it'll be bank jobs and wages snatches for those boys. (There is this one thing to be said for prison, as far as the young are concerned – besides all that knowledge and experience just waiting to be imparted – it teaches you to get on with your fellow man. There isn't room in prison for self-indulgence. It's what makes your average villain such an easy-going bloke. Bit like boarding school, I suppose.)

Still, the R&R's a sort of service centre. It's where people like me and O'Malley go when we need a word with a bent copper or a business brief (a lawyer to you, a solicitor; you have legal briefs, we have business ones, creative fellows), some decent jewellery for the wife if money's short, or any general purpose villainy. Debt collection's one of the bigger businesses they do there. Sometimes people need to be taught a lesson. For £250 you can send them a warning, and follow it up with a visit, while they're out. It'll look like a burglary, except that nothing will have been taken, just kids' sort of wreckage – writing on the walls, all the furniture turned over, drawers ransacked, TV screen and stereo kicked in, shit on the carpets, in the bed and in the wedding photo album. They usually pay up pretty quickly after that, but if you have to, you can pay for a whole menu of measures of gradually increasing severity. Go through the lot and, at the end, the boys'll usually let you have the big finale for around two and a half grand. Not that anyone really wants the big finale. Except the undertakers.

One of the reasons the Rat & Rizla is so popular is its location – handy for the City and the print, but just in Hackney, just inside the East End, outside the operations area of the City Police, in the Met's Eastern Division. Our sort of people, a lot of them. They're not going to make any fuss about professionals, not unless it's your turn, in which case they'll fit you up with a verbal statement and send you down for the job whether you did it or not. You have to be philosophical. Fair's fair. You have to take your holidays like a man and the boys in blue have a living to make as well.

The other reason is its lay-out. It's one big room with a long bar on the ground floor and stairs on either side of it (nice bit of wood, captain's balustrading, cut out of a Navy man o'war back in the 1850s before it was towed up to the Woolwich Hulks from Wapping to serve as a prison ship) up to a long balcony with a bar of its own and an unimpeded view of the bar below and the only doors. The upstairs bar is where the lads drink. They feel better, being able to see who's coming and going, and segregated from the plonkers down below.

Terry Wicklow was coming out as I went in, blue chalk on his fingers, click of balls in the background. He isn't a man it does to be rude to, so I had to pass the time of day with him. He's a funny fellow. Doesn't look very much. About five nine and slight with it, but wiry and light-footed. And he's still not a man you want to mess with. Terry kills people for a living. He's only ever served time once, and that was over a case where he was personally involved enough to get angry and careless. The seven year sentence was a bit on the stiff side for manslaughter in self-defence, which was still all the police were able to pin on him. (You don't get many witnesses volunteering in cases like that. Anyway, it was a private matter, within the family, so to speak. The stiffy was a minor villain who'd been jessing about with Terry's sister-in-law while his brother was on

34

the inside after snatching a lorry-load of cigarettes. There were those who reckoned he'd been shopped by his old lady and her fancy man. The law was waiting for him and his mates. Reckon Tel's brother thought so too. When he came out he carved his old woman up pretty badly. She disappeared, back to her family, up north somewhere. Just shows it doesn't do to go marrying outside your own folk. The pros' wives understand.) Anyway, by the time I'd offered him a drink, been turned down, asked him about his golfing holiday in Spain (he makes his day-to-day living running enforcer for one of the big firms; his guvnor's in permanent exile in Spain – one of the brains behind the big Brink's Mat gold bullion haul, a couple of years ago) and told him I'd see him up the Arsenal someday, it was five past.

I threw a bit of a wobbler once I got inside and up the stairs. It was pretty busy and I had to push my way past a bent brief I only know by sight and a D.S. – Detective Sergeant – on the Pentonville Road Force. They're the kind of people even I find it a good idea not to get too friendly with, because the brief is a big man in the long firm business and it doesn't do any banker's reputation any good being associated with long firm artists.

I'd better explain that. I know that all you lot who watch Rumpole of the Bailey on the telly will have worked out that every time that writer bloke Mortimer wants to get a brief off the scene, he packs them off to Birmingham or Bristol on a long firm fraud case, and I expect that like most people you'd guessed that was just a company fraud case that lasted a long time.

Wrong. Long firms are one of the oldest kinds of fraud there is. There are specialists in them, like that brief, who sometimes find it necessary to buy off the odd policeman who takes too close an interest in them. But they're also the way a lot of regular villains start branching out into white-collar crime. They're the stuff the Krays and Richardson mobs first got into, after scrap metal and the protection rackets. Basically, a long firm involves identifying some product you can shift fast for cash. Back in the fifties it was nylon stockings. These days it's more likely to be the fancy Italian knitwear, shades and leathers the kids who want to look like Paninari are ·into. That and stuff like cassette and video tapes. The long-firm registers itself as a limited liability company (so it needs at least one face who can pass as a legitimate businessman, which is why it's often seen as the first step up from strong-arm work), rents an office and warehouse space and starts ordering the product from honest suppliers. It pays them, too, building up a credit-rating. Then, finally, it puts in one big set of orders, takes delivery at its warehouse on a Friday, has all the stock out in the markets for cash the following morning, and the long firm operators and all their records vanish off the face of the earth, at least till the heat is off and they've found themselves another set of false names. The suppliers get burned. Very often the local bank branch where they've opened an account gets burned (they'll have made sure to generate an overdraft – like insider traders they believe in using other people's money.) All in all, it's a great deal too close to real business for a banker to want to get near to any of them.

Not that I'd have worried about those two if I'd realised who it was O'Malley was talking to by the upper bar. There'd been showers all that morning. The whole city was a bit damp, and in the R&R everyone was steaming slightly. There was that funny smell of damp, dirty serge and flannel you get when too many suits that haven't seen the dry-cleaners recently enough are wet together in a confined space. Most everyone there was fingering damp collars away from their neck and drowning the weather with a drink. O'Malley was getting himself round a stiff Bushmills, but the man with him wasn't. The man with him wasn't drinking or doing anything. He was just standing there, looking mean. Tall, thin fellow, dark hair, nasty mouth, black leather jacket, black roll-neck sweater, tight black cords on thin long legs. That rough, battered skin that looks as though a meteor-shower's hit it. He looked like a knife. Like a non-stick stiletto. Someone who wouldn't leave any traces. I did not like the look of him at all.

I forced my way over to O'Malley's side, and before he or I could say anything, the man with him said, in one of those Irish accents that sound like criticism, a voice from the border country, from Provo territory, 'You're late. You're out of order.'

I looked him in the eye, and then I looked at O'Malley. I played it straight. 'Who rattled his cage?' I asked.

O'Malley was sort of smiling, but he was sucking in his breath as he did so. He half-turned, blocking the space between me and the thin black duke and said, 'John Ford, will you allow me to introduce you to the Irishman.'

I nearly filled my pants.

I'd heard of him, of course. Everyone had heard of him. But I'd never clapped eyes on him before. Lots of people said they had, but I'm not sure I'd ever really believed it. Still, whatever anyone else had done, I should have trusted to my first impressions. I should have kept my mouth shut.

If a quarter of the things that were said about him were true, he was not a man to cross. I suppose he'd used half a dozen names so that in the end everyone just called him the Irishman, and he was, by reputation at least, the best hacker in the business. I knew of at least six major computer frauds, on both sides of the Atlantic and both sides of the Channel, he'd been credited with being the technician on. (In computer frauds, big is more than ten million dollars.) But that wasn't particularly what bothered me. What bothered me was the rumour he did contract work for the Provisionals. The Provos, of course, had been financing themselves for years off bank jobs and protection, but for a good few years now the word had been out that they were also into white collar crime, and the Irishman was their point man. To this day I don't know if any of that's true, but like everyone else I'd heard he had some serious muscle behind him. About a year ago he'd put together some crooked software for a trivial mob in Hendon. The deal was, they sold the software cheap to local companies – they fronted as a Software House – and the bent system authorised crooked payments on non-existent invoices to a bank account of theirs in Guernsey. Nice little idea, but they hadn't bothered to pay the Irishman his full commission, and bits of them were still turning up in Epping Forest, on Hampstead Heath.

So I wished I'd smiled. I wished I'd said Hi. I wished I hadn't been late.

I did the next best thing. I apologised. 'I'm sorry I'm late,' I told him. 'Got caught up talking to Tel Wicklow.' That seemed to do the trick, mentioning the name of a proper hard man, a respectable citizen. He didn't seem quite so ready to hit me any more.

He did turn on O'Malley though, saying, 'I told you. I don't take passengers.'

O'Malley was imperturbable, didn't turn a hair. He swallowed down the last of his Bushmills and said, 'And I told you I reserved my rights. Besides, he may have work for you himself. Now, will you stop playing the black man and earn that five thousand pounds I'm paying you?'

I don't know how he does it. It must be force of character, I suppose, because the Irishman just put his hands in his pockets and said, 'My van's round the corner.'

It was a pale grey VW shag-wagon with Shankhill Computer Services lettered in burgundy on its sides, and yes, I did look it up in Companies House a few days later. There's no such firm, but it looked legitimate. In the City, at least, it had the right kind of street cred.

O'Malley got in up the front with the Irishman. They stuffed me in the back. The odd thing was that in that decent-sized space (it was the kind of van that gets used as a minibus) there was just a small table with an ordinary television and a box with rheostat controls, the sliding ones you get on hi-fi equipment, on it, and one chair. I didn't have time to figure it out in the few minutes it took the Irishman to drive us round the back of IIIB.

You can only approach the front of IIIB's little building

on foot, but the back looks out on to a small court with one lane access to the street. The court gets used as the executive car park by the three London branch directors, O'Malley included. It's also where deliveries are made. (There's a back door.) O'Malley's parking space was empty as usual. Polly uses the company Jag, and Myles is a great believer in the London taxi. The Irishman pulled up in the vacant space. We could have been a perfectly normal delivery van. Then they got in the back with me. The Irishman connected the television to four car batteries in series on the floor, and took the chair.

'Right,' he said, rubbing his long dry hands together. I noticed he had stiff little bushes of black hair between the joints of his fingers. 'Security check.' He turned to Myles. 'You say your mainframe's a DEC?'

O'Malley nodded, adding, 'PDP series. All the peripherals are from them and their registered suppliers, too.'

The Irishman nodded sagely. 'Then you'll be having no problem with the main-frame. Digital, Sperry, Big Blue,' (I remember his using the nickname for IBM) 'they all build RFE baffles into their big boxes and peripherals.' I couldn't help asking what RFE was. He looked at me with something approaching disgust. 'Radio Frequency Emissions,' he explained. 'Electronic equipment this powerful radiates. That's the security problem.' He turned back to Myles. 'So, our only problem is the micros you've put in as intelligent terminals. Would they be networked by any chance?'

O'Malley nodded. The Irishman smiled. It wasn't a good smile. It stopped when he spoke. 'And are you going to be telling me what brands you've got?'

O'Malley shook his head. 'And what would I be paying you for? What I will tell you is that there's more than one kind. I didn't want to part-exchange the first machines we'd bought. I told the suppliers to build them into the system somehow.'

The Irishman smiled again. 'It's a mean old sod you're being, O'Malley.' He switched the television on. The screen turned into a noisy snow-storm. He turned the volume off, and began to slide the controls on the box beside it very slowly.

'Right,' he began to explain, 'it has an internal aerial. I've altered the rate at which the lines which create the picture shoot across the screen already so it's in synch with computer terminals, not broadcast television signals. I can amend that rate if I need to, but what I'm doing now is tuning it.'

Suddenly, the screen went solid, and text appeared on it. Myles and I both gasped. It was a dealing room screen, in the midst of executing a trade, buying yen, three months forward. The Irishman grinned. It made him look like a wolfhound. 'Epson PC AX,' he said firmly.

O'Malley nodded. He looked sick. 'How did you know?'

The Irishman was pleased. 'Now will you listen to the man?' he asked. 'O'Malley, those things are so powerful, you ought to have a broadcasting licence for them.'

'We got them for their processing power,' O'Malley murmured. He seemed aware that, in the circumstances, it didn't make much of an explanation. 'That and the fact you can lock the power off to make the machine secure when it's shut down.'

'Is that a fact?' He was proud of himself. 'Would I be right in guessing some of them will be off right now, it being lunchtime?'

Myles nodded again. I think he wished his head would drop off. 'All but one of them. That one.'

The Irishman kept on tuning. One after the other, five more dealing screens came up, all of them static, unchanging, a picture or memory of the last frame up before the machine was shut down.

'But how?' Myles asked, sounding as defeated as he looked damp. 'The power lock . . .'

The Irishman interrupted him. 'O'Malley, on a desk-top, everything leaks. The screen, the processor, even the plugs and sockets, even if they're disconnected. But if that's all your dealing room Epsons, perhaps you'd like some samples at least of the other equipment you've got.' The answering nod was unenthusiastic. He started tuning again. It took a little while before another screen came up. It was the draft of a letter this time. 'Olivetti,' the Irishman said. 'M series. That would be the secretaries.' Myles didn't even bother to nod this time. He just waited for the tuning to continue, for another screen to emerge.

'Oh bejasus,' he murmured when it did. 'That's mine from last night. I deliberately haven't used it all day . . .'

'IBM PC,' the Irishman interrupted again.

'Yes, I didn't want to trade it in . . .'

'Does anyone else use one?'

'Accounts and records use them too. They got used to them . . .'

'Then it's one of theirs, confirming what you did yesterday. I could surely pick up yours too, but probably not with this equipment and you did only want me to use the simplest stuff this time.'

It was my turn to say something. 'This is simple stuff?'

'Praise the Lord, yes. I built all this from second-hand components for under a hundred pounds. But the standard quality equipment would knock you back a little over a thousand. That'd pick up Myles's screen with a bit of work.'

O'Malley sat down on the floor of the van, gathering his coat-tails about him. 'How many people have this stuff?' he asked.

'Now you're asking,' the Irishman acknowledged. 'I know at least three people who are making a living in the City using this kind of equipment. Two of them are just commercial spies, tracking the other side's brokers during takeover bids. But one of them, now there's a smart young fellow, is trading on his own behalf. He has the grown up version of this equipment set up on the back-seat of his Jaguar -- no one's going to look twice at that car in the City -- with a cellphone, an acoustic coupler, a processor and a small hard-disc memory store. He doesn't need a printer on the premises. With that stuff there isn't anything he

41

can't get into. He just uses the information to help him choose what trades he's going to make. Smart fellow.'

'How do I stop him?' Myles asked.

'You don't,' came the answer, 'but I'll be having a quiet word with him meself. If he makes himself too obvious he could end up making life harder for all us working men, and I wouldn't fancy that.'

'That isn't what I meant,' Myles explained. 'How do I stop him, anyone, doing this to me, to my bank? And turn that damn thing off.'

The Irishman shrugged and did as he was told, before saying, 'There's a string of things you have to do.'

'Tell me.'

The Irishman sat back, enjoying himself. 'Well, now,' he said, 'the problem is the radio frequence emissions. You can't cut those out altogether, but for future reference you should know the US has much tighter RFE standards than the Brits do, so you might think about buying equipment built to American specifications in future. It'll cost you more, of course . . .'

'But what about *now*?' O'Malley groaned.

The Irishman grew gentle and business-like at once. 'You get hold of a firm called DataSafe. They make cheap little weejits that pump out a whole proper blather of radio noise. They'll be useful for a while, till the Brits get their general RFE standards up to scratch. Next you talk to DEC about the possibility of adapting and fitting their high scan rate screens. Other people make them too, but you may as well stick with the supplier you know. High scan rate screens are harder to read. Not impossible, but harder. You're also going to fit radio reflective glass throughout that building, if you can get the planning permission. It isn't pretty and it isn't perfect, but it helps.'

Myles sighed and asked. 'If I do all that, will it make me safe?'

The Irishman looked almost sad. 'Myles, I was able to do all this today because you have a tiny building, no real security, and the machines are hardly any distance away.

Maybe ten feet, most of them. Tomorrow, I'm coming back with the full equipment that I'd use on a bigger building – a directional aerial, a good low frequency tuner, and a proper variable rate monitor. And a memory. With that stuff I can bank any screen in the City, take it home and run it through some software I have and hand you needle sharp pictures. By the time I'm finished you'll never wear a herringbone suit again.' I suppose we must both have looked puzzled, because he explained, 'With the proper equipment, you get a herringbone pattern just before you tune tight into a screen. And with a directional aerial I can not only pick the screens off one by one, I can know which ones I'm getting and repeat the process another time.'

I guess Myles spoke for every banker and broker in the City. 'Shit,' he said. 'Is there nothing I can do about it?'

'Well, there is one thing,' came the enigmatic answer. 'What is it?'

'You go to a firm called Oceonics and you ask them to bring your system up to Tempest approval standard.'

'And what might that be when it's at home?'

'It's the Government standard for computers which have to be absolutely secure. Like the ones in the Treasury. It works, too. I know. I tried to crack the Treasury before the last budget.'

'How does it work?'

'Basically, they clad anything that leaks in metal screens and baffles, and then they test the shit out of it, adding more cladding till nothing gets away.'

'How much does it cost?'

'Now there's the rub,' the Irishman admitted. 'About as much again as you've paid for your whole system already.'

Myles stretched his legs out and shook his head wearily. 'Well then, I'm fucked,' he said flatly.

'Banjaxed,' the Irishman admitted, 'but I'd do the other stuff I mentioned anyway. It's like a burglar alarm. It won't keep anyone who knows what he's doing out, but it might discourage him. It might make him pick on something simpler. Why should he make his life harder than it is already?'

'Is that all?'

'For now, unless you think of moving. You could think about switching to a purpose built electronically secure building. Those architects can do that now.'

I didn't see that. I really didn't. There had to be a way. The usual way. When do you whack a feller you've been watching out for? Just as he's coming out through the door. 'No they can't,' I said. The Irishman looked almost offended and I almost wished I hadn't said it. But I had. And it was true. 'They may be able to stop or silence all the Radio Frequency Emissions, but they can't secure the weakest part of the system. The land lines. The computers have to be able to talk to the outside world, especially the trading room ones. You can get at them through the phone cables they use to do it. Even scrambling doesn't help, because everyone you trade or might trade with has to have the same scrambler, and a system that commonplace might as well be wide open.'

He looked at me, hard, then shrugged and said, 'You're lucky. You have a point.' He turned to O'Malley. 'Get me into the system, Myles, and I'll tell you how good your security software is, but as for tapping in itself, as for access, if that's what you're worried about, I know some about it, but you'd really have to talk to a gyppo.'

I couldn't help inquiring, 'What have gypsies got to do with this?'

The Doesn't-This-Boy-Know-Anything Look came back. 'The gyppoes have always been brilliant at staying in touch. You travel that far and that much and you have to be. Which means, that since the beginning, they've been the absolute best at tapping into phone systems and networks anywhere. No one touches them. Every night the globe's alive and crooning with their calls, and I tell you, the day a gyppo pays for a call, the end of the world is at hand.'

Myles more or less agreed. ''Tis true, but how do you get a gypsy to work honestly for one of the Meat? All things

44

considered I'd rather hire Telecom's phone-bugging department freelance. And they're not but a step away from here.'

'It's true, then?' the Irishman asked.

Myles nodded. 'They've all moved in to the fourth floor of the new City Telecom building.'

'They wouldn't come cheap.'

'And that's a fact. Not that I need them. Or rather, our friend here doesn't.' He inclined his head to me. 'Unless I'm much mistaken the system he wants to get into is simple enough. It's what needs doing then, that's difficult.'

The Irishman looked at me in a fresh light, with a new interest. 'Is it a little job you're planning then?'

I looked at him, a dangerous man, even in the dull grey light of the showery City winter, and, I don't know why, I suddenly felt lucky, felt full of it. I chanced my arm. Instead of answering his question I asked him another one. 'Tell me,' I told him, 'is it true you fed Bill Mackinaw through one of the mincers up at Smithfield?'

He gave me a look. The kind of look which could make a man wish he'd never been born. I'd overstepped the mark. I could sense O'Malley shifting. I remembered something else I'd heard. Something Tel Wicklow, hardest man I knew, had told me. 'Nah,' he'd said, 'leave it out. No one messes with the Irishman. The Irishman, he's the Left Hand of God.'

I hadn't known then what he'd meant, but I was getting an idea of it now. I back-pedalled fast on to the subject in hand, before it turned out to be my lights and liver. 'Actually, after what I've seen today, I think I might be. Planning a job, as such. I very well might be. How do I get hold of you?'

The Irishman laughed. He had bad blackened teeth. Hound's teeth. 'You don't,' he said. 'You get hold of O'Malley.'

I walked back to BHM through the continuing drizzle, reminding myself on the way that Guccis were no kind of footwear for the English climate. Steinitz was a bit peeved I hadn't warned him I might be late. I hate that kind of thing. I'm too old, too good, and too senior for that kind of treatment. I fobbed him off with talk about checking on some market gossip which I needed to act on right away. Which was true, after a fashion. I was thinking about that IBM PC screen of O'Malley's the Irishman had whistled up. It was the fact it was the Records copy screen, not O'Malley's own, which interested me. If it had been O'Malley's I'd have half expected him to put some garbage on it, but the fact it was on the Records screen meant it was a real trade, a trade he'd actually executed.

It was a three month interest rate swap, out of dollars into sterling. The underlying sum was thirty million dollars.

Put simply, an interest rate swap is the nearest thing to a gamble you get in the currency markets. Say you're holding ten million dollars for three months earning 8 per cent interest. Say someone else has sterling worth the same amount on deposit for the same time at 6 per cent. He's making less than you. But say you guess the dollar's going to slide against sterling in that period, so that 6 per cent of the sterling will end up being worth more than 8 per cent of the dollars. So you offer to swap your interest earnings with his. Both of you are gambling. You're betting sterling will rise against the dollar. He's betting the other way round. You're both taking a punt without having to bale out of your original positions. The nice thing about it is that even the one of you who's wrong doesn't do too badly because they still get the appreciation in the underlying currency. It's just a way of laying off.

Well, that was what O'Malley had done, and the fact it was O'Malley confirmed a nagging feeling I'd been beginning to have about three month US Dollars.

I got back to my terminal, switched it on, paused, inevitably, and started switching half our three month dollar positions into seven day and six month ones.

Anything for a breather.

CHAPTER THREE

In the end, I simply couldn't resist it. It was such a simple idea, and I was pretty certain now the Irishman could do it, could handle the electronic side. There were only two things left I really needed to do, if I was to play it safe, and no other way made sense: I had to get some kind of final demonstration out of the Irishman, and I had to go through every single operational stage of the plan and make sure I had everything I needed all geared up.

I started by going through my original source material again. I'd first got the idea from one of the most famous thefts of modern times: the Chase-Colombian blag of 1983.

Chase Manhattan Bank and Manufacturers Hanover Bank had, between them, loaned 47.2 million US dollars to Colombia, to pay for equipment for the military and the police force. So who said banking was ethical? We'll lend money to anyone we think can pay it back at a suitable price. Anyway, by May of 1983, the Colombian authorities had drawn down 33.7 million dollars. There was only thirteen and a half million left in the Colombians' current account at Chase Manhattan's London branch. That May, Chase got a telex from the authorities in Bogota instructing them to transfer most of that thirteen and a half million dollars immediately to an account at the Morgan Guaranty Trust Company in New York. The account specified belonged to the Zurich branch of a big Israeli bank, Bank Hapoalim. (Now do you see why I thought of it?)

The telex from Bogota was legally binding. It came through with the answer-back number of Colombia's central bank on it, which is the way a telex machine confirms that an incoming message is in fact coming from the number it claims to be from. And the telex was in the name of the Director of Public Credit at the Colombian Finance Ministry. It was true there were a few misspellings on the telex. It was true that normally all disbursements from the Colombian current account in London were confirmed by Chase's branch in Bogota. But stranger things have happened. A certain amount of licence is bound to creep in when accounts are managed at such long distances.

Chase transferred the money to New York.

What they hadn't noticed was that the day they got the telex, the day they transferred the money, was a public holiday in Colombia. There shouldn't have been anyone at the Central Bank to send the message.

Well, who checks their diary every day, just to find out if today's a holiday in Bogota?

When the Colombians, after the holiday, found out what had happened – and they always claimed there was no originating copy of the telex to Chase ever found at their central bank – they accused Chase of incompetence.

Maybe. Maybe not. The fact was that someone had got away with the best part of thirteen and a half million dollars, on a public holiday.

And yes, the investigators did go back to Morgan Guaranty Trust Company in New York. By the time they got there, the money had been transferred. So yes, they got in touch with Bank Hapoalim in Zurich and discovered that, as far as anyone could work out, most of the money had been transferred to a branch of another Israeli bank, Bank Leumi, in Panama.

That's where the trail ran cold, because Panama has bank secrecy laws. You can't sequester bank records, in Panama.

And I'd had sixteen million dollars altogether sitting in an inert account for two and a half years. Can you blame me for wanting to do it? Wouldn't you?

There was just one thing I was anxious to avoid. As I said, the Colombian trail ran cold in Panama, but that didn't stop the Colombians' domestic investigations. They talked to a lot of their own citizens who might have had information. A lot of those citizens got shot.

So I made only one promise to myself: I was only going to do it if I could get away free and alive. I had no idea when I started how close run a thing it would be.

I rang O'Malley at home in Aylesbury that Saturday afternoon. Polly answered. I did my stuff. I asked after the children. (Susie was off to her first gymkhana. Tom had a cold. I cheered and sympathised.) I asked her when I could take that boy up to Highbury, see the Gunners play, next. I asked her when she was going to pack off that insufferable buffoon of a husband of hers to Ireland for a weekend so I could slip down to the country and pleasure her like a gentleman. I'd acknowledged her inference that I needed a bit more practice before that happy day. Then she told me Himself was in the Music Room and I settled back and waited.

He does love machines does O'Malley, and he has a big and very beautiful house. A good thing too, for the very core of it is the Music Room he had built for himself. It's all wall, no windows. Even the door was acoustically designed. And it's sound-proofed. It has to be, because O'Malley has the most shattering sound equipment I've ever seen in private hands.

I don't know all the details, because he had the thing built specially for him. He's got top of the range Krell pre and power amps. He's got an Oracle Premier turntable, an SME 5 tone-arm and a Koetsu Gold cartridge. The speakers are a pair of Apogee Big Ones. The CD's a Cambridge Audio, and the cassette-deck's a Nakannichi. Just the equipment, never mind the bloody room, must have set him back the fat end of £35,000. That's why the room can't have windows. That weight of directed sound could bring a jet fighter down in mid-air at ten miles' distance. And do you know what he plays on all that equipment? He plays old Duane Eddy LPs and Buddy Holly singles, the originals, from the days when he was a lad in Dublin. On his equipment, you could mine coal and blast quarries just with the sonic boom off the scratches.

Anyway, it means that when he's locked in there, Polly can only reach him by a flashing light system he had installed. (Even down a phone line or intercom the burden of noise would be unendurable.) She has to wait for him to notice the light and disconnect the whole system before opening the door and coming to the phone.

It was a good five minutes before he came down, and I knew by then I really meant it. I hadn't changed my mind while waiting. I hadn't lost my bottle.

It was a short conversation.

'And what can I do for you, young fellow?' he asked.

'The Irishman,' I said.

'Indeed?'

'I need a demonstration of what he can do with telexes, computerised telex system.'

'He doesn't do demonstrations. You'll have to pay him, just to see him run through his paces.'

'I won't pay funny money.'

'I'll fix a price. What about equipment?'

'I don't want to use my own. Not yet.'

'All right.' There was a pause. Three beats. Then, 'Can I ask you just the one?'

'What is it?'

'You're thinking of the Colombian job, aren't you? Chase, 1983?'

'How did you guess?'

'I didn't guess. I taught you most of what you know, remember?'

I went back to my plans. The key to it was public holidays. The money had come to us from Venezuela. The whole point of issuing instructions on a day which was a public holiday there was to guarantee that there wouldn't be any conflicting instructions from Venezuela that day. It bought me twenty-four hours. But I didn't want to leave it there. I wanted more time still. The calendar gave me the answer. Christmas.

Christmas Eve was on Thursday and not a public holiday in Venezuela. But it was, by convention, a bank holiday. That meant I could get the instructions to BHM on the Thursday and the earliest the Venezuelans could find out what had happened was the following Monday, or Tuesday, counting on Boxing Day in Britain. What I wanted to do in those few days was not only get the money out of London, to some administration where it would be difficult to follow it, but also out of that second place to a third one. I knew what the third place ought to be. It ought to be Panama, because of its secrecy laws. Even so, I didn't want to leave it there too long. I wanted to get it in some form where no smart-arse lawyer or policeman could sequester it. That was a problem which could wait for a while. What had to be settled soon was where the money was to go between London and Panama. The more I thought about it, the more I was forced to accept there was only one conclusion: it had to be Switzerland.

I didn't really want it to be. The Swiss had been under too much pressure too often of late to relax their secrecy regulations. And Ferdinand Marcos didn't help. It wasn't just the international political clamour that made the Swiss authorities seize his assets and release details to the American courts, it was the prospect he might try to move the money himself. Those deposits were too big for the Swiss to want to lose them. So it isn't possible any more to be absolutely certain of secrecy if you open a Swiss account, but the trouble is, they've been doing it for longer than anyone else, and they've done it more. They have the expertise. I had to think if there were any alternatives.

I had a second problem, too. I had to think about how I actually opened the accounts. Part of me said the safest way was to go out and open them in person, but the investigators would be bound to check the travels of all the staff of BHM in London in the months before the theft. Flying out to secret banking havens in the months before would be too bloody obvious. There had to be a way round that. Something that fitted into previous, established routines. I had to think about that. I had to think about the fact that like a lot of people in the City, I don't really take a proper holiday. I take it all as long weekends. A lot of short breaks keep me fitter than one long holiday; and they help me keep a year-round tan. Was there any way I could use those habits in the time still available?

The one thing that was simple, settled and all above board was location. The Irishman would need somewhere to set up his equipment, and I didn't want it in my flat. I didn't want nosy neighbours identifying deliveries. I didn't want any kind of trace to be possible on the phone lines used. That wasn't a problem. Like quite a lot of people over the last few years, I'd punted all my spare money into the government's privatisation programme. After all, the government had designed each privatisation to guarantee the private investor an immediate capital gain. On top of the basic applications, like quite a lot of people in the City, close enough to the action to be able to risk it, I'd also done some trading on my own account on the day or two after each issue, buying and selling at quick small profits, to step up my overall gain. I'd put all those profits into a bank account in Jersey, but I didn't just leave them sitting there. The safe bet in London around the time of Big Bang was property with good access to the City. I'd had my Jersey bank as nominees use the money to buy a flat on my behalf in the Barbican. All perfectly legal, so long as I declared any ultimate capital gain on a property which wasn't my principal place of residence. Not that I wanted to sell it. Selling it would make it traceable to me, as it wasn't while the bank held it as a nominee. What it was, though, was empty and waiting to be used.

That made me feel a great deal better. We could make this one work. We could make this one fly. I settled down to think some more.

O'Malley rang me back on Sunday afternoon. He sounded pleased with himself. 'It's set,' he said. 'He'll do it.

Wednesday. He wants a K. He wants it cash, on the day.'
I suppose I hesitated for, oh, all of three seconds. For three
seconds I wondered if a thousand pounds wasn't too much
just to prove you could send a telex; but hell, if it worked
it was petty cash, and if it didn't was a thousand too much
to pay to realise you'd have to plan a different future?

'OK,' I told him.

This time he sounded relieved. There were just the
technicalities to work out. 'I take it you don't want
the demonstration to be run on BHM's system?'

I felt my heart accelerate. 'No I do not . . .'

'Don't worry, don't wet. I've set it up. We're using my
PC and acoustic coupler at the Eaton Square flat and we'll
be sending perfectly legitimate instructions to accounts I
manage at IIIB. We're going to have to do it at mid-day,
so we'd better make it all look above board. Book yourself
out for a two hour lunch with me. Bring your car in and
come and pick me up. The Irishman'll meet us at my place.
He says he shouldn't need more than an hour. There'll be
nothing to link any of it to you. It was just a day we decided
to have lunch at my place rather than in the City.'

I really didn't know what to say. O'Malley was being
wonderful. All I could really manage to be was suspicious.
'Myles,' I asked him, 'why are you doing this?'

He chuckled. Even his laughter has a brogue. Then he
said, 'I'll tell you after Wednesday.'

Steinitz wasn't so keen on my taking a two-hour lunch that
day, but there wasn't much he could say about it. Three
month dollars had been sliding ever since the Tokyo
exchanges opened on Monday morning and I'd covered our
arses. I pulled the hood down on the BMW, picked up
O'Malley, cut down on to the Embankment and went like
the clappers.

I will always remember it as a particularly good day. The
winter clouds were clean, the sun was out and even the river
looked blue instead of its usual muddy grey. As we whipped
past Waterloo Bridge, as white as a whale in the sunlight,

I even began to understand how people get sentimental about the Big City. The Irishman was waiting as we pulled up, strolling slowly round the square, looking like a cross between a tourist and the Boston Strangler. He sauntered over as we got out, and Myles let us in and up.

I'd phoned my bank in Jersey on the Monday and followed up with a letter and picked up the K in cash from their London correspondent bank that morning. The Irishman didn't so much count the roll of notes as weigh it, in his palm, testing its thickness. He wasn't in any mood to take in the hunting prints, the Ascendancy furniture or the paintings by minor Italian masters picked up on the Grand Tour, and I'd seen them too often, but I wish now I had paused a bit, because Polly won't allow any place she owns to look like rubbish, and it'll be a good few years before I see Eaton Square again. Instead, Myles took us straight through to his study. The Irishman went to the desk, sat down and switched the IBM PC on.

'Right,' he said, 'you have to tell me exactly what you want.' Both of them looked at me.

I swallowed and started. 'Myles has a telex facility on this PC. I want you to telex his bank with instructions on an account. I want their equipment to believe the telex is coming from a machine in the United States. We'll give you the number and answerback the message is supposed to be coming from. I also want their telex equipment, for the rest of today, to come through to this equipment whenever they telex that American number and for this equipment to respond to them and them alone with the American number and answerback. If any of that process leaves any traces in their system, I want those traces erased at ten-thirty tonight – five thirty in the afternoon Boston time. That's it.'

Somehow I'd expected him to react with dismay, to suggest it was difficult, was worth more than a thousand pounds. He didn't do any of that. He just pulled a floppy disk out of the supermarket plastic bag he'd been carrying and loaded it into the machine. Then he was silent for a couple of minutes, thinking, and occasionally keying in instructions. Then he turned to us and asked for the American number and answerback code. Myles slid over a piece of paper with them written on it, along with the message which was to be sent. The Irishman read it through and settled back in his chair and began to explain.

'I'm going to take you through this step by step so you know exactly what's going on. The first thing I have to do is to tell the telex software loaded into this machine that on any occasion in the rest of today that it receives a telex headed up by the number and answerback of Myles's bank, that it does not respond with its normal number and answerback, but with this American number and answerback, but it only does that in the event of a telex from IIIB. That will include the standard request for a confirmatory answerback IIIB's machine will ask for at the end of any telex from us.'

He keyed in his instructions and loaded them.

'The second thing I'm going to do is key in this telex message and load it, ready for despatch.'

He did so.

Then he sat upright and flexed his long fingers. 'The third thing I have to do is the hard thing. I have a prewritten program into which I simply slot the appropriate numbers. I'm going to use the acoustic coupler to hack into the part of IIIB's system, hard and software, which manages the telex operation, and I'm going to tell it that between now and ten thirty this evening it is not to process any telex numbers as they are typed. It is to wait till the number is completed. On completion it is to process any telex number except this one, this American one, according to the rules of its standing operating procedure. With this number alone, it is always to display the number and answerback as keyed in, but it is actually to connect to this number in London. Finally, at ten thirty tonight it is to delete all these instructions. Now do you understand all that? Is that everything you want me to instruct it?'

My throat had gone dry. I couldn't speak. I looked at

O'Malley and nodded. He nodded too. The Irishman licked his lips.

'Well, that's where you're wrong,' he said. 'There's hardly a computer system in the world where delete means delete. It normally means suspend from use. Take out of access. But a good enough hacker, a good enough fraud investigator, can access those inaccessible memories, and print them out and use them against you. The real bitch was a couple of years back when it even happened with one of those little hand-held Psion Organisers. Drug dealer. Thought he'd deleted all his records before the police picked him up. But he hadn't. The people at Psion unlocked the memory for the police. They sent him down. I have to instruct IIIB's computers that in this one instance delete means delete, and not just store. There is almost certainly a security system in place to prevent that, for obvious reasons. I have to write my way round it. Now leave me alone.'

The next twenty minutes were some of the stickiest of my life. There was nothing we could do to help him. As far as he was concerned we ceased to exist. All that mattered was the machine in front of him and the unseen machine a couple of miles away. His concentration was total. I still don't know how he did it. I don't really want to know. But the fact that he did it will always seem one of the most impressive things I've ever witnessed.

At last, he smiled and said, 'OK, let's send this telex.' Both Myles and I let out deep whoops of breath. I don't think either of us had been aware of breathing throughout all the twenty minutes. When it was done, the numbers and answerbacks we wanted issued and acknowledged, he turned to Myles and asked, 'How do you propose to test what happens if the bank telexes America?'

Myles just wagged his forefinger and said, 'Hold on five minutes and you'll see. But while we're waiting have a drink.' He poured us all a Bushmills. No one was turning it down.

Five minutes later he was on the phone to his assistant

at IIIB. 'Stiffy, O'Malley here. Look, I forgot to tell you. Old Winston in Boston phoned me at home last night and warned me he might be transferring twenty-five thousand between accounts today. Boston's been open over an hour now. Have we had any instructions? A telex? Just now? Well, there's good fortune for you. I don't feel such an eejit after all. For fifty thousand dollars you say? He told me twenty-five last night. I'm sure. Look, will you telex him back right away and ask him to confirm the amount? No, don't bother 'phoning, telex him. I want this in writing, there's a good boy. I'll be back in about an hour.'

He poured us all another drink. A couple of minutes later the telex came through. I will never know how I stopped myself dancing round the room. Myles sent the reply confirming the amount himself. After that, over a final drink, he put my mind at rest. 'Don't worry,' he said, 'I phoned Old Winston myself last night and asked his permission to switch funds around between accounts to check my new computer systems. You might almost say I was telling him the truth.'

The Irishman cut off the merriment. He turned to me and said dispassionately, 'The K was a favour to Myles. If you really have a job to do, my fee is 10 per cent of the gross amount. You provide the location. You provide the equipment. I'll give you a shopping list and instructions. And I need all the numbers – the telex numbers, the instruction codes, the account numbers – at least forty-eight hours in advance.'

I didn't like that bit. Giving him those numbers gave him a great deal too much control. 'Agreed to everything except the numbers,' I told him.

'Then find yourself another hacker.'

'Why do you need them? Why do you need them so long in advance? Why not on the day? You did all this in half an hour.'

He shook his head. 'America's easy. Britain's easy. So are France, Germany, Switzerland and Japan. And Hong Kong. Nowhere else is quite so easy. Canada's fairly easy.

China's moderately difficult. Chile's a nightmare. The more time I have to plan and prepare the better, but the less I know in advance the safer you feel. Forty-eight hours is a good compromise. Forty-eight hours I can handle almost anywhere on earth, and I don't know yet what you have in mind. Don't even think of offering twenty-four. It's forty-eight or nothing.'

What could I do, except agree? We wrapped up the loose ends.

'When are we going to do it?' he asked.

'Christmas Eve and the night before.'

'That gives us a few weeks. We'll meet next Wednesday in the restaurant at Walthamstow dog-track. Seven thirty. You'll give me the location. I'll give you the shopping list. And we'll sort out the money. I usually take half up front. Seven-fifty K.'

'I don't have three quarters of a million dollars.'

To give him his due, he grinned. 'I didn't think you would. I'll think it over. Give you my proposals when we meet.'

I drove O'Malley back through the fumes, the traffic and the thin sunshine to IIIB. Once we were on our way, I asked him again, 'Why are you doing all this, Myles? What is there in it for you?'

His reply was almost too quiet for me to hear. 'A lot of things.'

'What things?'

I understood two of his reasons. 'I'm bored for one thing. I've been doing it for fifteen years, John, and I'm bored. I've been thinking of going back to college, to teach this time. I've even thought of going back to the horses. I don't know what I'll do, in the end, but this is fun. This'll keep me busy while I think it over. You're another thing. You're not a bad lad. Polly says so, so it must be true. You've had your ups and downs, and it's about time it was your turn. OK so it's a crime. There's a French proverb – do you know it? – Great fortunes: Great crimes. Everyone ought to be allowed one crime in their lifetime. And I'll be a deal happier the day you're properly set up.'

I understood all that, I think, but there was something else, nagging away at him, something he had trouble getting out.

'We whizz it about, don't we, John? Computers, telexes, faxes, phones. We pipe the money down the lines, second by second.'

I shrugged it off. 'We always have done, bankers. Always in the forefront. New technology, new wheezes. You name it, we used it. Telegrams, telescopes.'

He grinned. That little mocking grin he sometimes has. 'And sometimes we screw it up. Like the time Citibank lost its cheque clearing facilities. Biggest bank in the world, allowance made for currencies, down for a week. Those early days after Big Bang when the program-trading machines drove the market crashing down three triple-witching hours in a row for no reason at all.'

I didn't see it. I didn't see what it had to do with me, with this. 'We all cleaned up our software after that, though,' I pointed out.

He acknowledged that. 'It's true. That is a fact. We cleaned it up, so the arseholes could go on using us.' He glanced at me and got to the point. 'Do you remember what I told you, John-boy, right back at the beginning, after the Maidens of Mercy?'

The Maidens of Mercy? I was hardly likely to forget. Little Irish kids' charity, IIIB had discretionary management of their investments, including their cash book. It was one of the ones Myles had handed to me as a portfolio when I joined him, to see how I operated, teach me the ropes. Well, one time, back then, I had a whiff of some funny trading between Swiss Francs and Italian Lira. I thought, get in there fast enough, make a killing. Trouble was, the trades on offer were bulk jobs. I needed to be able to trade about ten million dollars, in and out. So I looked at all the accounts I had discretion over and pooled them together for the deal. That included the Maidens of Mercy.

59

Well, it was a scam, wasn't it? Never trust any deal that comes your way out of Chiasso. Myles spotted that right off, going through my papers at the end of the day. Too late to get me out of it, but not too late to cover my back. He did some fast trading in New York that night – baskets of long-term bonds, mainly – and assigned the profits to my accounts. Took a hell of a lot of hiding from the auditors, that one. Less from the customers. They never really knew how close I'd got to losing them a bundle. When it was over, Myles tore me to shreds. I thought he'd have my arse.

I expected a going over for being stupid, being greedy. What I didn't expect was what really upset him. He told me, 'You should've left the nuns out of it, John-boy. Never mess about with the widows and orphans.'

'Yes,' I told him. 'I remember.'

He relaxed, sitting back and lighting up a half corona. 'Good,' he said, through a trail of smoke. 'Good boy. These were widows and orphans, I'd string you up. But they're not. We all know that. Deregulate the banking system, open up the nominee accounts, the off-shore holdings, and whizz the money around electronically at the press of a button, and who do we get? We get the arseholes. Sixteen million dollars, inert, discretionary owners unnamed, in what is for them an offshore high-yield account, they're not the widows and orphans. They're the funnies. They want the benefits of what we do, they have to take the risks. Seems fair to me, John-boy. It's funny money, and they're fair game.'

CHAPTER FOUR

They're strange places, dog-tracks. Even Walthamstow, which is now the premier track in Europe and has gone all up-market. Even has a nightclub of its own – Charlie Chan's – full of flossies in purple crepe and scarlet chiffon. More peroxide than Kodak. The thing about the tracks, though, is that people only go there because they love them. Twenty per cent of all bookies' revenues in Britain come from the dogs, but you'll never see a gentleman bookie going to the dogs. The Royal Family never go. There isn't any Ascot or Epsom. You may not get the mix of people you get at the horses, but at least you don't get any amateurs. You don't get any people who've only gone there to be seen, because it's the place to be.

They're a knowing crowd, your dog-track crowd: your better class of northerners, your sportsmen from the Big Smoke, your women who did their stint as kennel-maids when they were girls. They know their onions. They know how you fix a track (you stop the hare at the farthest bend from the stand, just for a fraction of a second; greyhounds are so stupid that the leading dog will actually hold back, never taking its eye off the hare, while the dogs behind him, masked from the hare by the leader's body, sweep past him and win). They know how you rig a favourite. (The easy way's to give him a gallon of water to drink ten minutes before the off – blows his weight and balance, but they're such sleek machines that can look a bit obvious. No, the best way's to send the kennel-maid in to give him a swift hand-job. After that he won't even want to spring out of the trap. All he'll want to do is lie there, puffing on a cigarette.)

I suppose you might think it's common, and maybe it is, but I love it. I feel safe on a dog-track, and there are a lot more like me. I feel I'm with my own, with people who understand me. I love sitting in the restaurant, ordering my scampi and chips, my chicken in a basket (wouldn't eat anything else at the dogs), laying my money at the tote stands at the back, and waiting for the moment, barely seconds before the off, when the crowd of really knowing punters, which has slowly been drifting forward, suddenly leaps up and starts placing money. A whole crowd in cloth caps leaving it to the last moment, acting in a kind of unison, trying to snow the bookies, trying to stop them shift the odds, all that. The cold hard yellow glitter of the floodlights, the dark recesses of the track, the deepening chill as the night draws on, and the guaranteed excitement every twenty minutes in the silky, sadistic plunging of the dogs. Nothing like it.

The Irishman was waiting for me, already downing a pint of lager, always a good sign. I'd been afraid he might be a Guinness man. Kind of professional Paddy. Once we'd settled down, got some bets on, ordered food, there was one question I had to ask him straight away. 'How much did O'Malley tell you I was after?'

He raised his left eyebrow. Sardonic, he looked. 'What makes you think he did?'

'Well, stands to reason, doesn't it? I didn't tell you, but you knew you ought to be asking for seven-fifty K up front. O'Malley's the only other person in the know. It had to be him.'

The Irishman smiled, trying to look human. 'O'Malley was right. You're not such a fool after all. I wondered if you'd noticed that. Yes, it was him. Yes, I know you're going after fifteen million.'

I looked about us, but no one was paying any notice to us. At the dogs you can get away with just about anything, short of screwing on the tables, swearing (it's a good night out, for respectable folk, remember – fur coats and no knickers maybe, but the fur coats never come off for you to check), or slagging off the Royal Family. 'So how are we going to do this?' I asked him.

He sank the last of his lager and set the glass down in front of him, signalling to one of the girls. He could be really polite when he wanted to. 'Miss, another of these if you wouldn't mind, and whatever my friend here's drinking.'

'Very nice of you, too. I'll have a lager.'

'Oh no,' he explained as she curved away, 'you're paying. The least you can do is cover my paltry expenses.'

This sounded like a new man. I couldn't help wondering if he was trying to wind me up or take the piss. I decided there wasn't any way of telling and played it straight. 'Of course, as I'm not putting anything up front.' He acknowledged it with another smile and a slight inclination of the head. Once the girl had brought us our drinks and food he took the lead again. All the while he held the chicken leg in his hand and stripped it with his teeth, fat shining on his upper lip. He looked like some kind of animal. A wolf, perhaps? Or a jackal?

He handed me a piece of paper, saying, 'That's the shopping list. It's quite short. It's very simple. And it's not at all expensive. So go to a big supplier, preferably one of the discount warehouses, and pay in cash. Leave not a rack behind. Then just leave it in the location. Don't bother trying to assemble it. I'll go in the night before and do all that. Where is the location, approximately?'

'Barbican.'

'That's good. That's very good. Now you just listen to this, and I'll tell you how we do it. Three days before the off, I'll phone you to confirm the job's still on. If it is, I'll tell you where to meet me the following morning. You will bring with you a letter containing the address of the location and the keys; the appropriate telex numbers and answerbacks; the applicable account numbers and any code numbers or words; and a draft of the telex I am to send, a schedule of likely events, and drafts of any further telexes you realistically expect I have to send. Remember, I am not a banker. You will have to tell me what I'm supposed to say and the kind of words I have to say it with . . .'

I told him they all sounded fine. He told me not to interrupt. He told me he wasn't finished yet.

'The envelope,' he explained, 'will also contain precise details of the planned money trail, so that I can decide where and when I am going to take my 10 per cent and notify the appropriate link in the chain, with all the correct account numbers and codes.'

That really was too much. I wasn't falling for that one. 'No,' I told him.

He looked pained. 'Now really, Mr Ford, you haven't any option . . .'

'I said no. No. No. No. No one gets to know the money chain. That is the only security I have.'

'I'm very sorry you feel that way, Mr Ford, because if you do, there's no way that you and I can do business. You'll have to find another hacker, and I doubt if, in the time, you'll find another one as good, or highly recommended, as me.'

He stood up and gathered his coat about him. He made himself look as though he was leaving.

He was bluffing. He had to be. He wasn't going to walk away from one and a half million dollars. Not like that. Not out of pique. 'I don't know your name,' I told him. 'That puts me at a disadvantage. It also tells me you know and care about security. You ought to understand my position. Let me make my position clear. You're right I'm not going to find anyone else as good as you. And you know what that means, cocker?' He stiffened. I suddenly realised what standing on your dignity looks like. 'That means if you walk away from this table now, the whole thing's off. I won't try and replace you, and I certainly won't come crawling after you in three days time. The whole thing will be off. There are some risks I will not take. That's how much my security means to me.'

I thought for a second I might have gone too far. Just once too often. Like I said, I'd heard a lot about him. No one in my business, my end of the business, hadn't. So I knew he had a motto, a little rule of the thumb. Almost like a Call Sign. And I was pushing right hard against it now. It was, 'No Surrender.'

He stood there, towering over me in a silence masked by roaring punters as the dogs swept round into the final straight. The tannoy was announcing the winner before he sat down again, saying, 'We understand each other very well.'

'Good. Now try this on for size. You will have to know the details of the first link in the money chain, because the details will have to be in the telex instructions you send to BHM. But that is all you get. You also get to specify any account, in any bank anywhere, you want your share delivered. Together we will draft a telex to the first link in my chain instructing them what to do with your share. You will send that telex on the day. You'll get your money the same day as me. And that way both of us know all the details on the first link in each other's chains. Mutual security. I will tell you precisely as much as you tell me. Shtum?'

He nodded once firmly and said, 'I think that will do very well.'

He didn't stay very long after that. I did. I had a lousy night with the dogs. Not a single winner. I had better luck with the girl who'd served us though. After she'd finished I took her up to Charlie Chan's. You know the form. Bit of gin, bit of dancing, bit of natter. Gave her a lift home in the BMW, and had her on the back seat in some poxy layby. Twice. I told you I loved the tracks.

I had to wait a few more days for more cash from Jersey, and then I went up to Brent Cross late night shopping. The Irishman was right. He had kept everything as cheap as possible. There was an Amstrad at the core of it, and he even apologised for the money wasted on the printer that came with it in an all-inclusive price. We didn't need a printer. I just handed over my notes at the discount store and carried it out in the cardboard box; loaded it in the car. The only add-on I had to pay for on the Amstrad was the second disk-drive he asked for but, frankly, I've had more expensive meals. All that left was the acoustic coupler. He'd given me a list of suggested brands and models and I'd just whizzed around a few stores comparing prices. I should have guessed his recommended model would come in, at one store at least, the cheapest of all the prices I was quoted. I had been worried about picking and buying software, telex software, but his final note just said the software was his department. I dropped all the boxes off at the Barbican flat in the early hours of Sunday morning, a time and day when no one stirs round there. I'd had a phone fitted there long before (you can never have too many phones) but it was one of those new key-pad types, and he quite specifically wanted one of the old heavy dial phones to mate with the acoustic coupler, but that was easy enough, because I still had one of those in the hall of the Fulham flat. They're great things phone-jacks. I just switched the two phones round. The new one looked happier in my real place, anyway.

It all seemed really simple. It all went really smoothly. But I have to tell you that through that week or so, one thing kept nagging at me; the offshore accounts. How was I going to open them, and open them in time?

Strange days. I was looking and feeling good. I was even enjoying my work. I was having a good time. I went to parties, got pissed, got stoned, got laid. And all the time my mind was ticking over, thinking: Switzerland and Panama? How do I get to them? Without leaving a chain of suspicion for the investigators to find.

There was another reason for the uneasiness of course. O'Malley. I hadn't heard from him in a while, and we were usually in touch every couple of days. If I'd been thinking straight, I'd have put the two of them together. I would have seen it. I would have realised that Myles would have an answer.

And when I finally nailed him in the Greenhouse, he did. He told me to go home that evening and watch TV.

I did as I was told. I got home late and switched it on and watched a couple of cool boys chasing villains in Armani suits. No earth tones, few words and a rock track.

Miami Vice.

CHAPTER FIVE

Miami is God's piss-hole.

The evidence of Paradise is there for any fool to see: blue seas, matching blue skies, both of them so rich and curved and gleaming you feel as though you're inside some aquamarine oyster glinting with pearls; beaches, palm trees, year-round sunshine, flamingos, and women with hips mounted on bearings, yearlings' legs, and tits like zeppelins. What more could a place ask for?

Well, not to be pissed on by God every day, for one thing. The evidence is in the atmosphere. The place was built on wall-to-wall swamp, all too inefficiently drained, and you feel it wherever you go. Step out of the air-conditioned offices, shops, hotels, apartment buildings and feel the sweat leap into your armpits like an oil-man's dream of gushers. The place is fetid, stinking and in perpetual decay. It reeks of corruption and chaos and death.

It's a fake, a fraud, a non-place, the accidental creation of con-men putting together rigs to part old crinklies from their money, selling them slices of bog in the sunny Everglades, where the sun never sets and the old never die. No wonder it's never got over its reputation for crooked dealing, sharp practice and swindles. It's like one of those brightly coloured Bateman cartoons you see in the adverts: amidst the acid colours of the tanned or peeling or merely reddened flesh, the bermuda shorts, the bikinis like incitements to riot, a thin little man in a grey flannel suit – The Man Who Didn't Break A Federal Law In Miami. Even before the TV programme, even before the Vice, even before the Cubans, the city was a kind of hell.

It was the drugs that finally did it, though. Miami's the nearest port if you're bringing drugs up by boat from the Caribbean, Central and Southern America. It's no distance at all from Nassau with its fully operational hot money banking centre, outside US jurisdiction. And, more recently, it's had the Cubans.

Fidel Castro's funniest joke.

In a sense, I suppose, the Americans had been asking for it: whining for years about Communist Cuba, about the lack of freedom, the prisoners, the absence of free enterprise. So a few years back Fidel just said: OK, all these people longing for freedom, for the reward of individual enterprise, you have them. You give them a chance. And promptly unloaded the jails, not just of political prisoners (a lot of those stayed inside, where he could keep them quiet – he may be a bastard, but he isn't a fool) but of any prisoners.

Which was right, really. There is no greater believer in free enterprise, in capitalism, no greater opponent of state interference (especially when it spells chokey) than your common or garden villain. He packed them into boats and set them off north, ditching his cigar, waving his hankie and giving them a couple of choruses of Good-Byee for good measure.

Well, what could the Americans do, but take them in, at their first port of call? Good, old honest Miami; where they promptly set up in small business, employing themselves and each other, not going on welfare, as street-pushers, distribution bosses, cargo-masters, shippers, enforcers and killers. Who could complain about that? All that lovely new trade and traffic pouring into the city, all those cash profits, ripe for laundering through legitimate banks, property development, and conspicuous consumption.

There's only one problem. It isn't much fun having the Guidos setting up crime syndicates in your neighbourhood, but I will say this for the Men In Suits: in the main, they're family men, they observe the decencies, and they have a family sense of structure, order, hierarchy. Whatever else the Italians bring with them, what you don't often get is them causing a public nuisance. They may shoot each other up in Pizza Hut now and again, but your ordinary punter, unless he's unlucky and gets in the cross-fire, is perfectly safe. He may get anxious. He may call for the D.A. to clean up the streets. But it's very unlikely he's going to wind up dead.

The Cubans aren't like that. They're like the other great liggers of the coke trade, the Colombians.

They are, in a word, mad.

It's the *macho* that does it. It's all individualism. The Cubans wouldn't know a structure if it came up and spat them in the face. The Colombians would tell it that they fucked its sister only the other night, call it a faggot, and cut its balls off. In their mind, rational things like carving up territories, agreeing on trade-offs, regulating routes, and settling compromises are the equivalent of telling them their weenie's shrunk, that they couldn't satisfy a woman with the help of half a regiment. A yanqui regiment. It gets them very, very angry.

Trouble is, not reaching compromise, not creating structures and organisations gets them very, very angry too. Not a day goes by without one of the boys believing somebody else is trying to rip him off, to carve him up, to make him look a wally. Offer him a steak and he'll think you're trying to tell him his old woman's put the horns on him. End up out of smokes and ask him for a fag and he'll blow you away.

None of this makes for a peaceful life.

But for the banks, it does mean Christmas comes every day. Yes, I know there's a law which says US banks have to report all cash transactions over 10,000 dollars. Yes, I know the Federal Reserve Boards have got heavy about enforcing those rules. But we all know that when the cocaine traffic through Miami alone is valued at two billion dollars minimum a year, when drugs are the second biggest industry in the USA (and the way the Japanese and Koreans go on building cars may soon be the first) then you can guarantee there will be briefs and bankers and accountants who will find a way to help their clients out of any little problems an unsympathetic government may create over the necessity of cash business in these days when the world is full of credit card fraud.

Miami, Nassau in the Bahamas, and Panama are the three corners of the Golden Triangle of the drugs trade. The real Bermuda Triangle is a hole down which law, professional ethics, political integrity, and simple honour all disappear in pursuit of one more dollar.

And one of the things you get in Miami are the correspondent and agent banks of Panamanian institutions.

Correspondent banking grew up in the good old days before the big banks, and a lot of smaller ones, decided they needed branches everywhere. All it means is banks in two different countries agreeing to transact each other's local business. If you bank in London, and want to be able to draw money in Singapore and your bank has no branch there, it'll set up the arrangement with its correspondent bank in the Straits, who'll do the same when they have a client coming to London.

The system still gets used a lot, because it saves on overheads, and because there are countries which don't exactly welcome foreign banks. For some reason the American authorities are suspicious of Panamanian banks and don't like them opening in the USA. In one way I can't blame them. Under US law, it's difficult for a local bank to operate across state boundaries. Things have got a little easier since the system was put in place after the Crash of 1929, but it's still not as easy as for foreign banks who get covered by a different set of rules. Can you imagine what would happen if a Panamanian bank were allowed to set up a network in the USA? It wouldn't be allowed to last long, but imagine in the meantime how many billion dollars could be whisked away from the Internal Revenue Service's prying eyes.

Despite all that, there are still American banks, especially in Miami, which operate as the correspondents of Panamanian institutions.

71

It was O'Malley who pointed it out; that I could go to Miami above all suspicion, and get a local bank to open me an account in Panama. Get them to instruct the Panamanians to open an account on my behalf in Switzerland. In their name. The perfect secret bank account system, and never been anywhere near a hot money haven.

The glory of Miami, for a foreign punter of course, being that it doesn't start ringing automatic alarm bells. It's a place thousands of people still go on holiday. Not to Miami, but Miami Beach, just up the way. The Lloret de Mar of the Southern USA. I regularly used to nip down from New York for the weekend when I was in the Apple on business. I don't suppose there'd been one year in the last ten when I hadn't tried to scag a long weekend there. I'd had a lousy year, so why shouldn't I try to get to Florida to get a bit of sun before Christmas.

It took a couple of hours quick work. With the Bankers' Almanac, the Euromoney International Bank Guide. With a telephone, to ask a few questions, set up the appointments, book the flights. And, most important of all, to ring a bank-note weighing manufacturing company in the USA to express an interest in their machines, to explain I was going to be in Miami shortly, and to ask if there was any bank in the city where they might have fitted a number of machines of late and who might be willing to give me a demonstration.

I was proud of that one, though I say so myself. Cash counting machines are useful in any bank, but if a bank suddenly starts ordering extra, you can guarantee that they are the kind of people who look with tender eyes on businessmen who discover their operations just happen to generate an unfortunate amount of cash. There isn't much that such an institution won't do to oil the wheels of industry, and grease the odd palm on the way.

I set the whole thing up for a long weekend a fortnight before we did the job. A fortnight was quite enough. I took the Thursday evening flight directly to Miami, going to the airport straight from the office to the usual chorus of cries of Jammy Sod. Jill, my secretary, even half-suggested I should have taken her, which did surprise me a bit. I'd never got the impression she was up for grabs. Not that I would have done, anyway. It gets too messy, pumping on the premises, and there isn't any way in the world you can maintain staff morale and discipline if everyone knows – and they always do – that when you should be thinking about their career development programme, the fate of six-month yen, or how to keep the equity-asset ratio steady for the next report to the Bank of England, you're really wondering if you can make that call to New York while she hoses you out under your desk or if you should wait till after.

So I got into Miami solo late that night, fresh as a daisy unfortunately. (Like most people, I get hardly any jet-lag going west, but coming east is like being worked over by the Inter City Firm.) I took a taxi straight out to the Hilton. This was meant to be a holiday, after all, and it had to look like one. I have a dangerous weakness for soft, hot, steamy nights beneath indigo ocean skies so I took half a Valium to make sure I got off to sleep and didn't end up prowling the bars. There's nothing quite like bars late at night, everybody a little punchy, blown and blue, dreaming of company, a little comfort in the clasp of another unnamed body, but I had things to do.

The following morning the sun came up like the usual kick in the teeth. I had room service send me up a breakfast of juice and fruit and coffee and realised as I sat on the balcony why I was doing this. I was doing it because I'd had enough of drizzle and greyness and worry. I was doing it for flat planes of white light bouncing off tropical buildings, for red and green roofs, pink pointing, high clouds and open skies and the long and unforgettable hiss of the sea. I got myself into my lightweight suit, made sure I had the cashier's cheque for ten thousand dollars drawn against my Jersey bank – it had just about cleared me out – and my passport for identification, and called down to the bell-captain to tell the doorman I needed a cab.

After due research, I'd chosen a little outfit called the Dade County General and Commercial Bank. They had just the right kind of whiff about them and, just as important, had proved to be the Miami correspondent of a Panamanian outfit called Banco Privado Centroamericano. I'd already had dealings with them for some of our Lebanese Muslim clients who had funds they needed kept out of scrutiny. Muslim clients? Us? If you think about it, for any not-too-devout Muslim, nowhere is safer from investigation than an Israeli bank. None of the faithful would guess you could be so blasphemous. I should have thought of that, too. I really should.

Still, that came later. For now I was bowling along between the palms in a white convertible stretch Lincoln Continental (you'd have to see one to believe it) happily remembering the telephone call to Panama in which I'd set up the fundamental arrangements.

The brighter ones amongst you will have been wondering about all these phone-calls. Wasn't I worried that they might be traceable, back to me? Well, I might have been, except that I'd made them all out of office hours, each from different call boxes. I suppose I should have just equipped myself with dozens of Phonecards, but I have to admit I did something else. Something naughty. Something I couldn't resist, to get my own back at those bastards who run the phone service. There is a two digit number which, if you key it at the end of the number you're calling, results in the call being logged by the Telecom computers as an Engineer's Test Call. No charge is made. Use it from a call box and not only does the machine return your first ten pence but it puts the call through free for as long as you like. I have a nasty habit of making all my international calls from phone boxes. And no, I'm not going to tell you what the two digits are. There are people out there who think I'm dead, and if they found out I wasn't they'd finish off the job. There are people out there who know I'm alive and would kill me if they didn't know I wouldn't be publishing this book if I didn't have enough to put them all away for a very long time if they move against me. The last thing I need on top of that is one of the largest, richest corporations in the world pursuing me for petty fraud and, if they find me, tipping everyone else off in the process.

The manager assigned to me proved to be a punk of maybe twenty-eight in a Hugo Boss suit, Cartier watch and Gianfranco Ferre everything else in an office which was all smoked glass, chrome, white leather sofas and Mexican rugs. He was welcome to all that, but the secretary was another matter. A cross between Fawn Hall and Donna Rice in a flimsy wrap-over chiffon frock and those self-supporting stockings over red high-heeled patent leather Fuck Me shoes. (If you're wondering about the stockings – she made it easy. Like lots of girls brought up to the outdoor Florida life she had less idea of how to walk well than a dustbin does. She strode down the long corridor with its fake marble floors and real tropical plants, flashing her pins with every step. Not that she minded my noticing. That's what wrap-over dresses are for.)

She sat us down with decaffeinated coffee for me and San Pellegrino for him. It came in a blue Perrier-bottle lookalike, and I had him down at once as one of those plonkers who gets sold on the packaging. I was grateful I was wearing my Michel Axel outfit. The business was straightforward enough. Panama had tipped him off. But you want to know, don't you? Almost everyone I've ever met wants to know how you set up a secret bank account. It's almost embarrassingly easy. I mean, that Imelda Marcos – she's not a rocket scientist, is she?

He flashed an expensive set of crowns at me, all straight wedges and quartz fillings, and asked, 'Have you decided what type of account you need?'

They always ask that. The whole routine is always almost identical, for the simple reason that the systems are all based on the Swiss ones. I had thought about it of course. The basic standard named account was no use to me at all. The last thing I wanted on this account was my name. A numbered account had its attractions. You fill out the same form as for a named account – the Agreement For Opening Of An Account Or Deposit and, if you want the bank to manage the account for you, the Special Clauses Completing the Agreement for the Opening of a Current Account and a Deposit – except that the account name is an agreed number or series of letters. You still have to sign the form, of course, but the whole point of the deal is that form is only ever seen by your specific manager or a designated alternate. Everyone else in the bank only knows you by the number. Your account can be handled in complete confidentiality. Even the account manager and his alternate, who is almost always a director, can only consult your master file in the safe by completing a signed, timed and dated control card, and they can only examine one file at a time. Any well-run bank that really worries about secrecy will also make you sign an agreement agreeing that you can't ever withdraw cash over the counter. If you did that, a cashier might be able to identify you, to match you to your number, the number you use as your signature. If you sign this supplementary agreement, you have to agree cash withdrawals in advance with your account manager who will make them privately in his office. If you do insist on counter-drawing rights they'll make you sign an agreement indemnifying them for the inevitable security and secrecy risk.

It's a great system and, especially when run by the Swiss or the Austrians, is more than enough for most people. They are much more secret than most people ever think about. Let's say you knew I had a numbered account, or suspected it. Let's say you're the tax man. To prove it, you send a small deposit to my bank to be credited to my account. If they accept it, the account exists. You've proved that. So they don't accept it. What they do is to write back and tell you I don't have an account with them but they're holding the money while they investigate. At the same time they let me know about the money. If I clear you, they accept the deposit and notify you, but if I suspect you, I only have to tell them. They send the money back, and you still haven't proved I have a secret account. And, obviously, all statements or letters to me go out in plain envelopes with the name and address written by hand so it isn't obvious it's a letter from a bank to a customer. Which is why some tax authorities (the technical term is 'bastards') routinely photocopy all envelopes from Switzerland and have them examined by graphologists working with computers, looking for similarities, trying to catch the bankers out.

I'd thought about a numbered account hard, and I would have been persuaded, if I'd been planning on doing an immediate runner. But I wasn't. That would only have made me Number One suspect. No, I was going to sit it out. Which left me with a problem. If my mail was vetted or seized and the dicks picked out an envelope with details of a numbered account, they'd assume it was mine, and so would any jury, and they'd be right. I needed to be able to claim it was an account I was acting as a postbox on, for someone else. A friend.

I leant forward and told the punk, 'Yes I have. I need an account under a false name.'

He reached into a drawer for the forms, mumbling, 'Sure.' I suddenly realised he was chewing gum. I must be getting old, because it really pissed me off. Maybe the old up-and-down English clearing bank training had really got to me after all. I don't like my money being handled by slobs. He put the papers in front of him and uncapped a fat Mont Blanc fountain pen. Once it was poised he shot me a smile and said, 'Now, what are we going to call you?'

I couldn't resist it. 'You're going to call me Sir,' I told him. His jaw dropped perceptibly. He reached for a tissue, too late to be surreptitious, and removed the gum from his mouth. I smiled at him and said, 'But the name on the account is Steinitz. Saul Steinitz.'

Well, it was the least the old sod deserved for complaining about the length of my lunches with O'Malley.

The rest of it was boring bankers' talk. All you need to know was that the punk was just a letterbox. The account was with Banco Privado in Panama. Only their General

Manager and this oaf were to know my real identity. Privado were to open a nominee account on my behalf with Bank Marius Mayer in Zurich. I could communicate direct, but all communications from the banks would come through Dade County in Miami. And for instructions from me to the banks to be valid, they would have to bear the name Saul Steinitz, the account number and an agreed code word. I'm an Arsenal fan. I couldn't resist the codes: for Panama it was Charlie; for Zurich it was George. The final instruction was about Zurich. The account there was just a front, with ten dollars in it. Whenever any other money came in to it, 90 per cent was to be transferred directly to the account in Panama and the other 10 per cent to another account, details of which would be delivered in due course.

That was it. That was all.

We were done. We were up. And we were running.

I know what you're thinking. You're thinking: Is that all there is to it? I could do that. Why don't we all open offshore bank accounts?

You're nearly right, but there is one thing you're forgetting. Opening and running a secret account is very easy, except they ask you one question first. They ask you if you have enough money to make it worth their while. No bank worth dealing with will accept a deposit of much less than a quarter of a million dollars. Some of the Swiss won't take less than a million. The best won't take less than ten.

I didn't have that kind of money yet, though I'd persuaded them I would have in a fortnight. They weren't entirely convinced. Which was what the cashier's cheque for ten thousand dollars was about. It was a first deposit, just to guarantee they'd get their charges, if nothing happened on the account.

Fancy it, do you?

I did. I fancied quite a lot else, too. I didn't manage the Hall-Rice lookalike, but I did pull a Canadian redhead at the hotel. She said she was a banker. I told her I was in pedigree dogs, which was nearly true. I'll sell a pup to anyone. And I water-skied and parascended, and while I was up there, hung from that big bag in the blue sky, I found myself smiling and thinking, 'All I have to do now is do it. All I have to do now is wait.'

CHAPTER SIX

The next few days were difficult. I flew back in on the redeye on Tuesday morning and went straight to the office. It's always a rough flight and I did manage to get some sleep on it, but there was the usual problem with people doing it for the first time and getting plastered and noisy on the plane. Any regular will tell you aerial dehydration's enough of a problem already (it's the pressurisation) without making it worse by boozing as well. You get pissed before you board the plane, and use the journey to sleep it off.

Once I was back though, all I could do was wait, and I've never been so hot at that. The important thing was to lead a perfectly normal life. What made that tricky was I kept wanting to slide over into excess: do two tracks of coke every hour, see O'Malley every day, whistle up a gobbler on the Gold Card every evening, have a heart attack every squash game (squash isn't a game that stops you having cardiac arrests; it's a game that helps you recognise them when they come), tell Steinitz his systems were shot every day instead of every other, and give him serious gip about his cash book.

Somehow, I managed to keep it all steady, on an even kilter, but I must have been wrecked, because when the phone rang at seven the following Monday morning, I had to scrape myself off the ceiling before I could answer it. It was the Irishman, good as his word. He kept it simple.

'Where?'

I gave him the Barbican address.

'That where you want it done from and all?'

I told him yes.

'When do I do it?'

'First telex the night before Christmas Eve, half past nine. You need to be on call that night and all the following day.'

'You should've told me it'd be such a long job.'

'You shouldn't take anything for granted.'

That seemed to please him. I could sense the dog-smile. 'Is the equipment in?' he asked.

'There and waiting.'

'Meet me there at eight tonight.' Then a click, and the dialling tone. He made it seem so easy. I'll tell you one thing, though: I went straight from the bathroom to the bog. I don't believe professionals can ever suffer from constipation.

I got through the day. I don't know how. I don't remember much of it. I do remember being more careful than I'd ever been in taking my views, in making my positions. But the time at the office wasn't the worst part. At least I had real things to do, real things to think about. The worst part was the time between getting back from the office and heading back to the Barbican. I'd thought about booking a squash court, but I didn't want to overdo it. I'd be playing the following day. I did call into Courts for a couple of Kirs Royales, but that only held me back half an hour. I couldn't take any more than that. The place was like a bloody funeral. Another Clearing Bank had announced that day that it was pulling out of market-making in Gilts – British Government Securities. That whole bit of the post Big Bang world was beginning to look distinctly dodgy. I told myself not to worry about it. It would all be behind me soon enough. Then I told myself I had to worry about it. Till it was all behind me, I had to worry about anything which affected my markets. I had to be seen doing my job. And a weakening Gilts Market ought to mean a softening sterling position, at least temporarily. I'd already shifted some call and short-term sterling that afternoon. Then I broke and ran. I had an hour and a half on my own at home. You'll understand the state I was in if I told you I couldn't even take a drink. I ended up watching Wogan instead.

81

The Irishman was waiting for me outside the flat when I got to the Barbican. I knew why he'd chosen the time. The show at the Barbican Theatre that night had started half an hour earlier. The exhibition had closed a half hour before that. And all the City regulars who had overnighters in the Barbican would all be changed and moved on by now as well. Eight o'clock was the first time there was no one about. No one to see him. I let us both in, and without saying a word he started upacking the boxes. I almost broke while he was assembling the kit. I would have gone out and found somewhere to buy a pack of fags, and I hadn't smoked a cigarette in years, except I kept thinking, 'No, no cigarette butts. Residual prints on the filters.'

I'll say one thing for him, it didn't take him long to get the whole thing up and running. He didn't bother to connect the printer. I let him run his checks on all the other equipment, including the acoustic coupler, before telling him to fit it up.

'I don't need it,' he said stiffly, a touch of pride in the voice.

'Yes you do,' I told him. One eyebrow went up. 'You'll see.' He did as he was told.

There was something else I was worried about. 'The coupler. When you were testing it, what number did you call? If Telecom can trace it, I don't want any surprises.'

His smile looked too like a sneer to make me happy, but it was a bit late to back out. He shook his head and explained. 'It was one of my numbers. I was calling down the balance of the software I'll need. But I change my numbers every month, you see. And my locations. And the software it's got loaded in it now tells Telecom's equipment to charge that call to my number, not yours. They'd have to trace my number, not yours, to track that call, and they have no way of knowing about me. Do they?' There was a flash of threat in the last two words. I didn't let that faze me, but I did agree. He put his long left hand out. 'The instructions.'

I shook my head. 'Not yet. The details of the account you want your 10 per cent transferred to, your instructions, and any codes.'

I'd expected some kind of fight. I'd expected some mouth. I didn't know if I should be pleased when I didn't get any. He handed me a folded sheet of A4 paper. The details of a numbered account in Geneva. Javert, Valjean et Cie. Codeword CIRCUITOUS.

'Access it,' I told him. He hesitated. 'I don't need a transaction. I just need to see acknowledgement of the answerback. That'll do me.'

He put through a telex instructing them to expect a credit transfer the following day from an account to be advised. It looked OK. When I nodded, he pressed the print button. A copy of the telex spilled out. He handed it to me, keeping his hand out for the original piece of paper. I let him have it back, of course. He wanted his handwriting back. 'You're really not a fool,' he said.

'Thank you.'

'Instructions?'

I took them out and took him through them. It was straightforward enough. A telex to go into BHM at 9.30 Wednesday night: 5.30 in the afternoon Venezuela time. The timing was important. The telex contained all the necessary, accurate, account and code numbers and authorisation names. It included a rider stating this telex replaced all previous instructions. That's a standard enough formula, but it covered me if the Venezuelans had sent a real telex between close of business London time and close of business local time. I'd be first in in the morning as usual, and would be the first to know, but I wanted everything looking right, just in case. It also contained the most important details, details of Banco Privado Centroamericano's account with Bank Marius Mayer in Zurich: the account number; the codeword, George. I'd also prepared a back-up confirmation telex he was to send on Thursday afternoon if BHM sent out a telex asking for repeat instructions. And warned him that if he got a telex

83

querying the instructions because Thursday was a local holiday, he was to blow the gaff and cut it. Disconnect everything. Destroy all traces. *Go*. That was the only query in the world which could spell trouble, could tell us to abandon ship. That was almost all he needed.

'This is fine,' he said, 'as far as it goes. But what about the detailed telex to Bank Marius Mayer, dividing the spoils?'

I smiled at that. 'It doesn't need a general telex,' I told him. 'They already have their instructions for my 90 per cent. All you have to do is notify them of the detailed instructions for your 10 per cent, transferring it to Javert, Valjean. I'll leave that to you.'

The Irishman grunted. I could tell he got my drift. He knew I was covering my back, finessing him. He knew there had to be a further stage in my money chain, designed to stop him shafting me. Even if there was some way he could telex Banco Privado without my knowing it, he didn't know the name my account was in, its number, or its code. But I didn't want him telexing Banco Privado without my knowing it.

'That machine,' I said. 'You're going to tell it to print out the time every fifteen minutes, and every telex that you send, and every telex that you receive. By six o'clock our time Christmas Eve, all this is going to be over. We're going to be done. We're going to be rich. If there are going to be any doubts from BHM they'll come before then. You need to keep this link open till then. This machine will be Venezuela till then. At six on Christmas Eve I'll be on my way to the squash court. I won't be going home first. But you will be going past my flat, with all the print-outs from this minute on. You'll put them through my letterbox. And when I come back, if there's anything funny about them, I'll be on to my banks. And if there's anything funny with them, before you know what's happened, half the regulars of the Rat and Rizla are going to be under contract to me, with half the fifteen mill as prize, and instructions to find you, cut your balls off, and nail them to your eyes. After you've talked.'

Not a flicker in his eyes. No movement in his mouth. No working at the jaw. Instead, he just stuck out a long hand for mine and said, 'Mr Ford, it's a pleasure to do business with you.'

Wednesday night, I hardly slept. I took two showers. I ate two breakfasts. I had the television and radio both on together. I got to the bank first as usual but somehow stopped myself getting there any earlier than usual. My eyes were tense. My ears were hot. My throat was dry. And my mouth felt like an elephant's armpit.

Usual procedures. Do everything by the book. Switch the alarms from red to amber status. They didn't go green till the little office and reception area which passed for our banking hall was open. Flick through the mail. Ditch anything that looked like a circular, for one of the clerks to vet, just in case. Put the real mail to one side to wait for Steinitz. Then go back to the telex room.

Two confirmations of transactions the previous day with New York. An enquiry about opening an account from a doctor in Boston. Looked like he was using a telex bureau. Transfer instructions on an account from Vancouver. Switching from sterling to yen. Smart move. An enquiry about various of our CD rates – Certificates of Deposit – from Hong Kong. What was that about I wondered? CDs are negotiable instruments, a sort of receipt for a deposit account. Say you deposit ten thousand dollars with us for three months at a given rate. We issue a CD to that effect. You can sell it. You can deposit it with another bank as security. You can use it almost like money, because whoever holds the CD at the end of the three months can present it to us for payment of principal and interest, no questions asked. This enquiry was for large sums. Why should someone want to switch so much money into bearer (whoever holds it, owns it – there's no register anywhere) negotiable form? Should I be worrying about Hong Kong? The usual

crappy enquiries from Tokyo. The slants ask about everything all the time, just for the hell of it, and you have to
answer every bloody one, because if you don't, you're off
the list and you'll never get the one in a hundred that leads
to an actual trade. All standard stuff. All boring. Except
for one telex (my heart is trying to punch its way out
through my eyes, nose and throat) between the ones from
Boston and Vancouver. It's from Venezuela. I seem to have
seen it before . . .

I go through it very carefully, in my mind. Telex name
and answerback are right. Account name is right. Account
number is right. Code word is right. Signatory is right.
Everything's right. Instructions to transfer fifteen million
dollars from this account to one held by Banco Privado
Centroamericano at Bank Marius Mayer, in Zurich.
Account details given in full.

A cough behind me. Steinitz.

Well, it's a nice day. Try to be cheerful. 'Morning, Saul.'

'Morning, John. Anything interesting?'

I manage to stop myself singing and dancing. Be as grey
as both our grey suits, his grey hair, my grey tongue.
'Mail looks flat but fat.' It's one of his phrases, reflected
back at him. At BHM we still use the old German system
Siegmund Warburg brought over with him. The directors,
and me (Treasury's worth a couple of bodies) open all the
mail together, note all its contents, suggest appropriate
action. That way nothing gets allowed to slide and all the
senior personnel know everything that's going on. No
surprises. Not that it's a problem in this outfit. The
senior personnel number precisely four. Embarrassing once,
though, when Cahane, the chairman, forgot to tell his
enthusiastic new young mistress to mark her letters to
him at work Personal, or Private & Confidential. Steinitz
found himself informing us on her behalf how wonderful
the old man's fat cock was for someone his, or anyone's,
age. He handled it rather well. Suggested it go on the
Public Relations file, copy to go to the Bank of England
with our next report, confirming our vigour. Cahane liked

86

that. Said he'd rather it was put down with our undisclosed reserves.

Steinitz is not so bad. Grumpy, finicky. Would straighten his pubic hair if he knew how. But for all the conservatism that keeps getting on my trolley, he's good. He can be cool under pressure.

Can I? 'Telexes?' he asks.

I shrug. 'Boring stuff, except for a couple. No, three. CD enquiry from Hong Kong. Inter-account transfer from Vancouver . . .'

'Out of sterling into yen, I suppose?'

'Yup. I expect they'll be sliding down their gilts positions soon, too. Rationalising.'

He shakes his head. 'No. FT this morning. They're doing a hardwoods deal with Japan. Acting as intermediaries for US sales. Helps them when their softwood market's soft itself. They're just getting ready.'

I'm impressed. Since deregulation, since the time when only this deal matters, this cut, no long-term views from either bankers or customers, it's rarer and rarer to meet a banker who keeps an eye on the industries underlying these money-transactions, tries to understand them well enough to take a long position. Is Steinitz Jewish or Japanese? They still do things like that.

'And the other one?' he asks.

I shrug. 'Not so good. That Venezuelan inactive call account. Instructions to transfer fifteen million dollars.'

I'd chosen the amount deliberately. Fifteen million dollars is the very edge of my personal limit for authorisation (for transfers, that is − it's a lot less for loans). Technically, I can decide on how to handle this without consulting him, but on the edge like this, courtesy demands you cover your back. Fifteen mill also leaves a cool million and change in the account. The kind of figure which reassures people. No need to panic if you've still got a million.

Steinitz makes it easy for me. 'What are you going to do?' he asks.

'Check it, first. Against the files. It's over two years

87

since we last had any instructions from them. Have to make sure the paperwork's in order.'

He nods, satisfied. 'You don't need to do anything till this afternoon, presumably, when their banks open?'

This is it. This is the crucial one. 'Not so easy. The transfer's to a Swiss account. Zurich's open now. Technically I should do it right away.'

'Are you going to?'

Why's the bastard leaving it to me? Go on. Be a boss. Help me out. I wait. But nothing. My left hand's horizontal. I turn it from side to side. In the balance. On the scales. 'Close call,' I tell him. I admit. It's time to make a decision. Go, go, go . . .

'I'm going to check it against the files first. If everything's in order, I'll telex Zurich and tell them to expect a transfer in the course of today. Then I'll telex Venezuela and tell them what I've done and ask them to confirm their instructions immediately at opening of business. That'll still allow me to make the transfer to Zurich before close of business. I don't want to get caught by the bank holiday and have them squealing about four days' differentials.'

Steinitz nods. 'That's what I'd do too. Raise it at Post Meeting today. Send the telex from me if you like. I'll countersign this afternoon if everything's in order. What does it do to our book?'

It's over. I'm in the clear. He's already talking about the consequences. Just as long as no conscientious bastard looks in the front of his *Financial Times* Diary, checks Venezuelan holidays. Answer his question.

'Well, we can cover it, of course. Your policy, to keep the spot positions healthy enough to accommodate a call on one of our inactive accounts. But I'd like to make it up at once. Pull back some of our short positions to call, and cut back our longer term positions pro rata . . .'

He nods again. He's looking like a fluffy dog in the back windscreen of a family man's Metro this morning. Just don't let him be any brighter. 'Any particular positions?'

We both of us smile. The conspirators' smile professional

money market traders give each other. 'I'm inclined to ditch some of our sterling for dollars. I'm not too hot on pounds just now.'

Steinitz looks ruefully down at his gut. The Steinitz diet has been the talk of the bank for months. His wife's told him to get into something resembling a respectable shape before their summer holiday next year, in Israel, 'where men your age have managed to stay in shape. Is it showing me up you're after?' Steinitz tries and tries but none of it seems to shift. He rubs his waistcoat and says, a little sadly, 'Me neither.'

The Post Meeting was a slow chore. I got through it by tuning out, by focusing on the thought of Jill helping one of the clerks dig out the Venezuelan file and checking the details of the telex against it. In an idle daydream it occurred to me that once this was all over, and I was no longer working at BHM, there was nothing, no sense of responsibility, to stop me slipping between those cool thin young buttocks, those lightly freckled legs. (Remember the old crack about minis? They let you get your hand on a girl's thigh without putting it up her skirt.) Nothing to stop me unbuttoning those primary blouses on sun-filled balconies in Miami.

The daydream stopped when I had to brief Cahane on the likely impact of shifting exchange rates on Israeli exports. BHM did a healthy trade in Bills of Exchange, and he was right to let it worry him. Steinitz and I slipped into technicalities for a while.

After the meeting was over, I went through the telex and the Venezuelan file myself, cross-checking, drafted the telexes to Caracas and Zurich and took the whole lot through to Steinitz for checking.

He took his time. He always took his time. He passed the telex to Zurich first. It was, after all, only a statement of intent. I took it out to Jill and told her to transmit (I should have said she worked for both of us). By the time I got back, he'd finished ticking his way through all the technicalities. He was chewing his lower lip. What now, I wondered? I didn't have to wait too long.

'I hate this stuff, you know?' he said.

'What stuff?' I asked politely.

He smiled and said, 'Not very bright I know, in an international banker, but I hate the demand for and provision of, secret banking. I always have done. Telexes, computers, faxes, just make it worse. I like to know my customers. I like to trust them. What is this stuff, do you suppose? Drugs? Probably not, or not so much, in Caracas. Bribes? A military slush-fund? A political cache? Do I really want to be handling this?'

I was practical with the old turd. 'It's money,' I told him. 'That's what we handle. That's why we're a bank.'

He wasn't listening. He was off somewhere. In his childhood maybe. In schule, dreaming of being a rabbi. 'They're Germans, you know.'

It was tough to know how to disagree with him without antagonising him. 'Well, not really. I mean, I know there were a lot of German settlers in the nineteenth century. German mining and railway companies. But they're Venezuelans now . . .'

He cut across me. 'Earlier, too. The Fuggers, the Augsburg bankers to the court of Spain, extracted the rights to the exploitation of Venezuela from the crown in the seventeenth century, as payment, the year no single vessel of the treasure fleet got through. I don't like Germans.'

'We aren't paid to like or dislike people,' I told him. 'We're paid to look after their money.'

I just wanted him to clear the file, but he kept rambling on. I was beginning to sweat. 'What if they're Nazis?' he asked. 'Neo-nazis? Militarists? What if they're going to use this money to slaughter innocent people? I hate this secret banking.'

I'd had enough. I blew my stack. 'Oh bollocks, Saul. Would you have denied German Jews, or Vietnamese Boat People, a safe place to hide their money? Money they could use to get themselves to safety? So what if bastards use it as well? What are a few bastards against giving people a chance to save themselves when the bastards come to power? We can't choose between them. If we do, one day someone else will. Someone who'll choose the Nazis over the Jews. Are those papers all right?'

He snapped back into the later twentieth century. On his way he nearly knocked me flying. 'They're fine. Frankly, I wouldn't really care if they weren't. If they can't trust their names to me, I don't really care if someone rips them off.' Blood pressure explodes, pulse off the wall, lungs sucking, bladder slacking, and me trying to look natural through it all. He went on, thank God, 'But these papers are fine. We probably ought to transfer the money this morning, but put the confirmation request through anyway. It'll give you time to ditch some of that sterling. I'll countersign it when we get the confirmation.'

I walked back to Jill's desk very, very slowly, and asked her to send the telex before lunchtime, so it would go through before the beginning of the Venezualan business day. I'd briefed the Irishman on Venezuelan business hours. I just hoped that he remembered. The last thing I wanted was him replying too early. Any time after two in London would be fine. I had to play it cool, though. I had to let Jill send it.

The Irishman delivered.

Six minutes after the opening of business in Caracas, if Caracas had been opening at all that day, the confirmation came through. Steinitz took it, initialled it, counter-signed the transfer authorisation and slammed shut the file.

I went back through to Jill.

She sent the telex.

Zurich gave us our confirmation.

And it was done.

I did get through the rest of my work, even if I got through it slowly. For the first time in my adult life I clock-watched. Closing down a football match when you're a goal ahead is another matter. So are Friday afternoons at school. Any afternoons. Most mornings.

At the stroke of 5.30 I was gone, with a wave at Jill and a shout of 'I am outta here!'

She surprised me by wishing me a Happy Christmas. We didn't make much of Christmas at BHM. I relaxed at last. I knew we were safe. There'd be no further queries or confirmations in and out of Venezuela now. And I wasn't playing squash.

I'd been telling the Irishman porkies.

It gave me half an hour. It put me half an hour ahead. To get to the flat. To be there waiting. Not for him, but for the print-outs. Or not.

I *was* due at the squash club at seven, for the Christmas party. The print-outs should be through the door by quarter to. If they weren't, I had to think about the panic button. If they were, I just had time to check them and destroy them before leaving for the club. One way or another I'd know.

6.32 they came through the door.

He must have motored.

A man after my own heart, as such.

They made a proper little thud. They were a proper little stack. I'd forgotten about the scale and wastefulness of printouts. Well, what's a few trees?

All the quarter hourly check times were there, from 8.30 Wednesday evening, to 6 o'clock on this one. A long, long list of four figure twenty-four hour clock entries, interrupted by only eight continuous pieces of text. Eight telexes. The first one to his own bank Javert, Valjean. The one he'd done in front of me. Then the first Venezuelan telex. Then the telex to Bank Marius Mayer with instructions for the transfer of his 10 per cent. Then the confirmation telex to his own bank to expect the money. Then their reply. The BHM's request for confirmation. Then the confirmation. And, finally, his own bank's confirmation of receipt of all moneys, as instructed: 16.49, Zurich time.

I'd thought about burning the papers of course. I'd

thought about acid. I'd finally decided those were all too obvious. There was a garbage pick-up Mondays. I tore the print-outs by hand and dropped them into one of the big black plastic pickup bags, along with eggshells, empty cans, rancid butter, the hard heels of old loaves, rotting vegetables, and newsprint.

Let the state destroy the evidence. Ash in a grate, or garden, or oven could be read. So could acid-attacked paper. But who could trace the contents of a single bag back to a single flat from all the filth in Fulham?

Let the Council do it.

Why else did I pay my rates?

I changed my clothes and ran.

Did I feel like fifteen million dollars?

I don't know, to tell the truth. I still don't. What does fifteen million dollars feel like?

I only know I got pissed and pulled a tottie. I only know I got gobbled in a car-park.

And then it really started.

CHAPTER SEVEN

Christmas was quiet. I wasn't in any condition for excitement. I hate Bank Holiday weekends anyway. What's the point of time off if everyone else has got it too? I went to see the family on Christmas morning, up Highbury way. Well, the old woman likes it, and it would have looked a bit odd if I was the only bro who didn't make it. And I couldn't really be certain when I'd be seeing her again.

It was the usual family affair. Teenagers slouching around thinking all the grown-ups are plonkers. Lyn — she's Ted's wife, he's my oldest brother — getting pissed and trying to get off with anything in trousers. The old woman finally had to root her out the bathroom where she was feeling up a fourteen year old cousin. Lucky little sod. If she wasn't family I'd have slipped her a length years ago. No use as a wife, but she looks like she fucks a storm. Ange, my kid sister, was in a bit of a state. Her divorce was going through. It should never have happened. Us boys all warned her off when she got engaged that her Eric was a no-good. A right barrel, that one. Do anything for his mates. Do anything for a laugh. Did bugger all for his wife and kids. Even so, it shouldn't have got to a divorce. We could've sorted him out if she'd given us the word. People usually start behaving once the Ford brothers have taken them down an underground car-park and reasoned the whole thing out with them with cricket bats. That gets them on the straight and narrow sharpish. But she wouldn't hear of it. Said she loved him. Said she wouldn't hurt him for the world. What bloody good did that do her? Bit of pain helps some people see things that much clearer. What's love got to do with it, anyway? Love comes second. Third. After family. After money.

I worked through the weekend. That was good for me. Kept me calm. I was feeling pretty cool by the time I got back to work on Monday, as part of the holiday skeleton staff. I'd got it all worked out, see? What I'd kept in mind through all the planning of this blag was statement dates.

We were due to issue the six-monthly statement on the Venezuelan account on the last day of December. That statement could lead to one of a number of things. It was possible nothing might happen. It might be the account was really inactive – the beneficial owner dead, bunked off, or jacked it in, or nicked. If anything was going to happen it was going to happen soon after the statement was issued. If I got a good clear month without a whimper I was in clover. I could forget about the account holder. I could, without it looking at all odd, after three years in the job, give three months' notice, serve out my time and be off. I'd made a few plans over identity arrangements as it was. I wasn't sure I'd want to go on being me.

Alternatively, of course, the statement might set the cat amongst the pigeons. That was more likely, after all. Bring the Venezuelans down on our heads like thunder. There'd be uproar, investigations, the works, but I was pretty confident. I reckoned I was in the clear. The Irishman was good, and even if the investigation found the money-trail, the cash itself would be long gone. In fact, the cash itself would be gone this afternoon.

I'd set that up from the beginning, with the Panamanians. The trick was bearer bonds.

I've told you about bearer securities: whoever holds it, owns it. A villains' charter, of course. They really grew up out of something called the Euromarket. It started with dollars. Trading currency, the US dollar, which means there's a lot of it in banks outside the USA, not subject to US regulations. Not subject to any regulations really – sort of a multinational amongst currencies. And there are other currencies held like that too, outside their own jurisdictions, though in smaller quantities: deutschmarks, sterling, yen. Years ago, companies wanting to raise money started borrowing on those markets by issuing bearer bonds. An American company, say, would issue ten million dollars worth of bonds denominated in units of 10,000 bucks apiece, outside the USA. No US taxes to worry about. Mop up some of that pool of dollars outside the US, often at a lower rate of interest than they'd have had to pay out at home. No one was paying taxes on the money after all. They got the money gross. Obviously the banks and big investment institutions all piled into the market. So did everyone who had a cache of money they didn't reveal to the authorities. Soon every businessman in Milan, every dentist in Frankfurt, was salting some of his savings away in Eurobonds.

You can hang on to the bonds yourself. Sell a few when you need some cash, or take them into any bank in the world and use them as security. In the main, it's the best and biggest companies that issue Eurobonds. There are some exceptions, but it takes a bit of puff, a bit of financial sophistication to be in the Euromarkets. They're mostly pretty safe, and no one can trace them back to you. There's no register of owners.

You don't even have to hold them yourself. Lots of people don't. You can have them held in the central depository of AIBD, the Association of International Bond Dealers, in Luxembourg, either in your own name or a bank nominee's. AIBD hold the bonds, clip the coupons, and send the payments to your specified bank. And, so long as the paperwork is right, you can always go pick them up yourself from Luxembourg.

I'd made arrangements that, as soon as Panama opened this afternoon London Time, Banco Privado were to put twelve and a half of my thirteen and a half million into AAA, top-rated, recently-issued Eurobonds. I wanted recently-issued ones because the Euromarkets are now the biggest capital markets in the world − they beat the New

York, Tokyo and London Stock Exchanges to shit as a place for big companies to raise money cheap (after all, what they're getting is bondholders not shareholders; not people who are going to piss around with the way you want to run your company) and sometimes it gets a bit musclebound. It's a bit difficult to make a market, unload your bonds in a hurry. That doesn't happen with good, recent issues.

I'd told Privado to hold the bonds as my nominees at AIBD in Luxembourg, with the same identification codes as my account. The great thing about that was, if ever the investigation got too close, even if it got to Panama, even if for the first time in their history the Panamanian authorities agreed to freeze an account while inquiries continued, it needn't bother me. I'd only have a million in the account. I could just go down to Luxembourg, while on a long weekend break in Brussels say, and pick up my bond certificates. Dispose of them as and when I wanted. Perfect cover.

And I was in no rush. If the statement did lead to the Venezuelans going into uproar, and I guessed it would, what could happen? At worst, after the investigation, BHM could sack Steinitz, me, a few others as an example, as scapegoats. I should worry. Or they might just try to limp along, accepting no culpability, damaged by the scandal. It wouldn't be surprising if, a month or two after that, I decided my career prospects weren't advanced by being with a bank that made such fuck-ups and put my notice in, decided to move on. And one of the good things about being a banker, since deregulation, is that no one could really be surprised if you decided your best career prospects were abroad. You go where the heat is, these days.

So I was feeling pretty bloody smart that Monday with the skeleton staff. Jack the Lad. Cock of the Walk. Here's Mister Know-It-All.

I wish I had. I hadn't expected what did happen. No one could have. After all, as far as I was concerned, the Venezuelans knew bugger all about what had happened, had no reason to be suspicious, and wouldn't until statement date. So how could I expect a telex that afternoon asking for immediate notification of the status of the account?

I had to act as surprised as everyone else, of course, after Thursday's explicit instructions, but my guts were throwing wobblers. I was the one who drafted the telex back to Caracas. We got an answer twenty minutes later:

SUSPEND ALL OPERATIONS THIS A/C. NO REPEAT NO INSTRUCTIONS ISSUED BY US DEC 24. DEC 24 HOLIDAY VENEZUELA. CONFIRM IMMEDIATE RESTITUTION ALL FUNDS.

I'll hand it to Saul. He didn't panic. He told me to notify Bank Marius Mayer in Zurich of a problem with the transaction and telexed Caracas himself, informing them he couldn't reverse the transaction. Holiday or no, and checking that himself he saw it was ambiguous, all the paperwork had been valid and confirmed. He suggested they get in touch with Zurich and Panama direct. He was guessing I suppose that those accounts were run by the beneficial owners of the Venezuelan account, that they'd have the codes to get account information from the Swiss and Panamanian bank. As we did not. We hadn't needed and hadn't been given the authorisation code for the account in Zurich, because someone had already telexed Bank Marius Mayer with coded clearance to accept the money. I could see Steinitz wondering who the hell it could have been. Maybe the Venezuelans were trying to screw themselves to claim the insurance.

Myself, I did a pretty good job at playing the anxious, concerned, supportive Number Two and Jill went clucking around demented as though it was somehow her fault. And I was anxious, I suppose. I hadn't expected it all to blow up so soon. I kept telling myself the plan still held, that everything was under control. I did expect the next telex, telling us the account holders were flying their people in.

We were to expect them the following morning. What I hadn't expected was what they would look like.

They were Arabs.

Three of them. Couple of young guys. Twenties. Bum-fluff on the chin. And an older guy. Late thirties, maybe. Smaller he was. Big shoulders, chest musculature. A full beard. Swarthy. Looked as though he could have had a spell of smallpox when he was a kid. And one other thing. One thing so odd, that it really did lift the hairs on the back of my neck. He had one blue eye.

They didn't look the kind of people who could have the control of sixteen million dollars, but all the documentation they brought with them — Steinitz made me check it — cleared them, corroborated it. They looked too poor. They were wearing battered baggy old brown suits. Nylon shirts. No ties. Sandals. And those gingham Arab head-dresses. The Arafat look. Even Steinitz, who had an endless courtesy with customers, one of the things I admired about him, let a swift flicker of contempt pass through his eyes when I showed them into his office. The only smart thing about them was the brand new briefcases they were carrying.

I should have thought about the briefcases. They should have tipped me off. Where had they picked them up? In London, presumably. Why?

I spent the best part of the next hour ferrying the files in and out of Saul's office, Jill unable to keep her eyes off the door. He was being patient with them, insisting that holiday or no BHM had done nothing wrong, that it had followed explicit and authoritative instructions. But they weren't buying it. Voices were raised. Angry exchanges. It sounded pretty bloody. I wasn't even in there, and I could feel my chest tightening, but when it happened, it seemed to come without any warning at all.

Suddenly, an angry voice shouting, 'You did this. You are responsible. You are behind it. This is fraud. This is criminal. You did it. Jew.'

The red light on my desk lit up. Saul had hit the button

under his desk. He had had enough. He wanted them out. I started to get up and saw Jill doing so, too. The door was ajar. I could hear Saul saying, his voice steady but in what I knew to be rage, 'I suggest you take it up with a lawyer. I will accept any legitimate external investigation, but I did not become a banker to be insulted by . . .'

There was a shout, in some language I didn't understand, some final snapping of patience, and a blow, Saul gasping, and then a noise, a noise so loud it felt more like being hit than anything that came through the ears, and a horrible, horrible, long, choking, strangled cry, and the noise again, the noises. Again and again. And I realised it was gunfire, saw Jill, insanely, running towards Saul's door, and threw myself at her, dragging her down, covering her, as the three of them came out, swinging squat, ugly, black metal boxy objects, throwing their briefcases at people's heads to force them down. One of the young ones swung on us and pulled on his box. There was a spit of flame, the stench of cordite, the tops of two desks flying everywhere, splinters ripped out of their surfaces. Someone was screaming, face lacerated by flying fragments. The other young one turned, squeezed his trigger, spraying bursts of three, shredding partitions, ripping bits of masonry out of walls. The sprinkler system went haywire, sluicing water everywhere, into the smoke and the paper and dust. It all rolled together, the noise, the smell, the sudden damp, the rage, the urinous tang of fear, Jill sobbing beneath me, the echo of that long hopeless cry. And then they were gone.

I stood up blindly, stunned, on automatic pilot, wondering what the fuck had happened, how we'd found ourselves inside some war, and picked up a phone. No good. Smashed about by shotgun pellets. Another. Then another. And finally a dialling tone. I hacked out four 9s. An outside line, and the emergency services. I asked for an ambulance, and then the police.

I stumbled over to Saul's office. Jill had got there before me. She had curled up in the corner by the door, cradling her head in her arms and wailing softly, her chest heaving and rising, her mascara streaky on her face, tears and snot mingled and shiny on her cheeks and upper lip.

The desk had been all but blown apart by a shotgun blast. All the glass had shattered, crackling and bright underfoot like morning snow. The papers had gone everywhere. So had the blood. Streaks of it, and thicker jets, on the walls, the floor, the woodwork. Saul's chair had tipped back with him still in it, smashing his head against the wall. Half his jaw had gone, broken teeth white in all that red. There was a gaping hole in his chest: a mess of bone, blood, tissue and clothing. But what I mainly remember is his eyes. One of them was closed, contused, swelling, already yellow and purple, like a boxer a couple of days after the fight. The other one was still half open, rolled up under the lid. All I could see was an almond of dirty yellow, already and forever glazed.

I do my damnedest not to remember the rest of that day too clearly, but it keeps on coming back. Everyone got in on the act, especially once I explained why the Arabs had come in: the City Police, the Serious Crimes Squad, the Fraud Squad, even the Sweeney. They held us at Cannon Street nick, questioning us there in underground rooms yellow under fluorescent lights and naked bulbs. It seemed to go on forever. It seemed the longest day of my life. It was early evening before they'd had enough, for now. They weren't going to hold any of us. They weren't really interested in the possible fraud. It was the Arabs they were after. But even after they let the others go, warning them they'd be questioned again, they hadn't quite done with me. There were a couple of other people who wanted to see me.

They weren't British. They weren't fuzz. If I'd been more in control of myself I'd have told them to naff off. Not that they would have listened.

He started it off. Tall, wiry, handsome bloke, in his fifties. Looked uncomfortable in a suit. I found out why soon enough. 'You're in trouble, Mr Ford.'

I picked up the accent. Un-English. Un-German. Hebrew. What were the Israelis doing getting involved in this? I didn't ask the question. I was too busy looking at her.

I should have felt guilty I suppose. Saul dead, blown away, because of me. I should have had my tail between my legs, but looking at her I didn't. Somehow Saul's death made the feeling even stronger. If I could have had my way I would have reached out then and there and spread her across the table and, without waiting to find out if she was ready for it or not, just put it in. Just put it in and spilled the whole day out of me, into her, into one long come, into oblivion.

She was lovely. Medium height and dark complexion, glossy black hair, those big, long-lashed brown eyes that throw your desire, your hunger, back in your face, and the kind of figure men kill for. That wasn't it, though, really. That wasn't all of it. It was the way she stood completely still, perfectly poised, just watching me, giving nothing away. No pity, no amusement, no contempt. Nothing. Total self-sufficiency. Absolute self-containment. She was, I swear, the most beautiful thing I had ever seen. And that wasn't the tiredness, the exhaustion, the fear or the anxiety talking. It was real. In the middle of all the waste, the death, the drudgery, the godforsaken greyness, she shone.

The geezer kept talking. 'You don't have to talk to us, Mr Ford, but I think you ought to.'

I looked at him, dully. 'Who are you?'

He sat down, lit himself a cigarette, offered me one, shrugged, and almost whispered, 'Mossad.'

I went straight over to the door of the holding cell and started hitting it. Trying to beat the shit out of it. Trying to beat me out through it. The pair of them just let me get on with it, just watched me do it. It felt like they were laughing at me behind my back. I started kicking the door as well. Eventually, someone strolled up to the other side of the door and pulled the hatch. Not a woodentop. Not uniformed branch. A DS by the looks of it, Detective

102

Sergeant. Looked like a soul boy with a spot and weight problem. He was chewing gum. These past few weeks I'd been surrounded by people chewing gum. Got right up my nose, if you take my meaning.

He had a way with words. 'Yeah?' he said.

'Get me out of here,' I told him. 'I don't have to take this . . .'

'Yeah,' he said again. 'You do. Get back in there sunshine, do the business. You're not walking till we're ready.'

I didn't understand it. I didn't know how we'd got to this. I would have to find out. But for now I could only surrender. I knew better than to go on banging on that door. I knew better than to ask to see my brief.

I didn't breathe, for a bit. I felt my heart sighing. I suddenly realised just how tired I was. I'd very nearly had enough. The last thing I needed right now was Israeli Military Intelligence. 'What do you want?' I must have sounded hopeless.

He was surprisingly sympathetic, gentle, for a soldier. 'Tell us what happened.'

'I've told the police, over and over . . .'

'I know. I've seen your statement. I'm not supposed to have. We have no legal status here, except as friends and allies. But tell me, please, face to face. There may be something, some detail, we can understand, we alone can make sense of.'

I sat down in front of him, hands on my knees, and tried to look him in the eyes. I couldn't quite make it. 'This is a freakshow,' I told him.

He nodded, just the once, as though he was too tired or shagged about to manage more.

It was time to be reasonable. 'Look,' I told him, 'I don't know what's going on. I don't know how I got into this. I certainly don't know what you're doing mixed up in it. I don't know what Israeli Intelligence is doing operating in a London Police Station, and I don't know why our boys in blue are playing along. I think I better know. I think someone better tell me.'

She told me, the short form. 'There's been a fuck up,' she said.

I didn't look at her. I looked at him. At last he unwound a little more and told me as much as he was prepared to say, for now.

'We warned them,' he said, 'your authorities. We warned them we'd monitored terrorist movement in and out of London, that we'd noticed an increase in activity. Not the official people, the ones at the safe house. The unofficials. Our enemies. We warned your people to expect something, to increase surveillance, and they ignored us. Now this.'

He shrugged, and I thought I caught the edge of a strange shrewd smile. 'The strange thing is, this wasn't one of the groups we'd been monitoring. This lot are new arrivals. That doesn't matter. Your people look foolish. They have been foolish. We have offered to help them stop looking foolish. Which is why we have a free hand. There are things we can do they cannot. There are laws we can ignore which they can only flout with difficulty, because we are deniable . . .'

She interrupted him. She scared me all over again. She said, 'Which is the best news you've ever had.'

So I told them, all the events of the morning. It was becoming a routine, a performance, a number. It was ceasing to be real. Only one thing kept nagging at me, one thing I didn't understand. 'When we heard the first shot, everyone froze, except for Jill. She moved. She headed for Saul's office door. She headed into danger. I stopped her. I had to. Damnedest thing I ever saw.'

The woman spoke again. She had one of those low, warm, brown voices — voices like the sound of satin being slipped from skin. 'Not really,' she said. 'She loved him.'

Now she was talking out of her arse. I let her know it. Disbelief, almost laughter. 'Jill? Saul?'

She cut me off with a sort of sad smile, her eyes a little cloudy saying, 'They'd been lovers for years.'

Well, what do you know?

Less than I thought, apparently. 'I still don't get it,' I

told them. 'I still don't see how you lot are involved . . .'

He was cautious. 'We have enemies, Mr Ford, and they have money, a lot of it, which means they have to keep it in strange places. We like to know where it is. Saul was one of us, Mr Ford, and he was watching that Venezuelan account. Our first sign of trouble was when he notified us of a transfer. We thought it was for real. We came in to see if we could work out what they were planning. We didn't have it marked down as a theft, so we weren't expecting their reaction. And nor, I think, were they.'

The woman took over. I was glad. It gave me an excuse to stare at her. 'That puts you in danger, Mr Ford. They over-reacted. They killed the one man who they thought knew where their money had gone. If they want it back – and you saw how much they wanted it back – then they'll come after you next, as his assistant. As someone who might know.'

She looked at the man. I got the impression they might almost have rehearsed this. It was his turn. 'If I were you,' he said, 'I would be worried. You could ask for police protection of course, but they're not experts at it, and the anti-terrorism squad is overstretched as it is. If I were you I'd be looking for help. We can offer it to you. I've discussed it with the local authorities and, in the circumstances, they're willing to turn a blind eye to our involvement. At the very least I think you should accept our offer to have Major Stern here babysit you.'

He glanced at her, and she shot me one dazzling smile, like heartbreak, saying, 'Rachel.'

I won't say I wasn't tempted. I was. Those Arabs were still out there. I was mixed up, a little crazy, lonely, confused, and I could have done a great deal more than babysit with her, but there were too many loose ends left by the day's events. I hadn't expected things to move so fast, so far. I wanted to check the castle walls, the network. I wanted to know the money-chain was safe, secure. I couldn't help believing I would be all right as long as the money was. The money was what everyone was after. Except for Mossad. And the Arabs couldn't afford to kill me. I might be the last point of access to their dollars. I had to have time. Time to myself. Even so, I asked the nagging question.

'Two things,' I said, trying to sound tougher than I felt. 'Just two things. Who the fuck were those guys? And who the fuck are you?'

His eyes were sad. Pale brown with little gold and green lights in them. Pale eyes in the dark, death mask of a face. But he had that shrewd look on again, that almost-smile. 'I, Mr Ford? I am Colonel Effrem Rabin of Mossad. And they are the PLO.'

I told them they had to let me sleep on it. They weren't too enthusiastic about it. I wasn't wild myself, but I needed the time. They could get me at the office or Cannon Street nick first thing the following morning. Cahane and I had to start getting things back into shape.

I didn't go back to the flat. I knew better than that, though that caused a few problems in itself. I never got round to calling my answering machine, so it was a bit of while before I discovered the worried messages from O'Malley, and from my brother Frank on behalf of the family, wondering what the hell had been going on.

I checked into the Savoy Hotel, mainly because I knew where its pay-phones were. It was time for a few free long-distance calls.

Zurich was closed by the time the police let me go, and it took me a bit of time to get myself sorted out, checked in, and through to Panama. All I wanted to know was that the money had got through, the Eurobonds been bought. Using a phone-line wasn't that safe, but the call couldn't be traced to me and I could identify myself to Banco Privado. I knew all the names, the account numbers, the codes.

It must have been about nine o'clock. I was just standing

there, thinking, at the call box half way down the stairs to the main restaurant. I'd hung up on Panama a good ten minutes before and I felt like death.

They hadn't got the money. So of course they hadn't bought the bonds.

How could they have? They were glad I called. They were a bit annoyed about the late change in procedure. The telex to Switzerland on Thursday, quoting all the Zurich numbers, all the Zurich codes, changing the payment instructions. No, of course they couldn't give me the details of the new instructions, not unless I gave them the new code I'd telexed to them. I could sense the sudden panic, the uncertainty as to whether I was the real account holder.

I hung up on them.

It had been the one loophole. To be absolutely safe, I'd have needed to invalidate all instructions on the Zurich account which didn't arise from Panama. But I couldn't have done that or there would have been no way Zurich could accept the initial deposit. Not without telling at least one other person what the Panama code was. Zurich had had to be independently operable.

The print-outs, I kept thinking. The hard copy. Then I realised. It had to be a fake set of print-outs. I'd have spotted it at once, if I hadn't been so jubilant. The telexes to his bank in Switzerland. The print-outs didn't make any sense. According to the print-outs the telexes to his bank had gone from the fake Caracas number. But they couldn't have. There was no trace of his having reprogrammed his own bank's telex. They'd have had no way of replying. And yet there had been replies. The print-outs bore virtually no relation to what had really been going on that night in the Barbican.

I felt like death, and someone stuck the muzzle of a ·44 Magnum in my temple.

It was her. Rachel. She had to say it twice before I took it in. 'If I can do it, so can they. I think you need that babysitter, Mr Ford.'

That was just about my limit. That was just about my crow.

I had the PLO out looking for me.

I had Israeli military intelligence door-stepping me.

I'd killed my boss.

I had a death threat poking in my ear.

And that bastard Irishman had stolen all my money.

Part Two:

The Middle

CHAPTER ONE

I knew exactly how bad I felt just a few minutes later, up in her room. That explained a lot, too. Her room. Explained what she was doing wandering around the Savoy past midnight without so much as a by your leave. She was legitimate. A guest. Not that that means too much. I'd flogged in there often enough in the early hours to use the phone and got away with it. You can get away with almost anything almost anywhere so long as you've got the brass for it. All it takes is bottle. That and the speed to duck. My brother Stan worked that one out years ago, pulling birds. Just go up to them he would, in the pub, on the bus, in the old sharp whistle and cheeky grin and say, 'How about a fuck, then, darlin'?' Got away with it too, God knows how many times. A lot of them would laugh at first, but get them laughing and you're half way in. 'After all,' he used to say, 'what can they do to you if you ask? Say no? Laugh? Belt you one?' They could belt you one, which is why you have to have the speed to duck. Don't want to hurt that pretty profile. And always keep your crutch out of kicking distance. Not a bad way to live a life.

And what I'd not been doing. But the reason I knew just how bad I felt was that I was lying on her bed watching her move about the room in those tight clothes of hers (I'm telling you — like ferrets in a sack) and I knew as certainly as anything that I didn't have the energy or guts to try it on. I ask you, was it fair? Locked away in a double room in the Savoy with a beautiful woman and I was about as much use to her or anyone as a kaleidoscope to a blind man.

Not that she was even thinking about it. She was Little Miss Efficiency and, like most efficient organised people, she could only tell me what I knew already.

'You're in a world of shit,' she said.

I had to tell her. 'You have a talent for the obvious.'

She shot me the kind of glance they use to stun cows with before they hook them up by the feet in the abattoir (I've always wondered about that: Do calves have calves?) and said, 'I'm not the only one.'

Now what did she mean by that, I wondered? I'd been counting on everyone downgrading the money, what with the killing, the shooting, the goons in dishcloths. Could she be thinking of it now? There didn't seem much point in worrying about it. I had enough on my plate. I let this one slide. She had other things on her mind in any case.

'Has it got through to you yet?' she asked.

'Has what got through?'

'The fact that you're in a world of shit.'

I thought it over and admitted, 'It doesn't smell too good.'

She nodded, in what looked like relief. I liked that. It might not have been me she had been worrying about, but I could pretend it was. It had been a long time since anyone worried about me. There have to be Australian Fords somewhere on the other side of the world (it's not as though we haven't produced our fair share of villains, clanking down to Brisbane in their chains) gritting their teeth in the midst of a sandstorm, bobbing their corks and telling the world, 'No worries.'

She sat down on the bed beside me and slapped my thigh. I wasn't so keen on that. Bit too old chums together for my taste. Then she said, 'They're going to come after you. They have to. Where else do they have to go? Who else can help them find out where their money went?'

There was an easy answer to that. 'The Chairman,' I told her.

It seemed they had considered that already. She shook

112

her head and said quietly, 'No. I don't think so. If they can't find it, they might try to kill him, just for good measure, but they aren't fools. They've already made it pretty plain they know they have to deal at operational level.'

If she was trying to get the wind up me she was doing pretty well. 'So what am I supposed to do about it?' I asked her, showing a fair degree of hump. 'Just sit around waiting for them? What are they going to do? Liberate my Left Bank? I like my Left Bank. I like all of me. I want all of me left alone. I'm a one man independence movement. A separatist for me.' I took a rest after that. I never was much of a one for eloquence.

For a second, I almost thought she smiled. Not a nice smile. Not for me, at least. The kind of smile you might flash a kid still kicking up a fuss about going up to bed long after it was tired. Then she said, 'You don't have any choice. They're coming whatever you do. Your best bet is to have us around to help you. We know them. We know the way they work.'

I couldn't help myself. I slipped on my South Afrikan, Afrikaaner redneck accent and let her have it. 'Yew European liberals make me sick. Yew don't understand them like we dew. They're our keffers. All of us grew up with these blecks . . .'

She stopped smiling. She looked me in the eyes and asked, 'Have you ever killed a man?' I didn't move. She went on: 'Do you have any idea of how to deal with a man who's snapping the safety off an M-16 while another man has a garotting loop round your neck and your head's spinning and your eyes are watering because they came in behind a CS grenade? Do you know how to do that? Do you?' I shook my head. She nodded hers. 'I thought not. That's what I meant. It doesn't matter what you think of us. Of Jews, of Israel, of the Palestinians. It doesn't matter and I don't care. What matters – what matters to you is, How do you stay alive? How do you get out of this still able to walk around and hold a conversation? How do you do that

113

without us? Well, I can tell you that. You can't. We're the only hope you've got.'

I felt shagged all over again. Not mad anymore, not really. Oh sure, if I could have got my hands on that Irish bastard right then and there I'd have had his lights and liver. Not even really embarrassed. I'd felt a bit of that, down by the 'phone. You know, the kind of embarrassment you only get when someone pulls the rug just as you're in the middle of doing something smart. All that pride, all that pleasure, blows up in your face. The real red face, wet-eyes number. The perfect slicing pass off the edge of your boot curling out across the pitch to your wing-defender and that quick skinny little forward just gets up in its flight path and heads into an open goal, the very second you and your lads have started the run up into midfield. The sweet little punt into softening bonds with a fattening spread before any of the market notices, and suddenly the price tumbles and you're looking at a capital loss instead of an income gain, and you know you've been stitched up by the only other player in the market who set the whole thing up to limit his over-exposure. You've been giving it to her for ninety minutes strong, one hand wriggling her boobies and another finger up her arse, and you're both hot and wet and about ready to tip over and she whispers, 'Do you think you could move it around as well as in and out?' The time you get away with a fistful of millions and some little shithead gets them off you . . .

No, even those embarrassments were easing and over. I just felt wiped out, wiped over, felt wasted. I just wanted to lie down right where I was and go to sleep and never get up. I wanted the whole bloody thing to be over.

But she, she just looked down on me with those big brown eyes of hers and murmured, 'Well?'

Well. Well. Well, what was I to do? What choices did I have? Either I could roll over, or I could roll over and play dead. And if I did that, she was right, I'd be dead for real soon enough. Go with the flow, I said to myself. Just go with it. Just roll.

'So what do you want me to do?' I asked her.

She smiled one of those insufferable little smiles women have. One of the ones that says, 'I told you that'd happen if you didn't wear a raincoat/get it serviced/eat your spinach . . .' One of those smug, bitch, glances. Then she said, 'That's better. I'll telephone Effrem.'

He arrived about thirty minutes later. The desk rang up first. It didn't sound as though they liked it, visitors in the early hours. And even when he got up to the door they had this funny pattern of intricate knocks worked out they had to go through before she'd open up for him.

I didn't wait for him to start. I didn't want a lecture. Instead I asked, 'OK, so what is it I have to do?'

He sat down. She didn't. I noticed that. Did she take nothing easy? Probably not. Rabin himself looked as tired as I felt. I wondered what he'd been doing, working on, this late. Tracking the Palestinians? But how? He pushed the thought aside with a voice as low and gentle as sleep itself, sitting in a chair in the Savoy Hotel, his elbows on his knees, his hands together and his head bowed low, not looking at me. He might have been praying, but what would he have been praying for? My life? His? Theirs?

The way he started wasn't exactly reassuring. 'There are some things you'd be a great deal better off not knowing, but we don't have time for that. Not now. Not any more. So you just listen and remember everything I tell you, till all this is over, and then forget it all.'

I never would forget it. You can tell. In the end, I'm glad. I wake up sweating some nights about having been told too much about people who will kill to keep their secrets. I'm not going to tell you all of it. I am going to tell you enough so that they'll know, if anything happens to me, I remember it all, and there are other ways besides a book like this of leaking it. They wouldn't like that, so they might behave.

He started ticking points off his fingers. 'We have thought for a long time this was a PLO account. That doesn't tell

115

us much, though. The PLO is a holding company for eight constituent organisations. Arafat's the chairman because he leads the largest single member group Al Fatah, but he doesn't have majority power or anything close to it. Which is why the others keep trying to kill him. Only Hussein of Jordan has a harder time. The other reason he has a hard time is the money. The PLO, the holding company, invests the money. About four billion dollars of it.'

That did surprise me. It must have showed, because he went on to detail where it came from, and how Mossad knew. I'm not telling you that. I'm not telling anyone that. Not yet.

What you need to know are the broad outlines: the collection of Arab conscience money from everyone from the Libyans to the Saudis; and the investment of it, in Australian sheep farms, Brazilian coffee plantations, the Eurobond market, you name it. Those bastards are rich.

Rabin went on. 'Conservatively invested that four billion must bring them forty to sixty million a year. That's a lot of arms, Mr Ford. That's why we want to know all we can about the money. Forty to sixty million scattered round numbered and nominee accounts around the world. If we can break out the details of some of those accounts, we can get some action, the way the Americans are now with drug profits. The banking system is designed to hide money, you know that, but with enough political will, and enough evidence, we might be able to freeze their money, some of it at least. We could begin to starve them out into submission. So the first thing we have to do is prove this was Palestinian money. That it was Palestinians who did this. We have to remind the world who the bad guys are, but we have to find them first. But there's something else.'

I'd been afraid there would be. I did as I was meant to. I asked him what it was.

He explained. 'The PLO's a holding company. Some of the money it invests directly, but much it invests for its member organisations. They insist on a measure of independence, so they need their own money. They'll tell you it's for their welfare systems – hospitals, schools, camps. But most of it's for guerilla training. Most of it's for killing Jews.

'This account had been inert for a long time, which means that it was being kept for something. Something special. Something big. Now suddenly they want it. Whatever they were planning is afoot. We need to know what it is. That involves knowing who it is. Who are they? PFLP? Marxist PFLP? Black September? We need to know. Which means again, we need to find them. Then, when we've found them, found out who they are, found out what they're doing, we can make you safe. We can kill them.'

'No,' I told him, 'not for me. You wouldn't do that for my sake. You'd do it because of what they did to a Jew.'

I suppose I was trying to shake him up, make him angry. I suppose I've always been uneasy round the headmaster type and always felt a need to rattle them. It's one of the reasons I've always liked and respected O'Malley, I think. He's the same type – at least he can go *mano a mano* with them every inch of the way – but it doesn't show. Whatever I was trying to do, it didn't work. He just turned away from me again and said, 'What would you have us do? Avenge everyone? We have our hands full, and our hands tied. We can't make up for every ugly, squalid, stupid, little killing, and you wouldn't want us to. But you should be grateful for what we can and will do, because until they're dead you have a death sentence suspended over you. We're going to save your bacon, Mr Ford.'

It was the *bacon* that did it, that kicked the heart out of me. I knew what he was telling me. I wasn't kosher. I was unclean.

I finally got round to asking the big question. 'So what exactly is it you want me to do?'

He looked at Rachel and she answered for them both.

'They may be crazed,' she said softly, 'but they certainly

aren't stupid. They know that if anyone can find an answer to the mess their money's in, it's going to be an operational banker, and that only leaves you. They have to come to you. We can watch you, and when they come we can find out who they are, but that probably isn't enough, for you at least. We already know they're trigger-happy. We have to find a way of keeping you alive through all of this. The easy way is by making them think you might give them what they want. And what they want is their money. So the more actively you're seen to be pursuing those funds, the more chance you have of staying alive and the longer they'll be out in the open. It works for both of us. All we want you to do while we cover your back is to turn detective. You can do that, can't you?'

There was an unspoken 'even' in there somewhere. 'Even you.' It set my teeth on edge.

There wasn't much I could say against it though. What other offers did I have? And besides, I had to turn detective whatever happened. I had to find that filthy, stinking, paddy bastard and all my lovely money. I also had to find some way of doing it that didn't make it too obvious I must have nicked it in the first place. I won't say I wasn't scared. I was. If this had been a building site I would have been shitting bricks. But I had to trust their muscle. They were the only strong-arm team around and I knew after what had happened in the office I needed any army I could find. No, what worried me more right then was tracing the money and covering my back on the banking side. I could only see one way out of the hole. Only one man who could help me. I did my best to put on an honest, exhausted face. I hadn't had a lot of practice, but it seemed to satisfy them for now. They didn't raise a squawk as I told them, 'I can't do it alone. No one could. All right, I'll believe you'll do what you can to keep me alive, but this whole transfer business is a bitch. Getting information out of the Swiss is like pulling teeth . . .'

Rachel gave a sick smug little smile at that and said, 'I've had to pull a fair number of teeth in my time.'

It turned my stomach. 'It isn't the same,' I told her. 'Working over frightened little suspects in a darkened room is a whole lot different from scaring information out of bankers. Do you think I don't know that? What do you take me for? Some pisspot from a public school? We have pigs too. Pigs like you. Proper pigs. Pigs that stitch up verbals, send people away because it's just their turn, pigs who can't seem to help making suspects clumsy, so they keep walking into doors and tripping down stairs. And what good does it do them when they shift them to the fraud squad? When they have to take on people who live in suits and do their business with a terminal instead of a sawn-off or a two-by-four? I'll tell you what good it does them. The square root of fuck-all. It's the same for you with this. You can pimp and pose and posture all you want, but there isn't anything you can do to help on this one. I need someone else. I need a banker.'

'There are bankers at BHM,' Rabin interrupted.

He got a snort for that one. 'Not any more there aren't. The only other one they had is dead. What they've got left are filing clerks, pen pushers and salesmen. And I told you, I have to have a banker.'

They seemed to surrender at that. 'Who do you want?' Rabin asked.

One guess, right? You've got it. 'I want Myles O'Malley of IIIB.'

'Why him?' Rachel asked. A suspicious bitch that one, right enough.

'Because I trust him. What other fucking reason would I have? Do you think I trust you? Really? Do you think I trust anyone while a bunch of dinges in teatowels are running round trying to blow me away and while someone bloody clever walked right through all our systems and stitched up millions?'

That interested Rabin. 'Was it clever?' he asked.

What was it that prompted my reply? I don't know. Vanity? Acting the outraged, ripped-off banker? Trying to defend the systems of my institution, the oldest response

119

of bankers since the dawn of time? Who can say? But I guess that most of it was vanity. I wanted them to know how smart I'd been, even if I didn't want them to know it was me who had been smart.

'Clever?' I exploded. 'It was brilliant!'

Rabin nodded. 'That was what I thought. It would be interesting to know who did it. Someone on the inside, some other Palestinian taking a cut of all those assets? Or have they been working with someone else? We know there's been mutual arms buying going on by the Palestinians, the Irish, and the Afghans. Castro's been buying for the Colombian cartel and the Chinese are selling to everyone. Have they been banking together, too? Did one of those other groups try to get clever with the money? That would be valuable information too.'

I hated every single word of it, and can you blame me? The last thing I wanted was them looking too seriously at where the money had gone. And anyway, while we sat talking, I'd been working out what my one and only hole card was. 'No,' I told him.

'What do you mean, no?'

'Just what I said. No. Your bimbo here was right. I'm in a world of shit. I know that now. But there isn't any reason I have to dig myself in even deeper. And I have a price. My price. You're going to pay it.'

'We've paid your price,' he said emphatically. 'We've bought your life.'

'Bollocks.' It stopped him. He wasn't used to being talked to like that. 'Just bollocks. I didn't ask for any of this. What did I do? I went to work for what's supposed to be a Swiss bank. And what happens? I find it's holding laundered Palestinian assets. It's backed by the State of Israel, and it lives in Mossad's pocket. Is that my fault? Is any of that my fault? No it isn't. If this was a real bank, instead of some rinky-dink toytown spy store, the most I'd be dealing with right now is the City Fraud Squad. These fuck-ups are all your doing. I don't have any choice. I have to go along with you. But you're not getting any more out

120

of me than I strictly have to give you. I'm not the CIA. I'm not one of your little buddies through the looking glass, and I'm not sitting around in your filthy world any longer than I have to. I'm getting out. I'm getting away. When this is over I'm going where none of you clowns can find me. Which means you're going to have to pay my price.'

To do him justice, I think he understood that. I think he got the point. What he asked was, 'What is your price?'

I gave him the long pause. The Dealer's Pause. The 'I'm not worried, this is easy, just thinking through the details' pause.

Then I told him.

'I want the money.'

She moved. She squirmed. She would have kicked the sentence through my teeth if no one had been looking. But he didn't. He seemed to understand. He shrugged and said, 'It isn't our money.'

I wasn't quite sure that was an answer. She was. She wasn't having any. 'We can't do that,' she told him, ignoring me, but lunging forward and poking the air for emphasis. 'Those are criminal funds for us to confiscate. Think how we could use that money.'

He waited for her, not so much to calm down, as to get uncertain, of him, of his intentions, of the situation, before saying, 'We could use it, yes. But we've never had it so we won't miss it. I don't really care who has it so long as it isn't the Palestinians. And he's right. We are asking a great deal from him. If he can bring us our enemies and find out how and why all this was done, that's good enough for me. The money is a price we can pay. I wish that all our orders came in so cheap.'

She wasn't happy about it. I wasn't her favourite person. But she wasn't used to disobeying orders. If I'd thought about it, that would have scared me stiff right off the bat. But I wasn't into thinking mode. I was just trying to survive.

Which was why I told him, 'There's one more thing.'

She turned away in disgust. He merely asked, 'What is it?'

121

I nodded towards her. 'She thinks I'm just a streak of piss, which doesn't give me much reason to trust her. She'd hang me out to dry as soon as look at me. She'd sell me to the Palestinians herself if she thought it would do any good. So I work with you. Just you.'

He shook his head. 'That isn't possible.'

'Yes . . .'

'That isn't possible.' He wasn't someone you'd want to argue with. 'And you have nothing to fear. If she makes a mess of this she has to answer to me. And I promise you, no one in the universe wants to have to answer to me.'

I could believe it. There wasn't anything I could say. His final remark was addressed to her in any case. 'I leave on the first flight in the morning. You can reach me through the Golden Sunset War Room if you have to. Try not to have to.'

They looked at each other. I didn't recognise the look back then and I'm not sure I can describe it now. Trust in his eyes, I think, and something like worship in hers.

Whatever it was, if I'd known what he was up to then, and had known where she and I were headed, I think I would have topped myself on the spot. Because they hadn't even started.

CHAPTER TWO

'Myles?'

'Fordie, where the hell have you . . .'

'Shut up.'

He shut up.

'Right. Now cancel whatever you're doing and meet me in the Rat and Rizla at eleven.'

'What are you saying, my boy? It's shitting gold this morning. I'm missing points and spreads with every word. Tell me what this is about and maybe we can deal.'

Oh very good, very convincing, O'Malley. As though I could say a damn thing over an open 'phone line, especially when all the City already knows there's been a bloodbath fitted in my office.

'Stop pissing me around, Myles. Just be there. You have other floor traders. This'll be to your advantage.'

Long pause. Maybe an inch or three of panic.

Then: 'All right. Whatever you want. Always glad to be of service, my boy.'

He was there, just before opening, inside. The R&R wouldn't keep O'Malley sitting on the doorstep. He's much too good a customer.

Rachel took me over there. She had no intention of leaving me alone. I tried to hold out for some kind of armoured limo, all shatter-proof glass and toughened steel-plate. Well, isn't that the kind of thing these secret service types are supposed to have hidden in their brollies? Press a button on their fountain pens and one pops out all fired up and ready to go? I never did find out if the

Israelis had one in London or not. She pleaded security.

'I'm not taking anything we'd have to park,' she said. 'First of all because I have no intention of dropping you off while I park. Till this is over I go everywhere with you. I babysit you . . .'

'Change my nappies?' I asked hopefully.

I'm not quite sure if the look was contempt or disgust. I always have difficulty telling those two apart. What she said was, 'Keep your diapers to yourself. And second, we're not taking anything that can be booby-trapped while we're out of it. Or even watched so we can be followed afterwards or machine-gunned on the spot.' I had to admit she had a point. 'We don't even want you kidnapped. At least not yet.'

All I managed to that was a sort of gargled shriek. 'Whaaaa?'

She sort of smiled. She wasn't a great smiler. Pity. She had the cheeks and teeth for it. I suppose she thought it made her look unserious. Less the hardened killer. Bit of a bitch, really. If she'd softened up a little, she could have had my hardened killer any day of the week.

'It is possible,' she said. 'You do realise that? The time may come when we have to put you under surveillance and let them pick you up so we can trace them back to their operational station. And their commanders.'

I could have done with less enthusiasm. She could at least have had the good grace to make it sound as though she was not looking forward to it. Then she got practical again.

'No, I think we're going by taxi.'

She got her way. I was getting used to her getting her way. Even so, the whole thing felt daft to me. Tooling through the London streets in a regulation black cab while somewhere out there a bunch of people were looking for me, planning to practise a little touch of radical interventionist surgery. Without an anaesthetic. I'd rather have had the armoured limo.

We sat in and through the usual East-West traffic jams,

clogged in the Strand and Aldwych, almost stationary in Fleet Street, the fast hopeless tool up Farringdon Street and the desperate cut through Smithfield where idle lorries and empty crates – long after the market was closed for the day – created a halfwit one-way system that slowed us down even more, then out round the back of the Barbican, down London Wall, the customary horlicks by Moorgate (he should have cut down Gresham Street, but you try telling that or anything like it to a London cabbie, fat with the Knowledge and his smug little licence), ached round the Liverpool Street one-way system, and finally found ourselves hacking left up Bishopsgate.

On the way, more as a way of keeping my temper with the fat bald git up the front of the cab than anything else (have you ever noticed that about cabbies, the fat ones, the ones with the big coil of blubber hanging over the backs of their shirt-collars, that however white and pasty they are, the lardy roll behind their heads is always red, like it got sunburn or something? I wonder why that is?) I told her a bit about the form.

It came as a bit of a relief, that. She and Effrem had had me under their thumbs ever since they hauled me out of the pig-pen. It was some kind of consolation to be taking her into an environment she knew nothing about, where she had to rely on me for her bearings. And the more I could keep it that way the better. Whatever else I had to do, I had to angle them away from me as regards to any suspicions about who half-inched the fifteen mill in the first place.

First thing I did was to warn her off. Tell her that, whatever it looked like, the R&R was home-base for the hard men and I didn't want her trying anything tough and fancy. Second thing I told her was a bit about O'Malley. Built him up a bit. Cross between old Nathan Rothschild, Sherlock Holmes and Professor Moriarty. Not far from the truth, either. If ever there was a poacher turned game-keeper, it's Myles. I also told her that she had one little problem. I told her the only way to crack computer thefts like this one was to be prepared to go illegal yourself. I got a bit of a lump in my throat and a red flush when I said it, because I had a horrible feeling it was going to be true, and I had no idea about how to set about it yet, and if O'Malley came up with any ideas I had a feeling I wasn't going to like any of them.

Anyway, what I told her was that, although Myles was the only man who could help us, who could help me, he wasn't going to be prepared to advertise what he knew about illegal procedures. She could keep an eye on us, but he wasn't going to let her sit in on the detailed planning and procedure.

That was the way it turned out, too.

Myles was waiting for us in the upstairs bar, only person in the house at that stage. He was leaning over the bar, canted above a straight glass of Guinness, looking cool as murder in a double-breasted herringbone suit. He barely hoisted an eyebrow when he saw us. I picked up a slight air of uncertainty about him, but no fear. That surprised me. Almost anyone else I'd ever known, including me, might just have been a little bit afraid of a friend they knew who was in the middle of a major robbery and a machine-gun killing showed up demanding help. But not Myles.

I should have expected it, I suppose. Irish. They can be wild or stupid or a bloody nuisance, but they don't seem to build fear into a one of them. Most people, you can piss on their shoes and they'll get annoyed but you play the heavy and they'll back away. Not the Paddies, though. It doesn't matter what you do to them, they just keep on coming. It isn't that they don't know when to stop. It's more like no one's ever told them you're supposed to stop. They don't have any way of understanding it. That was what made the Irishman's motto so alarming. He meant it. No surrender.

I was glad of it right then. I needed all the support I could get, and Myles was a man who had the balls for it. If I'd stopped to think about it, though, I might just have got more frightened myself and bailed out while I

126

still could. There was another Irishman involved in this, after all.

Myles fingered to the barman, saying, 'Another Guinness here and a Bushmills and . . .?'

He looked at me and Rachel. He looked funny. He looked kind.

'Grouse,' I said.

'. . . and a Famous Grouse, a large one. Make that two, in the same glass. The boy looks like he needs it.'

Before the barman could say anything I added, 'No ice. Water on the side.'

Myles looked to Rachel. 'Orange and club soda.' He didn't look too happy about that – he never had seen the point of going to a bar to drink anything but liquor – but he nodded a confirmation of her order to the barman and palmed a tenner under his glass.

Business done, he turned to face us and said, 'I don't believe you've introduced us, John-boy.'

I tried to do the honours. 'Myles O'Malley,' I said, 'And Rachel . . .'

She cut me off. 'My name isn't important,' was all she said.

O'Malley was persistent, in a kindly way. 'Oh but I'm afraid it is, my dear. I never do business with people whose names I don't know.'

She smiled at him. 'I find that hard to believe. I thought bankers did business with numbered accounts and nominees every day.'

He bowed from the waist in a half-acknowledgement. 'It doesn't have to be a real name. Simply a means of identification. A mutual convenience, is all. I surely wouldn't dream of asking the identity of your principal, your beneficial owners. Interpol? Fraud Squad? Mossad? None of that matters to me.'

They were smooth, the both of them.

All she did was bat her eyelids, and pause, and finally admit, 'Stern.'

He extended his big right hand. She took it, as he said,

'Rachel Stern. A very great pleasure to meet you, I'm sure. Myles O'Malley at your service.'

I coughed. 'My service, Myles. Mine.'

Our drinks had arrived. I floated a little water into the whisky. It settled, curling into little glassy fronds.

O'Malley bowed again. 'Indeed,' he said. 'Perhaps you'd better tell me what all this is about.'

I took a deep pull at the whisky, holding it in my mouth to let it warm my throat before letting it down to warm the rest of me. Then I tried to tell him and warn him all at once.

'You will have heard about a little fuss at BHM yesterday.' He nodded. 'Well, it seems to have been about a transfer we executed at the end of last week, from an inert account to an account in Switzerland. It seems our instructions were fraudulent. Our visitors yesterday were trying to express their dissatisfaction with our systems. They want their cash back.'

He nodded again, as though to say that sounded perfectly reasonable. 'How much was it, may I ask?'

'Fifteen million dollars.'

This time he sighed. That *was* reasonable. 'Do you happen to know who your visitors, or at least the beneficial owner they represented, might have been?'

Rachel fielded that one. 'The Palestine Liberation Organisation,' she said, as though they were the most ordinary outfit in the world, which, in her world, I suppose they were. 'Or more exactly, one of its member organisations.'

He managed to avoid shooting any kind of glance at me, especially one which might have read You Silly Little Bastard. He simply became very practical. 'And you say the funds were routed to Switzerland?'

I took that one. 'Yes. To an account in Bank Marius Meyer, Zurich.'

'And the authorisation, the instructions, were in order?'

I took another swig at the Grouse before answering, 'Well, yes . . .'

He picked up on it straightaway. 'But?'

I told him what he knew already. 'But the instructions as per usual came from Venezuela. Only trouble is, they came in on a Venezuelan bank holiday.'

'Which nobody bothered to check, am I right?'

I pretended to get angry. 'Well, of course we didn't, Myles. This isn't New York we're talking about. Not Tokyo. This is fucking Venezuela. Anyway, you know as well as I do, any serious bank in town is forever getting instructions from these Rin Tin Tin Republics that take no notice of their local holidays. Holidays are for peasants. The people we deal with are round the clock, round the year capitalists.'

He flapped a hand as though to cool me down. 'I grant you. I grant you that. But this time you have gentlemen claiming to represent the beneficial owners who are attempting to repossess their assets. Which isn't so usual. How did you get your instructions?'

'Telex.'

'Can I see them?'

I looked at Rachel. 'We can get them,' she said.

'You can get them,' I specified. 'I'm not turning myself into a practice target until we know exactly what we're doing.'

Myles stepped in. 'Whatever. Bank holidays and telex sound like a cut-out to me.'

'What's a cut-out?' she asked.

I took that one. I didn't want Myles looking like the only man with a brain round here. Well, you live in hope. 'It's when someone gets between the account-holder and the bank and cuts out the communication system to represent himself as the owner.'

'Is that easy?' she asked.

Myles backed me up. 'No, it isn't. There are relatively few people good enough to do it.'

'Well, that reduces the frame, then. Makes it easier to find out who did it.'

I wanted that particular turn in the conversation halted.

129

'Myles, I'm less interested in who did it right now, or how it was done, than in finding the money and getting it back. I'd like to save my skin.'

She looked disappointed. Myles just looked curious, the disinterested curiosity of someone facing a serious challenge to his skills. Like someone facing XQJZRKY at Scrabble. 'Easier said than done, if it's holed up in Zurich.'

'But can you do it?' What was Rachel trying to do? Feed his ego? He didn't need any help.

'Most things are possible, Ms Stern.' He said Ms. He was careful about that kind of thing. The most scrupulous crook in Christendom. 'But it isn't easy. And it isn't legal.'

'But you will help us?'

'I'm not sure about the Us, Ms Stern. If I do help, I don't want any witnesses I can't vouch for. That includes you. If I do it, I'll be doing it for John-boy here. So you tell me something, Ms Stern. If I don't do it, what sort of actuarial risk does my young friend here represent?'

There was a little moustache of orange and soda on her upper lip as she said, 'If you don't help him out, he might as well be dead.'

I was getting sick of the smug way she said that. To Myles, however, it seemed to represent no more than he'd expected. 'Then I had better try to do whatever I can to help, had I not?'

She smiled. She actually smiled. It was like the sun coming out on a summer day in England. A miracle, and a joy. She even went on smiling as Myles said, 'But you will understand, I hope, if I do not publicise my actions. And you will not mind if I ask for a private word with my friend.'

I don't know how he does it. I never have. He could charm the knickers off nuns. I'd expected some kind of fight, but she just hoisted her arse and her glass and went off to a table at the far corner of the bar. As she sat down and looked back towards us I tried to shoot her a look. One saying, Behave, Don't Get Us Into Any Bother. The place was slowly filling up, and I knew what this lot would be like with a bird like her parked off there on her own. Honey in a bear-pit. I knew she could handle herself. I just didn't want her to do it too well. I'd had enough aggravation for a lifetime in the past two days.

O'Malley leaned tight in towards me and said, 'Well, thank you very much, John-boy. That's all I needed. That's what I want right now, to be inside a war.'

That much I had expected. I let him have it. 'Shut the fuck up, Myles. You don't begin to understand this one . . .'

'Don't I?' If there had been any Ss in there, it would have been a hiss. 'The rat goes down and tries to take the ship down with him.'

'Can it, Myles. I'm not a grass, and I'm not a whinger. This is not what it looks like.'

'Then what is it?'

'He stitched me up, Myles. He wallied me good and proper. It's bad enough it's Palestinian money and I've got Israeli goons dancing all over me. But you introduced me to him, Myles. The Irishman. And he stitched me up.'

He seemed genuinely taken aback, which was something. I had had my suspicions. It had just occurred to me O'Malley might be in on it. Two Paddies together. Not that I really believed that. He was a mate. And a rich one. Still, I was relieved. I filled him in. 'The bastard had to have my Zurich code. Insisted on it. To transfer his 10 per cent. But 10 per cent wasn't good enough for him. He used the code to override my instructions and transfer the whole fucking lot. I've got people trying to kill me for money I don't even have.'

Myles is fast. He had most of the picture in an instant. 'What's your deal with her lot?' he asked.

'Live bait. I hang around to tempt the Palestinians out. They roll 'em up, I get to keep the money if I can find it.'

'So they don't suspect you?'

131

'Not yet.'

He nodded and clicked his fingers for another Bushmills. 'When you did the deal with the Irishman . . .'

I remembered something he'd said to Rachel, so I asked him, 'What is his name, Myles?'

O'Malley just shrugged. 'Which one? Whatever, when you did your deal, his 10 per cent, you must have known where it was going. Where's his account?'

'Javert, Valjean.'

'Geneva?'

'The one. That's my problem. How the hell do I get into them? I'm not the American government with a drug indictment issued for him.'

God bless O'Malley. I should have thought of it myself. 'Not necessary,' he explained. 'His 10 per cent was moved at the front, yes?'

'Yes.'

'What was your confirmation all the deals had been done?'

'Delivery of the telexes to me.'

'Showing a 10 per cent transfer to Javert, Valjean?'

'Yes.'

'So they were dummy telexes. No sign he'd shifted the lot?'

'No.'

'How much time did he have?'

'Very little. I kept it very tight.'

Myles paused, for maybe a beat and a half, then he saw it all. 'Did you ever see him feed anything to Geneva?'

'Yes, when he was setting the whole thing up. They responded.'

'Well, thank the Lord for that. It means it's a real account. In which case he will have had an immediate transfer mechanism built in just the way you did to clear the cash out as soon as it arrived.'

That I could see. That made sense. 'Then the money isn't there any more, and I'm shafted. Stone cold trail.'

Myles shook his head. 'No, not necessarily. He wouldn't have had the time to fake the codes to his account in Geneva. Which means you still have them. You can use them. You

132

can put yourself in the same position with Javert, Valjean as these Palestinians are in with you. You send Geneva instructions about the funds. They tell you the funds have fled. You play the aggrieved owner. It's just possible you might be able to shake the destination of the funds out of them.'

I could see a problem. 'OK I've got the codes but they won't be enough. He's bound to have had some system whereby the telex answerback for the instructions matches. How do I fake his telex number? I'm not a hacker.'

He's got one major thing over me, has Myles. He knows when not to be too clever. 'No, I don't believe it. No way he can build in that extra precaution. He moves around all the time. Changes locations, numbers, identities. He can't have a telex answerback security system. The codes have to do it on their own. It must be that they accept instructions wherever they come from so long as the codes are in place. You could wire them from Wigan if you wanted to. All right, the money's gone, but at least it gets you a location. It's a start.'

He was right, but there was another problem. 'Yeah, but Myles, you know how I have his codes and so do I. But I can't tell the Israelis that. What do I tell them?'

He thought about it, hard. Then he said, 'You dummy it through me. They aren't bankers. You know what civilians are like. They all think it's like something out of Dallas. I play JR. I say I'm doing the heavy in Switzerland, calling in my favours. We make it look as though the Irishman did it all. Sent the money to Zurich, then Geneva, then wherever it's got to now. He's the villain, you're the hero, I'm the hard man. I can fake that much. What I need right now though is the real stuff. I need the telexes, with his codes on them. Where are they?'

I went weak. I went cold, then hot, then cold again. 'Oh Myles. Oh Jesus.'

He looked really concerned. He looked anxious. It felt almost personal. 'What is it? What's the matter?'

'I threw them in the trash.'

CHAPTER THREE

'Pull yourself together, John. How's the rubbish disposed of in your building?'

'Central chute, into a skip, council collection Mondays. Day before yesterday.'

'When were you last in the flat?'

'Yesterday morning, first thing.'

'Do you know for certain there was a pick-up Monday?'

'No, but come on, Myles . . .'

'Come on nothing. Monday was a holiday, John. This is London. And you're in Fulham. Anything to do with the council and we're in with a chance. Those bastards couldn't organise a fuck in a brothel. I need your keys and I need some kind of identification in case I have to pass as you. I'll pick up some clothes for you while I'm at it. You look disgusting.' I gave him my keys and driver's licence. 'Wish me luck,' he said, 'if only for your own sake. Now, where can I reach you?'

'Savoy, they've got me holed up there for the moment. Room's in her name. But I don't know if they plan to move me. You'll have to check with her. Aren't these people supposed to have safe houses and things?'

He looked at me pityingly. 'I think you've been watching too much television, John-boy. Still, let's check it out.'

We checked it out. For the moment it seemed we were staying where we were. If we did get moved around it would be to another hotel. She told Myles that if he lost touch with us he was to 'phone a number at the Israeli Embassy leaving a number where he could be reached and she would get back to him. He told her he was going off to call in favours in Zurich. She seemed to buy it. She even took it quite well when he warned her not to let me anywhere near the BHM building until he had a clearer picture of what was going on.

It was not until he had left and I had had another necessary drink that she got round to asking, 'What was it you gave Mr O'Malley, John? I saw you slip him something.'

I was angry with her. Myles gets a 'Mr' while I'm only John, like some bloody lackey. That was what stopped me answering her straightaway, and gave me the time to think up a cover.

'The keys to my safe-deposit box, and authority to open it. Someone has to have it. Just in case you mess up on the job. Just in case I die.'

We spent the next few hours holed up in the hotel room, me flat out face-down on the bed wishing this was over, and her pacing up and down as though she had a tiger in her drawers.

It would be a while before we found out what was going on during those hours, but we found out some of it around three o'clock when she finally got cage-fever.

'Do you have a telephone number for Mr O'Malley, John?'

This time, I let her have it. 'Try, "Do you have a number for Myles, Mr Ford?"'

'Don't be ridiculous.'

I counted to ten under my breath. If I hadn't done that I would have hit her. And if I'd hit her I guess she'd have broken my arm. I always knew numbers were power. Or at least safety.

'Yes,' I said finally, 'I have his direct-line number. I'll give him a call.'

It wasn't Myles who answered, though. It was Stiffy Durrant, one of his boys. (So called because he always had one. Kept half the tarts in London going on a retainer-basis.)

He sounded pleased to hear me. 'Ford, thank God you called. Did BHM get hold of you?'

135

'No . . .' I tried to think of a way of explaining, and ducked it. 'No, I'm tied up. Police and stuff. What's the matter?'

He hesitated. People do when you mention the fuzz. Then all in a gabble he said, 'We were just talking about it, calling the police, ourselves, didn't know what to do . . .'

'Slow down, Stiffy. Just slow down. Take a deep breath and tell me what's going on.'

He did as he was told. 'We've hardly seen Myles all day. Went out this morning. Said he had an urgent appointment, but he'd call in if he was going to be tied up. He called about noon. Said he'd be a couple of hours. Sounded fine. Checked on our new CD placing. Told us to get in on some of this new Dai-Ichi Kangyo issue. Then about twenty minutes ago we got another call on this line. Some foreigner. Wog accent. Said he had Myles. Said if we ever wanted to see him alive again to get hold of you. Get you to call this number he gave me. We've been trying to get hold of you, but BHM . . .'

I didn't hear his babble for a bit, though she snapped me out of that when I told her, and made me take the number.

But all I could think of was, Oh Christ what are we into now?

Oh Myles, what have I done?

She was livid.

'Why didn't you tell me? Why didn't you tell me he was going to your apartment? We knew they were bound to have it covered. We were going to do it ourselves when we were ready. We were going to send you home to smoke them out. But we were going to have you covered. We were going to set you up properly. We were going to be ready to take them. As it is, you've handed your friend to them on a plate. What did you think you were doing? Why didn't you just tell me?'

I didn't have an answer for her. There wasn't anything

I could say, not without saying a great deal more than I intended. What I did know was I had to find a way of helping Myles, and she looked the only way I had. I did the best I could.

'We weren't thinking. He was going to get some clothes . . .'

That only enraged her more. 'Clothes. Clothes! You sent him into a trap to get you clothes? You wanted clothes, we'd have got you clothes. There's a tailor's right around the corner. There's one across the road. For clothes, you did this?'

I was worried enough not to have to feign anger or upset or embarrassment. It just spilled out of me. 'I know it was stupid, I know what I've done, but I'm not used to this. None of us are. We don't live in the middle of a war-zone. We didn't ask for your war to come spilling out on to our streets. We didn't expect it, we don't like it, and we're no bloody good at it. But it's done, and I want it undone, and you're the killer queen round here, so you just tell me how to do it. Whatever I have to do, I'll do it. But I want Myles out.'

She thought that out. Looking back, I think she must have liked it. Maybe just a touch of human feeling does it every time. She looked at me as though I was an idiot, but not as though I was a worm, not any more. And I meant it too. Whatever else he was, Myles was a mucker. We may have got into this together, but these consequences weren't any of his doing. He'd been trying to do me a favour, and I had to get him out.

'So what do we do, princess? What now?'

She began to do her job. 'Did they give you a deadline?'

'Doesn't sound like it. Not yet.'

'Then you get back to this colleague of O'Malley's . . .'

'Stiffy.'

She didn't smile. 'Tell him to go on manning that 'phone. Tell him to give us another direct line there where we can ring in on the hour, every hour. Tell him you're already dealing with the police and the Special Branch are likely to be in touch.'

'What are you going to do?'

She frowned. 'I'm an unofficial here, all our people are. That's the way your authorities wanted to keep it. I don't know if that's possible now. I'm going to have to get in touch with our people so they can notify your authorities and bring them in if necessary. Someone has to calm down O'Malley's people. I'll get those details sorted out. But . . .' She looked up at me with a sort of helplessness on her face, a kind of softness I'd never seen before, and went on: 'Look, how seriously did you mean it? How badly do you want him back?'

'Badly.'

'How badly?'

I didn't know how best to put it. All I could manage was, 'I owe him almost everything. If he calls, it's due.'

She nodded. She looked almost moved, despite herself. Then she asked, 'How long do you want him out?'

I didn't understand the question. I told her so.

She explained. 'So far as they know, he's just a friend of yours, who went to get you some clothes. They don't know he's working with us. If we get him out in one piece, if he still wants to, we can probably set it up so that no one knows he's helping us. So long as he was just a hostage, just a pawn, they'll leave him alone in future. But if they get the slightest impression he's working with us, then even if we get him out this time, they'll come back for him. They always do. There isn't any place to hide.'

I felt empty inside, and I knew why. I asked her anyway. 'How do we persuade them he's clean?'

She looked away. 'We can't. They won't believe Mossad. Or MI5, or Special Branch. The only person there's any chance of them believing is you.'

I swallowed. 'Does that mean what I think it means?'

'It might.'

It took her about an hour to set it all up. An hour and maybe a dozen phone calls. It was the longest hour in what had already turned into the longest week of my life.

You know the feeling. Last ten minutes of a match, up against a high-class oppo. They've got you bang to rights. They've got you where they want you. They've got the skills, the talent, the stamina, the experience. All you've got is balls and bottle and the hopeful ignorance of the innocent young. And maybe you've got the legs of them. You've got the years, a few years on them. So you've run them around, you've run them into the ground. You went out there, start of the ninety minutes thinking, 'Easy! Easy! Easy!' Because you're a kid, because you're dumb, because you're a dickhead. But you learn. They make you learn. And somehow, because you've got to, because it was how you were brought up, because you don't know any better, because it's all a question of face, you keep it going. You hold them off. You wear them down. And when they stick one in the back of the net you steal it back off them early in the second half, and you've given up any hope of winning by then, you're trying to hold the draw. You've got the point off them, just one, and you know you don't deserve it, but you hang on in there, because there's nowhere left to run and nowhere you can hide. And they throw everything at you. Even the goalie's up at the halfway line. They've got you where they want you and all you've got is guts. Even the legs have gone now. They had the brains. They paced themselves better. Your lungs are gone, they're aching out your chest. There's a gagging in your throat and the swell of blood behind your eyes and all you want is for it to be over, so you can fall down there and die, hanging on to the single point that's all that's left of your dreams and hopes and aspirations. All that's left of schoolday Saturdays singing, 'You'll never walk alone,' of jessing about in the changing rooms yelling, 'Play the man and not the ball,' and 'Referee's not looking, back row it starts cooking, get in lads start hooking,' and chanting like the little tykes you are, 'Ere we go, ere we go, ere we go.'

You've got a point against a better side, you've held them

to the draw, but they have ten men in your penalty box every second of the way and you've got ten minutes left of screaming pain, and jellied legs, and sinking desperation, and all you can think when you can think at all is, 'Please, Jesus, we can't lose . . .'

But you can. And you know it.

I'd thought I had it easy. I thought I had it under control. I thought that I was good. But I wasn't. Not good enough. And now it was showing.

That was the hardest part, right now. Having to face it. Maybe Myles could have done it. Maybe he'd have kept a better eye on the Irishman. Maybe he'd have kept a better eye on his back and got a swifter escape route organised. But I hadn't. And I'd dropped him in the shit and all.

You know how it is, when you've done something stupid, when you've done something wrong, and you've gone and got a mucker in trouble, and the time comes when you have to face it, face him, own up. You want to die, you want to slink away. It's like a knot and an explosion all at once inside your belly and your chest, but there's nothing you can do but face it, and the one thing you can guarantee is that it's going to be worse than anything you could imagine.

I lay there, on that bed, face down, head in my arms, head throbbing, not taking in her voice as it planned and explained patiently away, and I wondered, how is this going to end and who can I make suffer for it?

Isn't it always the way? You look for someone else to blame. You look for someone else to hurt. By the time the three heavies Rachel called arrived, I could only think of them as targets, as enemies. I wanted to load it all off on to them. I wanted someone to hate.

I'd hired a hacker, the best in the world, and I'd let him run my dodge unsupervised. I'd let him walk away with it. I hadn't had the brains to think through what could be done with print-outs and then I'd thrown the print-outs away. I hadn't put together a foolproof means of washing

140

my money out, and I hadn't thought through a quick escape, because I'd been too thick to see the owners of my money might be hairy bastards. I'd got myself stuck in the world of wired-up wallies, the funnies, the Secret Brigades, and I'd turned for help to the best mate I had, and sent him straight into a world of danger. I'd put his neck down on the block.

So yeah, I wanted somebody to hate and, bless them, when Rachel's three heavies walked into the room, the little tossers made it easy.

Three of them. I never did find out their names. They made it pretty clear the less I knew the better. Not something likely to build a boy's confidence. All I ever worked out was that the one with the beard who sounded German was from the Israeli Embassy, the fat boy was Special Branch, and the mincing queen was SIS. (I think I've got that right. I think he called it SIS not MI5. I know he was a mincing queen. Not that I've got anything much against faggots. Just patronising faggots.)

Anyway, it was the Mincer who set it off. 'We're doing a trace on the 'phone number,' he said. 'We thought it might be one of the lines at the new PLO office in Embassy Row. We have all those wired full-time. But it isn't.'

Rachel scowled. The Kraut gave her a look of irritation. She wasn't having any of it. 'Well, how am I supposed to feel?' she asked angrily. 'How would they feel if we let the IRA buy and operate an office and safe house in Tel Aviv?'

'They would not mind,' the Kraut informed her. 'Since the PLO have opened their office here, the authorities are sharing the proceeds of their 'phone-taps with us. We would do the same.'

That shut her up. But not the Mincer. 'Oh really, dear boy,' he whined, 'do we have to wash our dirty linen in public?' I wondered what kind of stains he had on his. 'Especially when the Stranger's Gallery is so overcrowded?' He nodded in my direction.

I didn't have any patience with him. 'Up yours, arse

141

bandit. I'm not here to be patronised by shirt-lifters. I'm here because I'm trying to help catch the bunch of thugs who blew my boss away yesterday. In the process, my best mate has got himself lifted and I want him out, any way I can. You got any ideas about how we do that, before I get tonto?'

Mincer tried the put-down. 'Keep your hair on, lovey.'

'Easily done,' I told him. 'It's my own. I'm all for a rug-free civil service. What's the matter, don't they pay you enough to get a good one? Or did Q screw up? I've stepped on better ones than that.'

He blushed deeper and deeper. I almost wanted to get up and lift the wig off. See if the red went all the way round his chrome-dome. But I remembered Myles, and the fact that the last thing I wanted was this lot going silent on me. We needed all the help we could get. That was when the 'phone went and calmed things down.

Rachel answered, and passed it over to Mincer.

When he hung up, he looked smug again. 'That was from our Telecom liaison group, in the City . . .'

I still couldn't resist it. 'Telecom House, right? Fourth floor?'

He pursed his lips, primping, 'You aren't supposed to know that.'

'Everyone knows that.'

He shrugged and turned away. For a minute there I thought he was going to freeze up on us all over again. He was too proud of his information for that, though.

'They tell me it's a public call-box. In a house. A boarding house. In Charlton. Very low-class.'

He kept on asking for it. I had happy memories of the old Valley ground. Whatever he might say, you used to get a better class of bundle down there. Not too many knives. Hardly any broken bottles. Only the occasional sharpened steel comb. No kung-fu batons and maces. None of the really nasty stuff. And plenty of room. Bigger than any stadium but Wembley and not much of a home crowd so you could always move away, or on, or up, or out. The only real problems I remembered was that some of them kept a particularly vicious kind of dog – alsatians, dobermans, pit-bulls, trained to harm. Happy days.

'We can't all have your advantages. Where do you live, anyhow? Blenheim Palace?'

The fat policeman cut us off. Good job, too. I might have got my eyes scratched out. The fat boy wasn't happy. Inter-departmental rivalry. 'We'd have needed a warrant to get that information,' he sniffed.

Mincer looked smug. 'Yes, well. Quite. Can't have people barging into other people's privacy just on the basis of natural suspicion and a couple of O Levels, can we? Oh, and the training course at Hendon. Not quite Cambridge, is it?'

He was asking for it now. In that little world he had made an enemy who would forever be running traces on him as a potential double-agent. He made two out of three after all: bum-boy, Cambridge – if he was brilliant as well he was almost bound to be a mole. It was almost in the rules. Job descriptions for the British Secret Service. It's always seemed to me a country's traitors tell you almost everything you need to know about them. The Yanks do it for money. The Brits for snobbery. Treason – the most private club of all.

You could see the fat man looking for some clever answer, but he didn't have the pace or brains for it. Still, if wishes had been deeds, he would have been Gore Vidal that afternoon, and Mincer, dog-meat. He got pompous instead.

'Still, this is where my people take over, isn't it? We'll put the house under surveillance.' He reached for the 'phone. 'While I'm at it, I'll put a team of marksmen on alert.'

Mincer rolled up his eyes. They don't have the best of reputations, the Met marksmen. I expect that was what Mincer meant when he murmured, 'Women and children first.' Then he spoke up, to my relief. 'I don't think that's going to be necessary. I trust we aren't going to have to

143

storm the place. And if we were going to have to, I think my principals would prefer the SAS did it. But as I understand our Hebrew friends' suggestion,' he half-bowed towards the Kraut. That's all we need, I thought, an antisemitic faggot, 'it won't be necessary for us to intervene, but merely provide a *cordon sanitaire*.' He pronounced it in the French way. Made it sound like Tampax.

Fat boy didn't like it. 'I don't see as it's any of their business. It's our parish. It isn't one of theirs as got lifted. And the kidnapping's a crime here, not in the Gulf.'

Mincer looked pained, but let it pass without correcting the fat one's geography. They aren't very smart, most of them, you know. Outside the City Force. Even the senior detectives are woodentops at heart. P.C. Plods with delusions of grandeur. Mincer tried to break it down so even his oppo could understand it.

'We aren't interested in making a crime of this. The last thing we want is a bunch of Palestinians on trial at the Bailey. Much less being convicted. Do you really think we want to put up with all the escape attempts and hostage-takings that would be bound to follow? Why make trouble for ourselves? It's bad enough having to cope with the IRA. If these people,' he indicated Rachel and the Kraut; she looked disgusted, 'are willing to find a way to take them off our hands, I for one would be very grateful to them. As would her Majesty's Government.'

That was what did it. That was what does it every time. The security services can always pretend to be party to the government's closest, most secret deliberations. I don't suppose for a moment it's true. I don't suppose they're bright or efficient enough to count. It isn't so long ago, after all, that they got so entangled with their automatic listening procedures bugging the phones of union leaders during the miners' strike, that they left the 'phones at the Soviet Embassy unbugged for a whole weekend. But there isn't any way the regular flatfoots can prove that, so they always end up rolling over and lying doggo.

'So what are we supposed to do?' the fat one asked.

Re-enter the Kraut. 'What we are liking,' he explained, painfully slowly, 'is services of surveillance. We are proposing Mr Ford should make a switch of himself for this Mr O'Malley, and that your Civil Police should monitor their movements thereafter. Our people would at the first opportunity intervene. With the minimum of force, naturally.' He pronounced it na-too-rallee.

I didn't like it at all. It was my turn to intervene.

'Look. I'm the one who's going to switch himself for Myles. I have some rights in this. These people have had fifteen million dollars lifted from the bank I work for. They're not happy about it. They know the British police are involved now, but they don't know I'm involved. As far as they know I'm on the lam. They don't know if I'm just scared, or if it was me that took the money. But the important thing is that they don't know you bastards have got me backed against a wall. So long as they don't know that, there's a chance Myles and I might get out of this alive. If they'll do the switch, if I can persuade them I'll do everything I can to help them trace their money, and if I can persuade them Myles is clean and needed on the outside to help me find the money, then it's possible they'll let him go and let me live until we find the money. If nothing else that buys us time. But if they get one whiff of woodentops, or Mossad, or SAS or any other bloody outfit, they're going to kill us both. And I don't want that to happen. So I don't want a small army of police around their house in Charlton. I don't want a sanitary cordon. The last thing I need is you lot making a spectacle of yourselves. If there's going to be surveillance, I want one, maybe two, really good operators doing it. Basically, I want her.' I indicated Rachel.

Part of it was a punt. If I could get away from the dish-cloths and the surveillance all at once, I might still be able to get safely away and have O'Malley in London help me trace the Irishman. Another part of it was for real. Too many cooks may not spoil the broth, but too many cops will spoil an operation.

'I can't agree to that,' the fat one told me.

145

Mincer was not so certain. 'I don't know. He could wear a wire.'

Rachel's scorn was wonderful to behold. 'Don't be ridiculous,' she snarled. 'They're bound to search him. As well give him a neon sign reading, Police Informer.'

Kraut came up with the answer. 'Perhaps . . . Perhaps close cover by one, or two, of our people, in radio contact with a looser group of your own. Cars at principal intersections, perhaps . . .'

Mincer liked it. 'That might work, I think.' A true civil servant. Never be too enthusiastic, just in case something goes wrong. It doesn't help to be committed. And fat boy had no say in the matter. He had one little gizmo left on his plate, however. He pulled out a little Sony Walkman, with what looked like a rubber cup wired to it. It was a rubber cup. He attached it to the telephone receiver, and said, 'I suggest we tape the call.' Then he explained why to the Kraut. 'It's possible your people might be able to identify the voice.'

There was something else they'd all forgotten. Or perhaps just never thought of. But I knew O'Malley. I knew it mattered that, whatever else they'd got out of him, the only 'phone number they'd got was the bank's. They didn't have Lady Polly's. O'Malley would sooner die than put his family in danger, and I knew I had to help him out on that one.

I had to make the second worst 'phone call of my life.

'Polly? It's John Ford.'

'Johnny, darling! How lovely to hear from you! I spoke to Myles last night in London. He was fearfully worried about you. Said he couldn't find you, after that horrid trouble at your bank. It was on the news last night. Dreadful pictures. I don't know why they're allowed to show them, when children will be watching, too. Where are you? What are you doing? Have you spoken to Myles . . .?

I knew what it meant when she was like this. I knew what it meant when she rattled on, nineteen to the dozen. It

146

meant she was worried. Not about me. She's a lady. She wouldn't worry too much in the end about the fate of the serving classes. But about Myles. About what he was up to now. What he might have got himself into. I cut her off.

'Polly, there's been a fuck-up. Just sit down and listen to me. That bunch at the bank yesterday are after me. You don't need to know why. I'm working with the police, is all. I spoke to Myles this morning. He went to my place to get me some clothes, and they picked him up. He's all right. We think they want to trade him for me. I'm going to do it. None of this is his fault and I don't want him suffering for it. But there is something very important. They may know he has a family, but we don't think they know who or where. That's the way we want to keep it. We don't want them trying to snatch you to get some extra leverage. I'm going to arrange some police protection for you at the house, just till Myles is free. But I want you staying where you are. I don't want you coming up to town, or calling the London flat, or leaving any messages, or doing anything to make yourself conspicuous. Please trust me. This'll all be over soon. Do you understand that, Polly? . . . Polly? Are you still there? . . .'

It took her a long time to answer. When she did, her answer was not encouraging. 'I don't know what you two silly buggers have been up to, Johnny, but if anything happens to Myles, I'll make you rue the day you were born.'

There wasn't much else to be said. Once all the arrangements had been made, I took Rachel up on her offer of clothes and a hold-all. Kraut did the shopping.

Then I made the worst 'phone-call of my life.

CHAPTER FOUR

I'd expected a different accent. Something thicker, more Middle Eastern. What I got was something that sounded almost American, or hyphenated American, anyway, with only an edge of the lift in the language, the rising to the end of sentences you get in native Arabic speakers. Rachel had told me to keep it simple.

'My name is John Ford. I was told to telephone this number.'

'Mr Ford. At last.' Perhaps it was the frame of mind I was in, but that sounded pretty threatening to me.

'You have a friend of mine, who has done you no harm.'

'That is true. We do have a friend of yours. And he is in no position to do us any harm.'

If it was meant to chill me, it worked. 'Let me speak to him. I want to know he's all right.'

'Be patient, Mr Ford. Be still. I have no intention of rushing this. I assume in any case this line is already tapped.'

I didn't know what to say. If I denied it, would he only think I was deep in the fuzz's pocket? Or was he second-guessing? And if he was, and I confirmed it, would that only cause him to over-react? I didn't have to say anything in the end. My hesitation was enough.

'I hope they're listening right now, Mr Ford, because if they are it will save you from passing the message on. We are armed, as you know very well, and we have no intention of being taken captive. We will kill your friend and anyone else we have to if any attempt is made to capture us. You do understand that?'

'Yes. I understand. What do you want?'

A sort of purr came into his voice, like a smile on its way to a laugh, as he said, 'We want our money back, Mr Ford. We want it now.'

Time to run the patter. 'I'm trying, but you aren't making things any easier. You may be angry, but we've been made to look like idiots. We don't like it when some wide-boy walks through our systems. But whoever did it was good, very good, and it takes everything we know to try to unravel it. And you people keep on fouling the whole procedure up. There aren't many bankers with the skill or clout to sort a mess like this out. You killed one of them yesterday and you kidnapped another of them today. What am I supposed to do? Whistle Dixie?'

He thought about it, but not for long. 'My people over-reacted yesterday, but not today. What is your relationship with the police and security services, Mr Ford?'

I tried a little anger. 'I don't have a relationship. I'm being kicked from here to kingdom come. They want you. I don't want you. I want the money back. I want my friend back. I want this ended.'

It seemed to make sense to him. 'The man we have, was helping you?'

'He was going to. I'm not sure he'll feel up to it after this.'

His answer was chilling. 'Oh, he'll feel up to it. He'll do anything we want, if only to prevent this happening to him again.'

I wanted to be sick. 'Don't hurt him. Whatever you do, don't hurt him.'

'I'll try, but that depends a little on what you're proposing.'

This was it. 'You want your money, right?' His silence was acknowledgement enough. 'Well, all we know so far is that we routed it, as instructed, to a bank in Switzerland. That's why I need O'Malley's help. I don't have the power or clout to shake the information out of Switzerland. He does. He's no use to you where he is. I'm no use to you without him. If you ever hope to see your cash again, you have to let him go, and I have to be in touch with him.'

He was patient, like a grown-up with a kid. 'Oh no, Mr Ford, that wouldn't do at all. That wouldn't leave us any control, or anything to bargain with. We still have to get out of this silly little country after all.'

I think I'd have given everything I had to avoid saying what I had to say next, but nothing would have been enough. Old London Laws. Don't grass. Don't whine. And don't leave your friends hung out to dry. 'Then let's do a switch,' I said. 'Me for O'Malley. He can do the business on the outside. You can keep me in touch with him by 'phone. Together we can sort this out and find your money. You'll still have a hostage till it's over. And we'll all get to walk away.'

Why did that feel like wishful thinking?

Because it was, old son. It was.

He thought it over some more. Then he said, 'That might work. You'd be prepared to do it?'

'What option do I have?'

'None.'

'I want to talk to him first. I want to hear he's all right.'

There was the sound of some swift soft jabber away from the mouthpiece, a couple of thuds, a dragging noise, something in English I couldn't make out. Then O'Malley, saying, 'Fordie?'

There was something odd about his voice. Something thick and clotted, like a boxer with a post-fight tongue, too big for his mouth. 'Myles, are you all right? Are . . .'

'I'm OK, John-boy. Really. They just got in my face.'

I wanted to say, 'It's all right, Myles. It's almost over. I'm coming for you,' but they snatched the 'phone away from him and I never got the chance.

It was the same voice again, saying, 'Very well. The details.'

Time to fake it again. 'Where are you?'

He was too smart for that. 'No. Not here. That's none of your business.'

150

'Then where?' I thought a second for myself. 'I'm not going down any back alleys where you can stiff us both. It has to be somewhere fairly public, fairly open.'

He was gentle with me. 'That won't do the marksmen any good. It doesn't matter how good their lines of fire are. We'll still have guns trained on the two of you.'

Fear made me angry and anger was the right response. 'Do you think I'm dumb? Do you think I'd go for any piss-ant scheme like that? I'm not in this for the penny-antes. I want to get out of this alive. Him too. And screw the cops, screw you, and screw the money.'

It seemed to reassure him. 'Do you know a place called Redhill?' he asked.

'Redhill!' Well, I ask you. Not the Riviera is it? A windy ghetto for those not good enough to make it up in town. Still. 'I know where it is. South of a river is a bit beyond my manor. Surrey's beyond it.'

'I hope not, Mr Ford, for all our sakes. There is a new shopping complex there, opposite the railway station.'

'Yeah, I know it.' I did. BHM had put some money into the development.

'Good. There will be a certain amount of traffic there, on the road between, this evening, but not too much, outside the rush hour. It should suit both our purposes. Be on the station side of that road, opposite the shopping centre this evening at eight o'clock. We will come by car or truck. We will make the switch at the traffic lights. And Mr Ford, we will be armed.'

I explained it all to Rachel's heavy mob. The fat one was least happy.

'Redhill,' he said, screwing up his face and looking the way I felt about it. 'It's outside the Met's authority. Our case, though. Grey zone between us and Surrey Constabulary. I have to let them know in case we get into a hot pursuit inside their parish. Don't like it. Never like getting the village bobbies involved.'

Mincer tried to console him. 'It shouldn't come to that.

The last thing we need is hot pursuit. Mr Ford might come to some harm. We will need their assistance for loose surveillance, however. And we will need to select a radio channel common to them, the Met, and whatever equipment Miss Stern may have. What I will do is arrange to have our people secure the house in Charlton round about the time Mr Ford is making his switch in Redhill. That way, if they are so foolish as to return, we should be able to end this little matter then and there. I assume the Embassy will wish to participate?'

A nod from the Kraut. There was something else on my mind. 'The radio channel,' I said, 'make sure it isn't one of the regular police bands. They're bound to monitor those.'

Rachel drove me down in a banged-up Ford Sierra. Inside though, it had radio equipment that looked like something off the Starship Enterprise. That would have been good. I wish we could have just beamed Myles up and switched to Warp Factor One and lit out into hyperspace. But it wasn't going to work like that. It never would. She didn't say much on the way down. We had it all worked out before we left. She was going to drop me off round the back of Sainsbury's so, if they asked, I could say I'd parked back there and walked down to the station and the traffic islands. There was a side road came into those traffic lights, under the railway bridge. She'd be stalled fifty to a hundred yards up there on the bend round the hill, faking some futt in her engine. The local pigs would be warned to leave the area and her alone. She didn't tell me where their second vehicle would be, and I didn't want to know. It seemed to me the less I knew the better.

Funny thing was, the less she said, the more sympathetic she seemed. I think this Daniel in the Lion's Den routine must have done me some good with her. Hell of a way to pull a woman. Money's so much easier. There was one question we had not sorted out, though.

'What about Myles?' I asked her. 'If this works out,

he's going to be stuck in the middle of Redhill with no idea what's going on. Is someone going to babysit him?'

She frowned. 'I hate these rush jobs. The loose ends are the dangerous ones.' She picked up the radio handset, pressed a button and said, 'Maccabby One. What arrangements do we have for the barter? I can't pick him up without making myself visible. Who's to do it?'

She pressed the button again and a voice I did not recognise said, 'Foot patrol, but not till you're well out of there. It's taken care of.'

And that was that.

There was a crush outside the station, a crowd trying to dash across the road at the new roundabout. Tarts mainly. Eighteen-, nineteen-, twenty-year-old birds from town. You get a lot of them down the old Surrey railway towns – Croydon, Purley, Redhill – dormitories now, most of them, or dumps. At best, employment catchment areas for town or Gatwick Airport, or the big boring office blocks from Croydon to the South Bank at Southwark. At worst, places with no real reason for existence any more. They try. They try to stay alive. Wine bars open and fold. Bad restaurants and pubs-with-meals try to crack the Berni Inn and Trust House Forte market (avocado with prawns; chicken, steak, or scampi; choccie mousse or Black Forest gateau; house red or white; gin, whisky or lager, and Irish coffees and cream liqueurs; all the blokes in whistles, all the birds in polyester party frocks; 'and they give you so much to eat. It's *reeely* good value.') and mainly fail. And each of them has at least one big nightclub. The Redhill one had changed its name. The Millionaire. Used to be an Odeon. Most of them were converted cinemas, redeveloped after the bingo boom burst. You know the type. Black fake lacquer walls, flashing lighting, one cheap laser, one of those mirrored balls twirling in the ceiling, and a shit-house like an abattoir.

The girlies head south to them when they've had enough of town. It's sad. They think because they've got to Surrey

153

they'll meet a better class of bloke. What they find is the usual suburban hop-head, after a pint, a poke and a rumble. On a big night those places turn into a cross between the Gunfight at the OK Corral and a fourteenth rate bordello. Not that it stops the birds. Hope springs eternal, I guess.

Friday, Saturday nights you get the sixteen-, seventeen-year-old slags who've been poking boys at school since they were twelve and have finally got bored with talk of nothing but football, villainy and scrapping, sick of them passing out in a beer-haze on top of them after a couple of clumsy strokes. Those are the nights you get the serious aggravation. Rest of the week you get an older crowd. That little bit harder and more cynical, but still hoping, underneath all the make-up and the sneering, all the put-downs with the girls from the typing pool who've come down with them ('Nah! That one's all marf and no trahsers . . .', 'Wot, im? While there are donkeys on the beach?', 'Well, another night for the Magic Finger, girls . . .') that this time they'll find the one. The trainee bank manager. The computer salesman. The one with the top-of-the-line Escort or, dream of dreams, a Volkswagen Golf GTI Convertible, an expense-account, a couple of credit cards (the old plastic passports) and two weeks holiday each summer in Yugoslavia. (Their kid sisters still head for Spain and pull the local waiters aloft them. Or to Club Med, where it isn't the sex that gets them down by the end of the holiday. It isn't the fucking. It's all the beer and vomit.) You want to know how to get pulled at one of those places? Pretend to be a travel agent.

I must be getting old. Ten years ago, more, it would have been a pleasure to light out of that crowd with a truck-full of those darlings. They travel in packs. That's all right. Gives a likely lad a choice. Get a couple of bevvies down the second best looker (the best looker's always too full of herself to come across), cop a feel on the dance floor, quick grope in the corridor, a bit of teasing ('Come on, darling, leave it out. I have.'), a bit of pressure ('Don't shag about, love. I'm not leaving with a stiffy.') and give her a quick one across the back seat in the car park. (Never in a lay-by. You might have to drive her home.) But even where I was going, I didn't fancy it tonight. The fumbling. The fat, white, greasy skin. The smell of Malibu, cheap perfume and desperation.

I had the wit to think, I must be getting old. I rated this neck of the woods when I was a kid. Usual reasons. Big hard boy down from town pulling the girlies. But not just that. There was that concert hall back up at Croydon. Fairfield Halls. Used to leg out there for gigs some nights, and a spot of aggro. I remember sloping off to a Slade gig there once. Had a bird who fancied Noddy Holder's hair, and they weren't playing Hammersmith that tour. Don't ask me why. Maybe they didn't like the way the lads up in the balcony pissed down on the heads of the punters below. Never stopped the Quo.

It's a naff part of the world. All that really squalid sixties building. Even the new stuff looks crappy to me. Tacky shopping centres, and cheap metal and glass skyscrapers funnelling the wind down roads too wide or busy to cross, even if there wasn't a barrier down the middle. No wonder the little bastards who live there vandalise everything they see. Gang signs in the bus-shelters. Street-signs buckled off or round. Piss on the floor of the public 'phones and shit smeared on the hand-sets. Not that there's any excuse. The little horrors would foul up Buckingham Palace if you moved them in.

I stood against a howling wind under dreary red street lights facing the traffic lights and the shopping centre. I had my collar up and my arms crossed to keep my jacket closed and tears streaming down my face from the cold, and I wondered what I was doing.

All I ever wanted was to be rich. Is that a crime? God knows what I'd done was common enough. There was more than one tale of banks paying the perpetrator off to keep his mouth shut. It's bad for the reputation when someone ligs you out of millions. Makes account-holders fear you're not secure. Nothing's more likely to cause a run on a bank, and a run is precisely what makes a bank unsecure. A self-fulfilling prophecy.

It wasn't only computer thefts either. There had been that lad in Switzerland a few years back. Quiet, responsible boy who had finally been put to work in the bank's safe-deposit box vault. Over four years he had carefully cracked every box whose owner hadn't been in over a two year period. Best estimates had put the take at ten plus million dollars. No one checked. No one guessed. Twenty-two years old and he resigned and lit out to Italy. Took up with some bird down there. When owners finally started reporting missing valuables, the bank reimbursed them. Hushed it up. Then he gets homesick and comes back to Switzerland. The bank officials picked him up, took him back to the safe-deposit vault, beat him shitless, and took him back across the Italian border. Told him to stay there. They could do without that kind of publicity.

That seemed all right to me. So he was daft. But ten mill was worth a beating.

But this? This was crazed. There was a part of me that thought I'd be lucky to get out of this crippled. That wanted me to get out now and leave O'Malley to it. Whose idea had it been, anyhow? Who introduced me to the Irishman? And did what I'd done deserve the tender mercies of Mossad and the PLO?

But light out where and how? With what? To do what? Rachel had been right. The only way I was going to get through this was by playing it her way. She could get them off my back. I couldn't do it on my own.

I must have waited at those traffic lights for upwards of twenty minutes. Rachel was already in position up the side road, her car bonnet up and her playing with wrenches. It didn't look too convincing to me, but I was biased. I was preparing for disaster. I looked about me trying to spot the foot patrol that would pick up Myles, but I couldn't work out who it was. There were a few more people on the streets than cars on the road, but not many. A quiet New Year's evening.

A skinhead with a nut like a giant pimple came up to me. He was wearing the swagger and a tee-shirt against the cold, proving he was hard.

'Got a fag?' he asked. He gave me the look.

'No.' I eyeballed him back. I was almost ready for it. A rumble then and there. Something quick and violent to get the monkey off my back – the thinking, the anxiety. Some sudden act that might get me out of here, stiff me, unable to make the exchange. But he wasn't up to it. He was on his own. He was just a kid. And he was cold. He slunk away.

I stood on the island watching the thin approaching traffic and rubbed my hands together. I told myself how much I hated England in the winter. How, if I ever got out of this, I was parking myself somewhere like L.A. or Miami or Nassau in the Bahamas. Somewhere where a boy could still make a living as a banker and get a tan while he was at it. I wanted to come in out of the cold. I wanted to have a good time. What was so wrong with that?

There was a car approaching. Hard to make out the marque or colour in the thin light of the streetlamps and the narrow darkness of a winter evening. I made myself not look towards Rachel.

There was something behind it, tracking it too closely for real safety. A big dark shape in the night. I guessed a van. A Commer maybe. I was right.

They were idling, playing out the distance between us. I looked up at the traffic lights. They were shifting from green to amber. The car and van approached more quickly, sliding to a halt as the lights turned red. The passenger windows of the car were open. Whoever was inside shone flashlights in my face, the big ones, that dazzled me. I put up my hands to cover my eyes. That must have satisfied them. No gun. The door of the van slid open.

A voice I recognised from the 'phone said, 'Mr Ford?'
I nodded. Nothing happened. I said, 'Yes.'

Someone stepped down from the van and just stood there, unmoving. Blinking through the glare of the lights I finally made out Myles. He looked disgusting. His clothes were filthy. His nose was cut and his mouth looked as though someone had smeared it back across his cheek.

'You look like shit, O'Malley.'

He tried to grin, but it hurt too much. He said, 'That's what happens when you root in trash.'

Whoever was holding him by the scruff of his collar suddenly shoved him forward. He was unsteady on his feet and stumbled but he did not fall, still held up by the man who followed after him. A tall dark man in a sweatshirt and windcheater. A man bearing something black and boxy and semi-automatic.

He couldn't know that whatever he might do, O'Malley had given me a little lift. The trash. The trash.

I stepped forward. 'Let him go.'

Out of the corner of my eye I could see the lights shifting again. Someone in the car yelled something in Arabic. The driver of the van gunned his engine. The tall man pushed Myles out of the way, stepped forward and grabbed me by my suit-lapel and almost threw me into the van. He was still climbing through the door as it pulled away.

I tried to raise myself from the floor and turn to get a look at him, but as I turned I saw him lift the black boxy thing, and got no chance to tense before he brought it down across my neck and shoulders.

It didn't put me out, not that time. Not quite under. Through the van windscreen, between their bodies, I got a vague flash of Rachel looking startled in their headlights, and then we were cornering up the hill, and bearing left, and it got confused. But not before I saw something else – the driver's eyes in the rear-view mirror. One of them was blue.

It looked like we were heading out into country, well outside my manor. I saw a street sign saying Nutfield

Something and then it got pretty dark. It can't have been much later that we did a swift right, though, and I caught a flash of a sign reading Mid Street and I was well lost.

No more than ten minutes from the pick-up the van jerked to a halt. We'd turned off the road and I could see we were right out in the fields. Smell it too. But mainly I could tell because I couldn't see any lights. There was a metal five-bar gate in front of us. It was chained up. One of the men up front got out with a big pair of cutters. Go through that chain like butter. Then I saw the sign on the gate: Fire Crews and Emergency Services Only. No Entry.

Then I twigged it. Not that it did me any good, because this time they weren't taking any chances. They hit me again, and I went down.

CHAPTER FIVE

When I came round, I was surrounded by blackness. My body was jelly except for the crucifix of pain down my neck and back and across my shoulders. The world seemed dizzying and wobbly beneath me, and there was a monstrous roar invading my ears and everything between them. It seemed linked to the sucking in my throat and the thin cold air like needles in my chest.

I must have moaned, because the tall man beside me put his hand on my shoulder, as much in support as restraint. I could make out small lights before us, and dim shapes. But most of all what I made out was noise, a noise that acted on my whole body like a dentist's drill on teeth.

It must have been another half an hour before I got the bulk of my brain back and understood. We were in a plane. Nothing very big or grand. Six seater. Four of them. Me sprawled across the back two seats. Twin engine prop by the noise it was making. But a plane nonetheless.

I gagged, and started to throw up. The tall man took my lower jaw in his right hand and forced me towards a sick-bag. Tidy with it.

I tried to think, above the smell of puke, the noise of the engines, the pain in my back and the metal taste in my mouth. I should have guessed. But how could I have? Rachel and her heavies had not. Redhill. The old Redhill aerodrome.

No commercial service used it. It had always been too small. Bristow Helicopters had a factory there though, and private planes still used it, and a few executive charters.

Short hops by businessmen to Amsterdam and Paris when they didn't want or couldn't afford to be tied down to scheduled services. This lot could afford a plane. And it made sense to fly out illegally, at night, when the aerodrome was closed. No witnesses. No flight-log.

They'd had fifteen million on deposit, unused, for an age. So they could bear the cost of flying. But flying where? Where the hell were we heading? And why?

The tall man told me as much as he thought I needed to know. 'You only have yourself to blame, Mr Ford. Charlton was getting a little uncomfortable. I assume you had something to do with the stepping back of the surveillance?'

'I don't know what you're talking about.'

He sounded amused. 'Don't you? I rather doubt that. I'm not sure yet that you work for our enemies, but it would be very surprising if they had not put a hold on you after the unfortunate events of these past few days. We were watching out for the surveillance. We knew the patterns to expect. Our Irish friends had warned us, from the days they ran a bombing cell out of Charlton.'

Irish friends? I tried a little tabloid irony. 'What is this? Terror international?'

He smiled in the darkness. He had good teeth. I guessed he might be quite a looker. The Arab stallion type. The Sheikh. The Hawk. An image getting worn around the edges these days by all the fat petro-princes, buying up real estate and trollops. 'Nothing so grand.' He had to shout over the engines. 'We just have to find our friends where we can, and we don't have access to the regular channels.' He jerked me upright. It hurt like hell. Then he put the muzzle of his semi-automatic in my throat.

I hung tough. 'You aren't going to use that, not in here. You'd take us all down if you did.'

He acknowledged it, with what was almost courtesy. 'That's true. But you've already found out what I can do with it without pulling the trigger.'

I tried to nod, but my head wouldn't move. He wouldn't have seen it anyway.

He wasn't finished with me yet, however. 'We want our money, Mr Ford. We don't care very much how we get it, but we want it. There are those of my colleagues who hold you personally responsible. I'm not so sure of that. I haven't decided yet if you're a thief or a fool. It is possible, of course, you're both. Even so, I hope to be able to do business with you and your friend. But it has to be away from the attentions of your police and secret services. Hence Air Palestine.'

A sense of humour, too? Or was he just winding me up? Softening me up more likely. One of the others would do a hard man routine before all of this was over, then this one would be back all kind and witty and I'd be expected to blubber on his shoulder.

'There is a little detail you had probably better know, Mr Ford.' Why did that not sound healthy? 'We couldn't log a flight plan, the aerodrome being closed. We're flying low now, under the radar, and not feeding into beacons. Instruments and visual only. In a couple of hours we'll be landing at a little private airfield just south of Cork, to refuel. We can't do our journey in a single hop . . .'

Ireland? Refuel? I could guess what that meant. I must have murmered it under my breath. 'Costa del Crime.'

'What?'

I tried to shake my head, to cover it. 'No, nothing. My head hurts.' It hurt all right. The sudden activity was painful. What was in range for a smallish plane from Southern Ireland. Scotland, Wales and England, but why? Ulster. Get out of here. France. They could have flown direct. Or Spain. What did the Spaniards care? They had their hands full with their own problems, with the Basques and the Catalans. There was already a big wealthy Arab presence in the south, round Marbella. Good telecommunications to London. Or good enough. And no extradition treaty worth talking about with Britain. Hence Costa del Crime. Every London villain who made the big time headed south to retirement in Spain. Lie out in the sunshine. Let the fences and the dogs keep unwanted visitors out. Play golf, drink gin, bitch about the dagos, watch dirty videos and the BBC by satellite, and if you got really lucky, get photographed in the clubhouse with a gentleman. Sean Connery, perhaps. Or Roger Moore.

Anyway, he let it pass. 'You don't need to know our ultimate destination, not yet. What you should know is that we have rented the services of our Irish colleagues. They are a little nervous. It would be a disaster for them to have one of their airfields traced. Which is why, I am afraid, I have put you in additional danger by telling you where it is. If you try anything clever, you will have the IRA to deal with, as well as us. And by the way, Mr Ford, they're nervous, they're trigger-happy, and they don't like Englishmen. There isn't any chance of help from them. Don't even think about it. They're just as likely to kill you on the spot. I wouldn't like that. I want my money.'

I had to ask. 'Your money? Who are you anyway? Fatah? PFLP? Black September?'

He grinned again. 'Very entertaining, Mr Ford. Very droll.' At least he didn't blame me for trying.

After that no one said anything for over an hour, when the pilot, the ugly one with the one blue eye, turned round and shouted, 'Selim, Selim,' and pointed through the windows, indicating down. We were crossing out over the Irish Sea, leaving England behind. I saw the tall one scowl. I suppose because 'Selim' was his name. Not that I could do much with it.

My guess is that we touched down south of Cork some time round one in the morning. The depths of the night and the depths of the country. Not even the haze of an electric light anywhere for miles. We came down between two lines of oil drums filled with greasy rags, belching a viscous light and thick columns of smoke, black even within the darkness.

Selim and two of the others went out to help with the

refuelling. They left me with one of the youngsters, one of the punks. I remembered all too well what they'd done to Saul, and I took no chances, staying still and silent while a lean little murderer loomed over me with death in both his hands. From beyond the windows I could hear occasional barked instructions in a thick shamrock brogue, and I knew there was no hope out there. O'Malley notwithstanding, I was losing patience with the Irish. I didn't know then this lot would have preferred to do the job from Ireland, but didn't like the liaison between the British and Irish security forces.

By the time they finished the fuelling and off- and on-board checks they were getting tired, and perhaps a little careless. I heard Selim calling the other two in by name, though I couldn't tell which was which. Khalil and Nayef.

Take-off from a rough rural field was ponderous, painful and endlessly slow. There was a moment, just before the pilot banked away from trees, that I thought we weren't going to make it. Swissair it wasn't.

A wild grey winter's dawn was breaking, squally with showers and gusty with turbulence, as we came in over what I took to be the Spanish coast. Once we were in and over the pilot dipped low, still evading radar and turned out of the light, headed west, daybreak scudding behind us as we glimmered on through darkness, trying not to break cover.

That puzzled me. I'd guessed we would head south, towards the rich Arab colony on the Mediterranean, but if I had to put money on it my bet would be the estate we finally pitched towards – a pair of low hills, one fluffy with plane trees, the other bare, flanking a valley with an airstrip cut into it; I didn't spot the house at first, a low flat-roofed ranch-type spread over the brow of the naked hill – was somewhere south of Santander.

I'd also expected the place to be crawling – goons, guards and dogs – but as we bounced to a rickety halt no one appeared to greet us. It kept the place inconspicuous, but I wondered what arrangement if any had been made with the local authorities. Not that there would have been anything new about that. There have been smugglers working fist in glove with the locals from the north coast of Spain and the west coast of France as long as anyone can remember. No coast guard willingly worked the Bay of Biscay, some of the worst waters in the world, the sump of the North Atlantic where the waters guttered and swelled. I knew boys in the Rat and Rizla with iron guts and greedy eyes who ran Spanish brandy up by the shipload, mixed it with the cheapest French stuff and rebottled it as own-brand cognac for the cheap end of the club and catering trade.

Even so, I wasn't overjoyed to be in Spain. Oh, I'd been there often enough, down south – football tours, golf weekends and bonking expeditions, but there's something about the Dago brings out the worst in every Brit.

Why is that I wonder? Spanish Armada? I don't believe it. No, I reckon it has more to do with Brits getting to know it while they were building up the tourism under Franco.

Our lads, what they've always liked is a ruck and a bundle. And they're used to getting away with it. Face it, your average British rozzer comes from the same place as your hooligan. He's torn it up when he was a kid. Sometimes he still gets to, in uniform, and paid for it. He doesn't really want to bring in his own. There's a kind of silent agreement between our lads and filth. Your Spaniards aren't like that. Oh, they make a lot of noise, they wave the colours, but under the Caudillo the Guardia were a real enemy. They wouldn't just slap you about a bit, run you in overnight, in a good-natured sort of fashion. It was truncheons up the arsehole and electric cattle-prods in the goolies. Inhibits the fighting spirit. So our boys got to write theirs off as noisy wimps, fair game, as . . . well, as *waiters*. And waiters who poked our women, too. It isn't like the way we feel about the Frogs. It isn't hatred. Declare War

Now, We Wuz Robbed, The Hundred Years War Should
Have Lasted Longer, Remember Crècy, Poitiers, Agincourt
and Waterloo loathing. But it is contempt.

You know, no wonder the wogs all hate us.

And I didn't even speak Dagostani, so breaking out was
out of the question. How would I ask for help?

That was a long way off, however. Selim bundled me and
my bag off the plane and started pulling me towards the
house.

It was a longer walk than it looked from the air. I was well
jiggered by the time we were over the brow and almost
running down the incline to the house.

They may have had four billion dollars to play with, they
may have had the money for a nice spread in northern
Spain, but they didn't believe in interior decoration. A
basic kitchen, some couches, a few single beds – all under
dustcovers – and a lock-up breezeblock basement. Guess
who ended up in the basement.

I must have slept. I must have passed out. When I came
round, brighter, stronger sunlight was sloping through
the narrow barred-up window tucked into the wall just
under the ceiling. It was Selim who roused me, with
some bottled water, pitta bread and chutney. Not the
best meal I've ever had, but I was tired, and beaten up,
and famished. When I'd wolfed it down he said, gently,
'It's time you came up. It's time you tried to call your
friend.'

They had a single, old-fashioned dial-phone with its own
number ripped out of the dial. Even so I wondered how
much it must have cost them to fit a phone this far from
a major town. I wondered if it would work.

Selim dialled the international code for London then
handed over to me.

'What time is it?' I asked him.

'It's ten. The Spaniards run their clocks an hour ahead

166

of London. Nine there. If your friend hasn't abandoned you, he should be waiting for your call.'

I dialled Myles's direct line at IIIB. He answered before I heard a single ring.

'Yes. Hello . . .'

'Myles, it's John.'

Then Selim leaned across the 'phone and cut me off.

He smiled, and it was no longer a pleasant apparition. 'That should stop them feeling overconfident. There's nothing like anxiety. Now, why don't you tell us what this is all about?'

'I don't know what you mean.'

He looked mock-sorrowful and glanced at the pilot, the older man with the blue eye.

He stepped behind me and placed his leather-gloved hands gently on my stricken shoulders. Then he pulled and pressed and backed me into a plastic bucket chair. Orange. Nasty. There was a stack of them in the kitchen.

He came in close behind me, lurking, and began to tease my hair, brushing it down with the edge of his hand, as though he was dusting a table, or waiting patiently to swat a fly. Then he leaned yet further forward, steadying himself by gripping my right shoulder. He polished my nut with his elbow, with the under surface, the back, of his upper arm. Then he did it. In a single movement he stepped back and pulled on my shoulder, tipping the chair on to its back legs so I was looking at the ceiling, and hoisted his crooked arm and brought it down, hard on my face.

I heard the nose-bones crack. I felt the blood fly, and the snot. And I felt pain. Pain like a red light blazing through my skull and down my throat till I was gagging and choking and throwing up at once.

Then he grabbed me by both the shoulders and hauled me from the chair and tossed me twisting face-first into the wall.

That was the only time he touched my face, or anything that would show. He was a professional in his way, and by the time he was done I wasn't sure I had any kidneys left.

167

When it was over, when they'd forced water down me so fast it came out through my nose, flooding out the blood and filth and I'd passed out again from the pain and pressure of it; when they'd mopped me down, and all my slops, Selim loomed over me and said, the good cop, the gentle cop, to the end, 'Why don't you just tell me how you did it? Why don't you tell me where the money is?'

The damnedest thing is, I wanted to. I wanted to spill my guts. I wanted this to be over. But I knew I couldn't. If I told them, they'd never believe the stuff about the Irishman. They'd never believe I couldn't get them back their money. At best, they'd kill me then and there. At worst there would be more of this. More pain. And then they'd kill me. I had to go on lying.

It took everything I had to speak at all, in whispers, and gasped phrases.

'I told you. Don't know. Don't know. Wouldn't be here if I knew.'

He backed away. He let me sweat. He went off with the pilot. Khalil. The name he'd used when he put a stop to the pain. He left me with the punks.

It was noon in London when they came back. One o'clock in Spain. They dragged me to the 'phone. We went through the dialling ritual. But before we did so, Selim said, 'My friend does not believe you. Still. He says a little more time alone with you and you will talk. And I? I no longer care. This call is your last chance to persuade me perhaps I ought to care. Oh, and whatever you do, don't tell him where you are.'

The numbers tumbled on the line. Then nothing happened. In the time when there should have been three, four, rings, there was silence. Then at last it started ringing. Four times. It wasn't until a fair while afterwards I realised what must have happened. They had a trace-tap on the 'phone and it silenced the first few rings, to buy them extra time in which the trace could work. None of that mattered for now, however. What mattered was my longing for O'Malley's voice.

When he answered, the line was hollow and distant, like the silence behind the sea-sounds in a shell, and his voice was haunted by an echo.

'John! What happened? I . . .'

I could hardly talk. I just about gasped, 'Doesn't matter.' Then I swallowed, and added as best I could, 'What news?'

Myles went business-like on me. He could have been negotiating a currency-swap.

'OK,' he said, 'take it from the top. I got in touch with Marius Meyer in Zurich. Trashed them.' (Bless you, Myles. Bless you, Fulham Council.) 'Finally, I threatened garnisheeing their London transfers and they spilled the beans. They had a pre-standing order to transfer any funds coming in from BHM to this account to another account in Geneva. With Javert, Valjean. The only identification I have so far is an account number and a transaction code: CIRCUITOUS. I've just been speaking to Geneva. They're giving me the same hard time as Zurich. But give me time. What I've done is use the account number and transaction code to instruct them to forward the funds back to IIIB. Now, if they still have the funds, they have no option. The code is binding. When it comes in we can transfer the money wherever our friends want it. But if they don't have the funds, they have to tell me. I pass as beneficial owner. And then I can cry fraud and threaten them with a writ in the Cantonal Court to find out where they sent the money. But it won't come to that, I'm sure. I expect to know one way or another by close of business today. Now, where are you? Where can I reach you?'

I swallowed again, hopelessly. 'Can't tell you that. I'll call you back at five your time.' (Pick it up Myles. Your time. I'm out of the country.) 'Just have the answers by then.' I took a deep breath. Then I added, 'It's a long shot, but if you have legal problems with it, get hold of the BHM solicitors. Talk to Buster Edwards. He's helped with stuff like this before . . .'

And then they cut me off again.

Think, Myles, think. Your time. Out of the country. Buster Edwards. The Great Train Robber. Who skipped the country. To Spain.

I hadn't noticed the pilot, Khalil, leave the room. I saw him coming back, carrying a telephone answering machine. They must have had it attached to another extension. They had the whole conversation, the preceding silence and rings, everything, on tape. Selim played it back, translating it for Khalil, and played it back again. And thought, and thought, and thought.

This time they didn't hurt me. This time they just let me sweat it out, in the basement lock-up, after showing me where the punks stood outside the house, scanning the skies and a distant road, winding through a wood, and showed me their guns. It was fear enough for anyone, on top of all that pain.

It was darkening when they hauled me out, and cold. A bitter, biting frost deep in my bones and injured organs, the ache of early scarring in my face.

They must even have had the trip of the dialling tumblers on the tape, and counted off the numbers, because when they sat me down this time, Selim dialled the whole number. As he waited over the early silence he said, 'In case you hadn't guessed, this is tapped. It won't do them any good, but be quick about it in any case.'

Myles was waiting for me. 'John, yes.'

'Surprise, surprise.'

He was gruff. 'I've kept this line clear for you. Couldn't keep you waiting.'

'What news?'

He hesitated. 'It hasn't been easy. I've had to threaten them with Swiss and British law. They've been trying to make me wait for a formal transaction statement.'

'So they have an address. For statements.'

'No, they were just jerking me around. Statements pile up in Geneva. Collected in person from time to time citing the code. So I telexed them an override to get

170

them to give me the details now.'

'And?'

'And, there was a set of instructions concerning an anticipated deposit of fifteen million dollars.'

'What instructions?'

Myles hesitated. I repeated the question. He answered at last.

'The immediate acquisition of fifteen mill in dollar certificates of deposit, bearer instruments only, issued by AAA bank or financial institution borrowers.'

'Well, that's it. Bingo. All we have to do is get the lawyers in to shake the CDs out of them.'

This time his pause was longer, but he broke it himself. 'It isn't quite that simple. I've been doing some checking. Spreading some jam around. Usual places, usual people. We both know a cut-out operation as smooth as this not pulled by an insider could only have been done by maybe half a dozen people.'

'Sure. But first things first. Let's get the money.'

'Just hold your horses. Hear me out.' I got the message. Whatever the reason – a telephone trace or something else – he wanted me to ride his pace. I could do that. I knew how. I listened. 'Stephan Hochhiem is holed up in Hamburg, keeping his head down since he tapped into the US Defense Department's specification system for that Arab arms merchant consortium. Maria Caridad was last seen in Cuba after she pulled the Cayman Islands job. Tim Wharf is in negotiation with the Fraud Squad and the Inland Revenue trying to hang on to as much of the hundred mill or so he must have taken these past eight years, and Jerzy Drabinski's dying in an AIDS hospice outside San Francisco. That only leaves the Irishman, who was around till mid August, but hasn't been seen since. It looks like him, unless we have a new generation at work.'

Nicely done, I thought to myself, through the red fog in my head, but what about it? I put it as simply as I could. 'So what? Let's get the money.'

Myles must have decided there was no point in being

171

gentle with me. He let it spill. 'We can't. He's clever, the Irishman. Geneva don't hold the CDs. Neither do AIBD in Luxembourg. He arranged for couriered delivery of the physical certificates to another branch of Javert, Valjean. To a safe-deposit box, with some physical code they won't tell me about, because if I'm the beneficial owner I ought to know. It's brick wall time.'

I tried to treat it logically. 'OK. OK. Point taken. But what do we know? Do we know who issued the CDs? Do we know what branch of Javert, Valjean?'

'Yes. That much I did get out of them before they closed down on me. It isn't good news. It's the Panama City branch.'

Why couldn't the little shit have chosen Vaduz? Or better, Monte Carlo. Panama was a good deal too Dago, and I couldn't go through Miami this time. There was my other question, too.

'What about the CDs? What do we know about the issuer?'

I think it was as close as I've ever heard Myles come to crying. 'I can't be certain yet, John-boy. I'm having a trace done our end. But I have my suspicions. We issued forty million in CDs that day as part of our normal funding programme. Biggest player in the market that day. I have a horrible feeling they're ours. I think they're IIIB's.'

'Myles, I'll call you back.'

'John-boy . . .'

This time I cut him off.

CHAPTER SIX

'You stupid bastards.'

Selim didn't like it. More, he didn't understand it. I tried to make it easy for him.

'If you had just come through our door and asked nicely the other day, instead of killing Saul, you could have had your money tomorrow morning. Now, God only knows what happens.'

Khalil, returning with the tape again, must have heard the contempt in my voice, and perhaps the despair. It left him looking ugly and dangerous. Selim restrained him with a wave of the hand.

'Explain yourself, Mr Ford.'

Easier said than done. I was sick, I hurt, I'd talked enough for this or any afternoon, and I was involved. But I was mad enough to try.

'You can listen to the tape. The short form goes something like this. We think a pro everyone calls the Irishman did it. No one knows his real name. He dummied a telex to us. We sent the funds to Bank Marius Mayer in Zurich. They had instructions to send them to Javert, Valjean in Geneva. And they had instructions to use the money to buy three-month dollar certificates of deposit. Those are bearer instruments. Hold the paper, own the money. Not registered, not traceable.'

Selim was patient with me. 'I know what CDs are, Mr Ford.'

Funny, isn't it? A man associates with people in dishcloths and you just assume he's stupid. I had to stop that. That was dangerous. I shrugged.

'Javert, Valjean bought the CDs and, on instruction, sent the paper by courier to their Panama branch to be held in a safe-deposit box. That's all we know. Not the number of the box. Not the physical code. Nothing. That needn't have mattered. If you'd played this by the rules, we'd have a chance, because it looks as though the CDs were ones issued by O'Malley's bank, IIIB. He could've tried to identify the serial numbers, gone to court with your evidence of theft, got a stop order on the CDs, put a warning out on the International Inter-Bank system and through Interpol and, at the very least, put matching funds into an escrow account and let you use that as collateral till the certificates showed up, or if they didn't show up, his year-end when he could have his auditors balance the whole thing off. But he can't do that now. Because he can't get an injunction on behalf of murderers. And I think I want to be sick.'

One of the punks brought me a plastic bucket.

I know Myles hadn't said all that to me, but he hadn't had to. I knew how it worked. After all, he taught me.

Selim set up the tape and played it back. He was silent for a long time after that. Eventually he explained it to the others. Then he was silent some more.

Finally he came back to me, looking gaunt and haggard, his pale brown eyes almost shifting into grey, he looked so tired. For a second there I almost felt some sympathy for him, but then I remembered what his people had done to Saul Steinitz and to me.

He squatted on the floor before me, unrepelled, the way most people are, by the condition I was in and the stink from the bucket, the thin mildew of stale waters that was all there had been left in me to come out. (Have you noticed that? The way people treat the sick as though it was their fault? As though they were disgusting?) He looked like an Arab, settled there. If we had been outside, he would have plucked at stalks of grass or drifts of sand and tossed them in the air to catch the wind and check its direction, as though that way he might catch some scent

174

he needed, drifting on the breeze. I could imagine falcons caw and striking. I could imagine him hooded in the little killers' leather mask, pricked with feathers and studded with jewels.

What he said got rid of daydreams.

'We don't seem to have any option We have to go to Panama.'

Part of me agreed. The closer I could get to the money the better. Another part had had enough, of this picayune picaresque. But I didn't have any say in the matter. The best I could do was stall.

'I don't see how,' I told him. 'What are we going to do for money? I don't have a passport. We need both for Panama. You're not going to get there in that thing we came in. What's its maximum range? Five hundred miles? Six tops? And what about you?'

He was sombre. 'We don't have a country, Mr Ford. It's what we want. It doesn't seem too much to ask. We used to have a country. But that doesn't mean we don't have passports.' He indicated each of them in turn, starting with himself. 'Syrian, Jordanian, Algerian and Lebanese. We take whatever nationality papers we can. Travel documents, too. It's only our most celebrated leaders who get to travel on diplomatic *laissez-passers*, on the passports of what will one day be the State of Palestine.'

'But what about me? My passport's still in London.'

He smiled. 'That needn't be a problem. This is Spain. It's Panama we're going to. These things can be . . . negotiated. But better not. I don't know where this is going to end. And nor do you. And thank you for not bleating, for not saying you'd done what you agreed to. I'm afraid you're in this to the end.'

I agreed by ignoring it, but, 'That still doesn't answer my question.'

He frowned. 'We have enough fuel dumped here to fly to Barcelona. There are daily flights to Panama from there.' (That alone was enough to tell me they had to run accounts in Panama themselves. How else would he know the schedule? Who was he – Thomas Cook?) 'In calmer circumstances, the easiest thing to do would be to have your friend make up a parcel of your papers and some clothes and send them to Barcelona by Iberia Air Freight. But the police would of course monitor such a package. We cannot risk such consequences. I'm very much afraid I'm going to have to hire the IRA again and have them break into your apartment. Where is your passport?'

No way out. 'Box file, behind the cassettes in the sitting-room.'

He nodded. 'I'll telephone. We'd better get moving. I dare say the authorities will be on us before too long.' He jabbered something at Khalil in Arabic. The only word I got was 'camera'.

Selim went off into another room while Khalil did as he had been told.

What he had been told was to fill the camera case. He did it in front of me.

It was one of those aluminium cases professional lensmen use, the solid ones with ridges. This was a big mother, with the usual grey polystyrene cut into shapes to take the camera-bodies, instruments and lenses. The lenses were the trick. They unscrewed.

There were two bodies in the case, four long lenses, and two smaller ones. They were the old-style lenses – glass in metal casings, except I guess the lenses themselves were really plastic not glass, to get the weight right. Because what he did was to fit black polyurethane inserts inside the unscrewed mechanisms, and into those he fitted small handguns, two of them, stocks into one lens apiece, the barrel and firing mechanisms into another. Then he reassembled the lenses. Neat. Very neat. I wondered how much they'd had to pay to adapt the camera equipment, and for guns that came apart so conveniently. The smaller lenses opened up to reveal black pockets for the ammunition. Then he put the whole lot together and snapped the case shut.

I could see it working. It would go through airport X-ray equipment and the metal of the case and the lenses would baffle the system. They'd never see the guns. My guess was that the lens mounts were lined with thin lead, just to make certain. Even if the authorities decided to do a hands-on check, what would they find? Open the case, it looked quite normal. Open the camera bodies and they would be empty. Pick up the lenses and they would be – what? Big, heavy, old-fashioned jobs, black as any other lens when you tried to look within. Only attempting to put a camera together and seeing the darkness in the SLR's viewfinder, the jamming of the shutter mechanism, would show that anything was wrong, and who had time to go that far, at a busy international airport?

Selim returned and flagged Khalil off to help the others with the 'plane. I let him know I was impressed.

'Where did that camera case come from?'

He dismissed it, sounding bored. 'Standard safe house issue. The CIA developed them, twenty years ago, gave them to Gaddafi. He let us in on the idea.'

I'm not easily surprised (do enough international banking and you lose the capacity for it) but that surprised me. 'The CIA? Gaddafi?'

That did not bore him. 'Yes. They backed him at the beginning. They make mistakes. They armed him, too. Most of the spare C-4 plastic explosive in circulation is from the shipments they sent him under cover. The marine barracks in Beirut was hit by what had been American PX. But you get the idea. We are fairly well prepared for most eventualities.' He got efficient on me. 'I've spoken to our Irish colleagues. One of their donkeys will fly in with your passport on the first flight tomorrow. I'm afraid, for form's sake, they will make it look like an amateur burglary. Children. Not that anyone will believe that, but I'm afraid you're going to lose your electronics. And I expect there'll be shit on the carpets.'

He sat down on the floor before me, his ankles crossed

and his knees pitched high, and put his elbows on his knees and his head in his hands. He looked exhausted.

Then he murmured, 'You say you think . . . your friend thinks, this was done by an Irishman?'

'That's his guess.'

He rubbed his eyes. I wondered if he had had any sleep. He did not look the kind who needed much. But something was bothering him. I'm still not sure it was what he spoke of.

'I mentioned that to our Republican colleagues. They were intrigued. They had no direct knowledge of this man, but they have reason to believe that something in the order of four million pounds was filched from INLA accounts over the past two years.'

INLA? Irish National Liberation Army? There had been stuff in the papers. Stuff about a power struggle within it. A blood-bath. An internal war so savage, so Irish, even the IRA had written them off. Was there something I didn't know about this? Did the Irishman make his living shafting terrorist bank accounts?

'Still,' Selim continued, 'he's our problem now. They made that very plain. But they did say they'd try to establish an identity. That might help us, no?'

'Who knows? What would he use his real name for?'

He put his hands up, in the universal gesture: Who knows? Who cares? Then he reached for the 'phone.

'You must excuse me. I have a call to make.'

It was a long call, and I don't know what it was about. I don't have any Arabic. He knew that. He must have known that. It was why he was willing to make the call in front of me. But it was still careless of him. I didn't get the whole of the number he dialled, but I got the start of it: 010 216. A long time later I would find out that was Tunisia. And as he introduced himself to whoever was on the other end, I got an approximation of his name. Something like Awa's Ear. Selim.

When he was done, and the others had come back in, he finished his arrangements. He told me, 'There's one thing

178

more. You have to call your friend again. You need a note of all the account numbers, names and codes he has. Well, you don't need a note, but you have to have him say them, so we have them on tape. And we have to make whoever he's working with believe we haven't gone far, once they find this place. Which means you have to tell him you may be out of touch for two or three days, but he is to stay by a phone you know at all times so you can reach him if necessary. We have to try to tie them down.'

I did as I was told. O'Malley sounded shagged, and sad. I wondered what he knew. I wondered what he had to feel sad about. That made me afraid. Maybe that was why, before they cut me off one last time, I found myself saying something soppy.

I said, 'Myles . . . if anything happens, tell porkies to Ma, will you? And the family. Tell 'em I ran off with some tart.'

I wouldn't have been able to. Run off with a tart, that is. Not after what Khalil did next. Not after his last little professional demonstration. He made me take my pants off – trousers, shoes, socks, boxers, the works. Then he pulled out a little weejit that really made him smile.

It was made of medium weight brass wire, a fair length of it, with a noose at either end. One noose went round my middle toes. Then he ran the wire round my foot and up my leg, taping it in place at the ankle and both sides of the knee. The other noose went round my family jewels, tight, and taped in place as well. They had to help me in my clothes, and that made Khalil laugh.

I had to hand it to him. It was light, it was invisible and, with that lot on, I wasn't running anywhere.

It wasn't until they had boarded me into the 'plane (I wouldn't have made it unaided) that I remembered to ask the thousand dollar question again. 'This flight to Panama. Just what are we going to use for money?'

Khalil turned out not to be the dummy I had taken him for. Or the ignoramus. He twisted round in the pilot's seat,

179

looking like the prototype for Malocchio, the Evil Eye, and shot me a wicked, snaggle-toothed grin as he pulled, from somewhere deep within the folds of his jacket, an American Express Gold Card, and said in halting, fractured English, 'Niffer liff howem wissart it.'

Most of the rest is detail. We jacked into Barcelona about midnight, one of the last 'planes in. Then we sat on the apron in a fine winter drizzle for the best part of an hour while Selim and Khalil took care of formalities. Stuff to do with parking the 'plane in a hangar as far as I could work out, and I would guess arranging for someone else to be able to collect it at a later date. If it was theirs, that is. For all I know it was rented and they were just ditching it. I don't know what they told the airport official, either; the one who kept eyeballing me, wondering about why I was so banged up. I was well beyond caring by that point. Exhaustion and the flight had got to me, the scabs and clots in my face opening up again as we had climbed so they had had to try staunching the flow in the end with oily engine rags. I must have looked appalling. I felt it. And there wasn't any hope of breaking free, the two punks flanking me all the time, and no one I could turn to, or if I could no way of talking to them.

What surprised me at the terminal, even through the disorientation of pain, was that one Iberia ticketing booth was still open. The punks kept me aside while the others made our reservations. I didn't hear the details. After that it was the credit cards again at the Hotel Booking Agency in the main hall and a silent taxi ride. Later, much later, I found a match-book for the Gran Hotel Sarria so I guess that's where we put up, but I don't really remember. I was barely conscious by then, and I don't imagine I'll be going back to check it out. All I remember is high ceilings and what seemed endless corridors, unfolding out of the darkness. I don't even know what I was doing with the match-book. Instinct, I suppose. Take everything you can from hotel rooms. I'm amazed I didn't walk out of there with a couple of shampoos and half a dozen bars of soap.

We were back at the terminal building by nine the following morning. I was feeling a little better after a night's sleep, but still not steady on my feet. We hadn't eaten either, and hunger had gone beyond the point of adding keenness to the brain and instead it was wiping me out. A kind of constant waking sleepiness that might almost have been concussion. Perhaps it was.

We waited at Arrivals first; or rather, Selim waited at the gate while the rest of us huddled on benches in the waiting area. I hardly saw the switch took place. It wasn't until I saw Selim turn and head back towards us with a nylon hold-all in his hand that I looked about and caught a glimpse of the rear-end of a short, muscular, black Irishman in a parka and jeans sloping for the stairs up to Departures as fast as he reasonably could.

Selim went through the bag, shuffling sweaters, shirts, a pair of jeans, and underpants, until he turned up the hard blue card of a British passport, no longer reassuring, no longer a pleasure. They waited for what must have been an hour before half-helping, half-dragging me upstairs.

It was in the queue at Check-In that I got my next surprise. 'This isn't a Panama flight,' I found myself whispering. 'This goes to Amsterdam.'

'Shut up,' Selim instructed.

It wasn't until we were on the 'plane, until Khalil had successfully passed the camera-case through all security-checks, that Selim explained.

'There isn't a direct flight to Panama on Fridays. Even if there were, we wouldn't have taken it, just in case you'd somehow managed to slip your friend some idea of our destination. This way they end up wondering how we're going to route and end up frittering away their forces.'

'What are we doing in Amsterdam?'

'Just changing planes. There's a KLM flight to Panama this afternoon. But it gives us another chance to bale out

181

if we have to. It's the easiest way of doing it, and easy enough to check out. But they won't work it out. If you have the ABC Airline Schedules and the Cook's International Train Timetables you're already a step ahead of every security force in the world.'

I asked him because I wanted to, because I was curious, not because I had any hope it might prove useful. 'How do you know all this stuff? You don't look like a terrorist. You don't sound like one. Where did you learn to speak English anyway?'

He suddenly roared with laughter, and had to smother it, as Khalil reared nervously in the seat before him, twisting to check us out. Selim waved him back, and the two in the seats behind us. But he still looked amused as he answered, 'Eton.'

I couldn't believe it. 'Eton!'

He nodded. 'And Yale. And Harvard Law School. I'm licensed to practise law in New York, and I kept my terms and ate my dinners and did my exams in London. Middle Temple. A year of pupillage and I suppose I could practise there, too. If I'd wanted.'

I don't know which offended me more: the discovery that he was a lawyer, because lawyers are arseholes; or that anyone with his background should be slaughtering the innocent. He seemed to understand. He went on without prompting, waving away the stewardess (you're not supposed to call them that any more, are you? Flight attendants? Waitresses.) who was trying to press plates of aggregate and a cup of tar on us.

'I was meant to be the one spared . . . all this.' There was an edge of exhaustion and despair in his voice at the phrase, as though what he had done and was doing had come to infect the whole globe. 'I'd hoped . . . I don't know what I'd hoped. Some foolishness. Some thought that one day my people would need builders as well as destroyers. Legislators as well as soldiers. And in the meantime – who knows? – perhaps there was some final bar of justice, some international tribunal, some court of justice, where I and

182

others like me could intercede for the rights of our people. To find some way of returning to our immemorial hills. Do you know what the most heartbreaking word in the English language is?'

I shook my head.

He smiled a bitter, twisted little smile. 'It's *home.*'

He was silent for a long while after that, but one word, one question, kept buzzing round my head, and in the end I had to let it out before it stung.

'Yes, but Eton?'

He sighed, remembering, a wry look in his eyes. 'I was lucky. My father was a doctor. Surgeon. Fifteen years in the United States and ten in the Gulf, repairing the indulgences of fat old men and the indignities of time, was enough to raise the money to educate his daughters and his youngest son, out of the necessities of violence.'

'What about your brothers?'

He shrugged. 'They are romantics. And they were old enough, as I was not, to see and understand the consequences of 68 and Hussein's strike against us in Jordan. And we have a, distinguished, relative it is possible to follow.'

I wondered who I was sitting next to. I tried to make sense of what his surname had sounded like. Awa's Ear? Who was this? An Arafat, or something?

But I'm an old-fashioned boy, and I was still offended. A lawyer, an Old Etonian lawyer, had no business doing what he was doing. Yes, sure I know bent briefs. My part of the world they're thick on the ground as leaves on a British Rail train-track in early November. Where I come from, the way it works is, there are people inside the system, people outside it, and the bent ones in between who weave a crooked way between the two. But whatever a bent brief might do — bribe a witness, try to knobble a jury, fix a copper — there are things they won't do. They won't kill anyone. They won't waste the DPP. They may be bent, but they're still lawyers. There are still rules. He'd broken every one of them, and he'd had all the advantages.

'Well, that's a pile of piss, isn't it?' I told him. It wasn't a question. 'What do you take me for? Some kind of liberal? Some kind of thick-witted, goody-goody twit? I know about lawyers. I know enough of them. While we're at it, my boss was a lawyer, until he got stopped being anything. He was like a lot I've known. He was a shyster, a dealer, an artiste. If he could drive a truck through legislation, he would. If he could tie it up in its own red tape, he would. He worked the angles, the percentages, the big grey zones. I grew up with the likes of him. Little lads from Golders Green not bright enough to make doctors but good enough not to let their mommas down completely. But whatever else he was, he was there for people no one else was around for. Him and all the others like him. "On yer bike. Get a kike," we used to say. Because they were there when the Middle Temple wasn't. But you, you go to Eton, you chew the golden dummy. And what do you do? What do you make? Besides a bloody shambles?'

Big speech. I hadn't known I'd had it in me. But he got right up my nose. The rich ones all do that. They all try to tell you how they suffered.

He sounded chastened. 'I never wanted . . . what happened . . .'

'Well, that's a fat lot of good, isn't it? Isn't that just too too noble . . .'

This time he got angry. 'Well, what are we to do? It's all right for you and your clever lawyers. You have a place where there are rules you can try to bend. But what are we to do? We have no place where we can guarantee other men won't come in with machine guns and change the rules. There isn't a tribunal where we can be heard. Do you know what changed me? What changed me was the camps in Beirut . . .'

He was at it again. 'Oh spare me, I've had enough of that as an excuse for Jew-bashing. What are your lot trying to do? Send them to Butlins?'

He took a deep breath, and said, his patience straining, 'It wasn't the Jews. The Jews let it happen, but they didn't

184

do it. That was what mattered. That was what made the difference. Do you know what we are to the world – and that includes the Arab world? We're a bloody nuisance. They wish we'd go away. They wish we'd vanish. And if someone chooses to give us a hand, who's going to stop them, if we cannot? I told you, it's all right for you. You have a place to call your own. We're sick of trying to behave as though that didn't matter. I'm sick of it. My father tried. My father gave up everything to do his duty as a doctor, to his people, in the camps. He died in Shatilla, healing the sick, operating on the wounded. They bombed the pit and rubble and refuse he called his hospital. So what are we to do? There isn't a Red Cross for whole peoples.'

What did he think? That I didn't read the papers? 'All right. All right. Even if I grant you that, how long have people like you been at it? Twenty years? Thirty? Blowing up anything and anyone in sight. And where has it got you? Thrown out of Jordan, Lebanon, even Syria. It's got you to Tunis and Algiers? Oh, very good. What is this, the long way home? Fact is, a bunch of kids with rocks in their hands in Gaza and the Left Bank have done more for the Palestinian cause in the past two months than people like you have done in a generation.'

He smiled, ruefully, and murmured, 'That is very much to the point, Mr Ford. The *intifadeh* is very much to the point.'

Now what did he mean by that, I wondered.

I don't know what I'd been hoping for at Amsterdam – an SAS reception committee? O'Malley waiting with a wee smile and a Queen's Pardon? My old ma with a kind word to make it better? Whatever, what I got was what you always get at Schiphol, and the last thing I needed right then, the best fucking transit airport in the world. What I longed for was Heathrow and a cock-up. What I got was Dutch efficiency.

And Palestinian, too. I guess I'd been hoping I might get free of them for a minute of two at least at Passport Control

185

when they went through the Other Passports line. Not that I could run, not wearing the harness. They'd thought of the queues already. As we came in to land, Selim handed me my passport and said, 'You're coming through the Other Nationalities queue with us. If the immigration official says anything to you, you just point at the length of the EEC passports line-up and shrug. That should do it. And remember, Khalil would like you to make a mistake.'

So I never did get to write the note with their names or some phonetic approximation of them and instructions to phone them to Myles, I never did get to slip it in my passport. Christ, I never even got to take a slash unattended.

All too soon, all too terribly soon for my liking, we were in a 747 bound for Panama and forward destinations. At least it was KLM. That was something, I suppose. Not Air Arrogance. (You have to say it with a French accent to get the true Air France ring to it.)

The long miles slipped away in the usual haze of bad film, bad food, bad air, until at last I found myself peering through the window waiting for the soft slide down through the Caribbean cloud cover into Panama, there before you knew it, the slip of the isthmus was so thin, its hold on reality so slight.

I'd been before a couple of times, as Myles's runner, back in the old days. He was good like that, chucking out the travel as brownie points. Not that anyone could like Panama. I'd seen the way other Central Americans grimaced when you called it a Central American country, and South Americans scowled when you called it Southern. Hell, it wasn't even a country. Cut out of Colombia by the Americans early in the century. It was what it had always been, a shipping point and a trading ground. It felt as though my life was up for sale.

Somewhere down there, on the Caribbean side (and Panama, funny S-shape that it is, is the one place where you go south-east from the Caribbean to the Pacific) Sir Francis Drake lay buried at sea, food for fish, after he and his rowdies made their last assault on Spanish treasure.

How had they done it, I wondered. Where did they get their bottle? Skimming the surface of the world in their coracles, taking on the greatest empire of the age, and more often than not winning. They were hooligans, I suppose. Millwall to a man. But I wasn't. No, not any more. I was beat and broken. No match for the Dago. No match for four stateless wogs. But I had to be. Somehow. 'We have time to finish our game of bowls,' Drake said. So they say. My arse. She might have had a right pair of bowls on her, but that was what he was doing as such. Giving her one for England. I wished I could, but I had a wire harness and four gunmen in my way.

The plane dipped and turned and, through the windows, the Pacific came into view. The Big Mother, which always felt a world away, because it was.

Somewhere, down there, lay my future, if I had one.

I tried to think what Myles might be doing to help. And Rachel. But it didn't work. I felt more like the Irishman. Sinn Fein. Ourselves alone. I wasn't sure I was up to it. Up to No Surrender.

That was bad enough. It would have been worse if I had known exactly what lay in store.

Before all this was over, I would have pulled a real bank job.

I would have done something much, much worse.

And I would have been through the worst joke in the world.

But that was later, when the Panamanians shut down all their banks.

Right now, though, I finally remembered what day it was. It was Friday. It was January the 1st. I couldn't think of any resolutions.

Part Three:

The End, And Then Some

CHAPTER ONE

Well, what can I tell you about Panama?

When God stopped pissing on Miami, he pulled the chain between the oceans, kicked the door closed behind him, and put up a notice saying, 'Cut Along the Dotted Isthmus.'

The only good thing anyone has ever found to say about Panama is that you can get through it really quickly.

But men cannot live by waterways alone. Which is why, as the ships poured through the waters, in a country with a pretty piss-ant agricultural sector (bananas is it, basically) they got into that serious sideline of freight and export-import, banking. Healthiest banking sector in the Third World. In 1970, they got rid of all their currency controls. And I really mean got rid of them – Panama is the only country I know that doesn't issue its own banknotes. It uses US Dollars instead, though officially they're referred to as Balboas. Even the coinage, which has different designs from the American stuff, is the same sizes, weights and denominations. Since then, they've found themselves with about a hundred and thirty banks, combined deposits somewhere between thirty and forty billion dollars. Which is about the only thing that anyone knows about them, and that's an estimate, because absolutely everything else about banking in Panama is covered by security legislation.

Which is, of course, where I came in. Maybe I should have stuck to reinsurance, the other game you get played round maritime banking centres. Insuring insurers, and the sweetest opportunity for fraud you ever did see. Because now, all those banking secrecy laws looked set to work against me.

I had just the one hope when we landed. It was just possible that, in all the chaos, rush and carnage, the flannel-tops had forgotten about the paperwork. Your British passport is one of under a dozen which will get you into Panama without a visa or a tourist card. At worst, they'll ask you to show you've got the money to keep the tarts of Balboa and Colon in the manner to which they've become accustomed. But my little chums weren't travelling on British passports. I hoped it was just possible we might run into trouble at the airport. Trouble that would let me stage a fit, a stroke, anything to get outside help. I reckoned my chances. I'd flown into Tocumen a few times before, acting as bag-man on a few funny little deals and knew my way around it. Nice airport. Very fancy. And one of the many where you're better off buying your duty free goods in town before you leave. Tough, too. Lots of security. They put sniffer dogs into the aircraft holds and passenger compartments, even, especially, if you're just in transit, for drugs. Which is a bit of a laugh really, considering for years now the military have been flying cocaine in and out of La Paitilla, the little airport on the other side of town, and out of the air force bases.

Still, when it came to the paperwork, I'd underestimated Selim, and I'd forgotten the little fact that most airlines that fly into the country are licensed to issue thirty-day tourist cards. They'd got their cards with their tickets.

But I only got the message that I was dealing with people who knew Panama and its ways at least as well as I did when they trotted me past the left luggage to the Avis desk, hired a couple of cars and drove us straight to the Hotel Continental.

I'd better explain that. With a few exceptions, a business hotel is just a business hotel. The El Continental is no exception. Air-conditioned, not too expensive, all the usual services. But what it does have, and its competitors don't, is location.

If you look in a gazetteer, it'll tell you that there are basically five major cities in Panama – Panama itself, Ancon, Balboa, Cristobal and Colon. What it won't tell you, and even maps don't really make clear, is that for all the agricultural land and the towns scattered around, for all practical purposes, the two ends of the Canal are the country. On the Atlantic shore, Cristobal and Colon face each other across it (and together they just make up the Spanish version of Christopher Columbus, a bit as though North and South London were separate cities in law as well as fact called William and Conqueror.) On the Pacific side, Panama, Balboa and Ancon all run into each other, strung out along the Via España. The city they form together is a bit like Los Angeles – the flash bits are all over the place, diamonds sparkling in a sea of shit. The El Continental at least puts you within easy reach of all of them. It's not far from the airport. It's a block and a half from the American Express office. It's an easy drive to the docks and downtown Panama, and not a bad one to La Exposicion and Bella Vista – all the places a business visitor is likely to need. And if you're into all that tourist stuff, it's not far from the old city, the ruins of Panama Viejo, though the place has other attractions besides a few old rocks.

So the moment we pulled up outside the Continental I knew they knew what they were doing.

At the desk, Selim proved he was a smooth bastard too. I'd already cottoned on at the airport that he spoke Spanish. What I hadn't really taken in was that he oozed charm. I don't know Spanish myself, but I know the difference between *quieseremos* and *quiero*. Between We'd Like and I Want. He used the right one. He was polite, and they like that in Latin America. They like a little formality mixed in with their macho. If you're going to operate in the region, two things you need – Spanish business cards, and a steady stream of *con permisos*.

The suite he got us was a group of interconnecting double rooms. As soon as we got up there I pretty much collapsed.

Not pretty and not tough, I know, but would you have done any better?

It didn't do me any good. I wasn't going to get any rest. Selim brought me round by the simple expedient of pouring a jug of iced water over my face. Then he suggested I take a shower. And then he came into the bathroom with me.

'Do you think I could get a bit of privacy round here?' I asked him, though I knew what his answer was going to be.

'No.' He pulled down the lid on the bog and sat down. I must have toyed with the idea of trying to drop him, do a bunk, for all of a quarter second. Then I heard the sound of Khalil unsnapping the camera cases and working his instruments together. No mileage in that. No mileage anywhere. Selim went on to tell me the obvious. 'Till this is over, you do everything with one of us present.'

I tried to sound unworried. 'No bonking for this boy, then.'

'Not for a while, no.'

I started peeling off my clothes. I'd guess it was deliberate. I'd guess I was counting on the fact that most people find it hard to tell lies to a naked man. One of the arguments for closing deals in changing rooms. I pointed at the harness. 'You going to take this off me?' He shook his head. 'You're going to kill me, aren't you?' I stepped into the shower, leaving the door open. Let the bastard get wet. I put the taps on high.

He had to shout over the noise of the jet. That's one thing you can say for Panama over some capital cities in the region. At least the water isn't hot and cold running hepatitis. What he said was, 'No.'

This didn't seem to be stretching his conversation skills much. I stuck my head out through the door. 'What the fuck do you take me for? I haven't got any hold over you. I can identify you. If you ever get your hands on that scrip I'm as good as dead.' I got back in and made more noise than lather. Consequence of the bruises on my body beginning to turn technicolour. He waited for me to get out and begin, very gently, to towel myself before he spoke.

'I've been trying to explain,' he said. 'I'm not a terrorist.'

I cut him off. 'You killed Saul.'

It seemed to hurt him, really cut him. He bowed forward, his elbows on his knees, rubbing his temples. 'Yes,' he said at last. 'Yes, we did. The others are of the old school. They don't necessarily agree with my way and . . . and I suppose you could say they're meant to be baby-sitting me. It's an ambiguous situation.'

'All right,' I told him, 'all right. Let's make it clear. When this is all over, one of them is going to kill me.'

He was firm at last. 'No. I'm not going to allow that. Letting you live when we don't have to, when it's not even in our best interests, might be some way of making up for what happened in London when the press pick it up. And I have to think of the press.' He went out to fetch me some clothes. I couldn't help wondering how much the others could make of what we were saying, and what they thought of us gabbling away in English. It didn't seem to worry him. He still wanted to explain, and I was a bit relieved by it. If ever there was a sign of weakness it's the need to make other people understand.

'You said the *intifadeh* had done more good for our cause than a generation of military activity, and you were right. It is making us, in the eyes of the world, what we have always known ourselves to be. Not killers, not murderers. Barely even soldiers. Just a people who are pushed around by men with guns.'

I let him have it straight. 'The only person round here being pushed around by men with guns is me.'

He nodded. 'Yes. Which is why I want you to go free. I want you alive to make the point that we gave you what we are not given ourselves. Which is freedom.'

He was quite a brief. I'd have hired him. But he wasn't interested in what I thought. He was just interested in talking.

195

'We can't win a war. There is no military solution. If only because we wouldn't be allowed to win. The one thing we have to realise is that a military victory for us would have to be a military defeat for Israel and that is the one thing the United States will never allow. But we are now, for the first time in forty years, beginning to win a moral victory and that can be translated into a political settlement.'

I don't suppose I was convinced. 'Tell that to Arafat,' I said.

He smiled. 'I have. But he knew it already.' I must have looked puzzled. He mistook it for interest. Frankly, the less I knew about the PLO the better, but I didn't have any way of shutting him up. 'There are people at the most senior levels of the military command who agree, who understand. Not all of them. Not their boss . . .' He nodded through in the general direction of his comrades. 'Not Habash. But even he was prepared to commit some money, this money, just in case there is political capital to be made out of the *intifadeh*. He doesn't want the PFLP to get left behind.'

I know better than to ask too many questions, but what else could I do? 'What is the money for then? Guns? Mortars? Plastic explosives?'

He almost laughed. 'No. With those we keep on losing. It is the disparity of the *intifadeh* which wins us friends. They have the tanks and the guns and the tear-gas. We have, at most, boys with rocks. We have a general strike. We have the dignity of old women. But the Israelis are clever. With the strike there is little enough money in the territories, and they control the supply lines. Prices escalate. People starve. Resolve weakens. But with fifteen million dollars we can buy food and drugs. We can extend the *intifadeh*, and every day it is extended, Israel's allies see a little more reason, more justice. And so does Israel herself. And the joy is, if we have the money, there is a limit to how much she can cut off the supply lines. Where we carry guns, they will kill us. But where we carry stones, they hardly dare starve us.'

He must have been good. I almost wanted the son of a bitch to have the money.

Which must have been where he wanted to get me because, once I was dressed and decent, he said a few words in Arabic to the others and sat me down in front of them and asked, 'Now, how do we get our money?'

I'd been scared he'd ask me that question, and not because I wanted it all for myself, though I did, still. It was because I'd been avoiding asking myself it. Because I was buggered if I knew the answer.

I thought about it a very long time before answering, and then I wasn't exactly encouraging. 'I don't see how we can.'

His next question made the whole thing sound like a board meeting. 'What exactly is the problem?'

That one was easy. I ticked off the answers on the fingers of one hand. 'The certificates are in a safety-deposit box in the Javert, Valjean branch here. We don't know what name it's under. We don't know the number of the box. And O'Malley told us there was some physical code as well. It could be anything – a passport, two matching halves of a banknote or a coin or a medal. Some other identifying mark. Three times over, we don't know what we're looking for. Three times over we don't have any way of getting them to give us access.'

He explained it to the others, who said nothing, looking to me like wise sheep. Then Selim started asking questions. Easy questions. It felt almost safe answering him. Like ping-pong.

'Where are these boxes kept?'

'There'll be a safety deposit vault.'

'Part of the main vault?'

'Unlikely. An annexe. They wouldn't want to be opening up the main vault every time someone wants to get their box.'

'And who would have access to this vault?'

'Different banks, different systems. But I'd guess the manager and a specific clerk.'

He mulled it over before asking, 'And if I have a deposit box and want to get at it, what do I do?'

I'm always amazed at how little people know about the basics of my business. 'Well, you'd go to the manager or the clerk, with your identification, which would have to be checked and, usually, complete a form. Then you'd be taken down to the vault, but not into it. Then your box is brought to you and you'd sign a log of the date and time you'd taken receipt of it. Depending on the amount of space down there, you'd either take it to a booth, of which there might be several, or a side table. You do your business, you lock it back in.'

'What about keys?'

'Two. Yours, which you'll have brought with you, and the bank's, both of which will be needed to open the box or, if it's a walk-in vault as they sometimes are, the door behind which an unlocked box is secured.'

'Are the boxes, or the doors, strong?'

'Not terribly, no. The main security is the vault itself. The two keys are just another means of making sure only the right person has access but, if you mean it, once you're into the vault, the boxes are pretty straightforward. The hard part would be knowing which box to go after. But I've explained that already.'

He nodded in acknowledgement. Then he thought his way through the problem, or tried to. 'There has to be a central list of the boxes and their owners.'

'Oh sure. The manager will have one, either in the main vault or in his own safe. But we don't know what name it'll be in, remember?'

Even that didn't put him off. 'Fine, but the one thing we do know is that it's a new box. It's recent. Either we want the most recent names on the list, or just the most recent boxes. The ones with the highest numbers, presumably.'

I wished, for my own sake, that it was as easy as that. 'We don't know it's a new box. He could have had it for years. It's a new deposit, that's all. At best we could hope to rattle the number of the box which has most recently had its owner in to deposit material shipped in from Switzerland. And even if it is a new box, most banks allocate them on a random-number basis, either computer or human generated. You can't tell from the numbers which are the most recent. You can't even tell from the outside which boxes are in use and which aren't, and even in a small vault you're looking at maybe two, three hundred boxes.'

That one really did slow him down, and gave me time to think how grateful I was for the pretty fair certainty that the Irishman would have lit out of Panama as soon as he'd made his deposit, if he'd ever been here at all. There are systems for third-party deposits. It occurred to me that that was what the physical identification, the physical code, might be about: authorising third party access. And we knew, O'Malley had said, the stuff had been couriered here without him. Whatever, the last thing I wanted was him on the scene as well as this lot.

Selim had another question. 'And these boxes are all the same?'

It was the smartest thing he'd said since they dragged me into the van. It was the obvious question. It had been staring me in the face. I think I must have grinned, because I found him smiling at me.

'No. No they're not. They come in different sizes and, as a rule of thumb, the bigger they are, the fewer there are of them.'

He went on smiling as he said, 'I think you're about to tell me something.'

Of course. Of bloody course. 'Fifteen mill, in Certificates of Deposit, O'Malley said. Fifteen mill.'

'Yes?' There was a lift in his voice, an expectation of pleasure.

'Well, CDs can come in denominations as small as a thousand dollars, but these won't have. These were a serious fund-raising treasury exercise for IIIB. They'll have been in ten denominations . . .'

'And . . .?'

'Well they're big, you see? They're security certificates. Fifteen mill at ten a shot is fifteen hundred certificates. They have to be in the biggest boxes. In one of them. I'll wager there won't be above a dozen that size.'

This time he did laugh, and clapped his hands together. And keeping them together as he grew serious again he asked me one more question: 'Are you sure, Mr Ford, there is no legal or official way we can gain access to the specific box?'

I shrugged. 'If O'Malley couldn't find a way,' I told him, 'then there isn't one.'

He dropped his hands.

'Well then, I don't see that we have any option but to rob a bank.'

CHAPTER TWO

For a few minutes back there, while Selim explained to his squad, I felt euphoric, like a cat with a stack of cream sandwiches, like the new boy on the team. Strange, really. I'd spent all my life avoiding blue-collar crime. I'd already stolen fifteen mill the gentleman's way and here I was setting about to do it like a thug, and it made me feel good. For a few minutes, my blood was up. I could understand why people did it for a living.

It didn't last long though, the feeling. Within a few minutes I felt like something different altogether.

I told you there was more than old rocks out at Panama Viejo. Well, for the Panamanians, what really counts out there is the crossroads on the approach. They love to gamble do the Panamanians, and what they love to gamble on most is a cockfight.

The Panama Viejo crossroads is where the big ones take place. I'd been out to one my last time in the city. I'm not sure how to explain it. Try to imagine all the excitement of a Cup Final crammed into a few minutes and a square of beaten earth the size of a sandbox. Imagine the excitement and uncertainty of the worst Saturday night bundle you were involved in focused on two animals by the hungry roar of a couple of hundred people, all of them with money riding on the outcome. Big, beautiful birds, wiry and mean beneath breathtaking plumage (it *shines* – greens, reds, blacks and almost-lilacs) surrounded by people every colour in the range from cream to Bournville.

Well, I felt like one of the cocks. Tense and nervous, ready for the off, the feeling on my skin that odd feeling you only seem to get round the Canal – combination of coolness (something to do with the current) and stickiness from the high humidity. A chilly sheen, like cold electricity.

But there was more to it than that. There's something about the cockfights that doesn't sink in until you see one, even if you're told about it in advance. They fight naturally, the birds, and the professional ones are specially bred for their aggression. They'd fight without encouragement, using the spurs nature gave them, and do each other serious damage till one of them backed out and left the hens to the big boy. But in the cockpits they don't fight with the spurs nature gave them. Instead, the owners strap on metal spurs – wicked things, about three inches long, curved like sabres and slick as a cut-throat. Those fighting spurs are the reason, as often as not, a pro cock-fight is a fight to the finish, till one of the bird's death. The blades are so big the birds can hardly move without razoring themselves, which only makes them angrier, more ready for the fray, slicing their own blood down their haunches.

The guy I went with tried to explain the fighting spurs as an improvement on nature and a purification of the sport. Me? I loved it. I loved the blood and the aggression, the brutality and death. But I wasn't kidding myself. Those spurs were just humans being humans. Piling on the agony for purposes of their own.

And that was what I was now. A fighting cock.

I'd come into this business with my natural affinities, ambitions and abilities, and somewhere along the line, for purposes of their own, other people, from O'Malley, through Rachel and Rabin to this lot, had started strapping fighting spurs on me, to do what I did for them. And now I risked cutting myself, getting myself killed, giving them their version of what they reckoned came naturally.

To tell you the truth, I was scared.

Selim wasn't going to let up on the pressure, though, not on his prize bird. He still had a lot of planning to do.

He turned back to me and said, 'The trouble is we have to assume that, if they haven't done so already, the authorities in London will work out we're on our way to Panama and start putting pressure on the Pineapple . . .' It was the first time I'd heard a foreigner refer to General Noriega, the local strong-man, drug-runner and nit-wit, by his Panamanian nickname (so called because he looks like one − not a pretty sight). 'And we have to assume they'll warn the local branch of Javert, Valjean that we, or someone very like us, are on our way.'

Professional exactness, more than any desire to keep him off-balance, being too off-kilter myself, wouldn't let that go through unchallenged. 'No,' I told him, 'it isn't quite like that. If I know the Swiss, they won't be working with the authorities yet. Even if the authorities are as smart as you say they are, and I reckon this is pretty much out of their league, then Javert, Valjean will still be denying the existence of any account or deposit box here while they check things out with the owner. At worst, there'll be an internal advisory to keep an eye on this one, and follow standard procedures to the letter.'

Selim dismissed all that. 'It doesn't help us at all. We're still under time pressure. Which means we're back to basics. How do we get in and how do we get out, and what do we face when we're in there? What are the security arrangements likely to be?'

That was one I could answer. 'There'll be a couple of armed guards at the door. Machine-guns. That's standard procedure in this part of the world. Inside, a minimum of one more armed guard, in a well-run institution, and this will be. The one inside could be a floater, pulled back down to the vaults when someone goes down. Then again, they may have a full-time armed guard in the banking hall, another in the security vault approach, and maybe another floater between the two.'

He thought it over for a while. 'So we're up against between three and five guards armed with machine guns?'

'That's about the size of it.'

'And there are five of us altogether . . .' I didn't like that five. There were four of them. '. . . with two handguns between us.'

I liked the talk of handguns even less. I knew it was easy enough to buy arms in Panama. With enough dosh you could buy them straight from the army and its more crooked armourers. Or the bookies at the cock-fights could set you up with a contact. Ditto most of the smaller freight agents. They could put the word out for you. But the less we had to do with shooters, the more I'd like it. 'I thought you weren't a terrorist,' I told him.

'I'm not. At some stage we're going to have to use the guns for intimidation. If we get that right, threats alone should get us the guards' weapons, which will make me feel a great deal safer on the way out, but I'd rather not have to use them. Not again.' He had the good grace to remember Saul himself this time. He thought some more. 'What if two of us were to go in to see the manager tomorrow to open a safety deposit box? Legally. We fill out the papers and he takes us down to the vault?'

I shook my head. 'Not in any well-run bank that I know of, no. It's one person down to the vault at a time, even if they come in together. At most, where there are several booths, more than one booth might be occupied at a time, but customers will only be allowed in or out of them and the vault area solo.'

I admit he was impressing me. He was smart. He got it at once. 'So if we want to get more than one person down there, we'll have had to make our intentions plain already, in the manager's office?'

'Yes.'

'So we'd be bringing him out under duress into a banking hall with at least one and maybe two armed guards in it, two more outside the front door and maybe one in the vault?'

'Yes again.'

He had his response ready. 'The two at the door needn't

be such a problem. It's coming into the hall and finding a loose cannon waiting for us that's worrying. We need to have someone waiting in the banking hall, ready to deal with that guard, as we step in with the manager. Which means they have to come into the bank at the same time as us or ahead of us.'

I liked all the talk of us even less, but I let it go for now. Selim was still mulling over his problem.

'He mustn't obviously be with us, but there has to be something for him to do. Something unsuspicious. Look at brochures?'

I wanted to laugh, but I was so tense it came out as a sort of high-pitched hysterical keen. Like Luton fans when they see the Shed approaching. 'It's not a High Street branch. Come in with your cashcard, take out fifty quid. It's a Swiss bank in a tax haven. He'd have to have something to do.'

'Such as?'

'Well, it would have to be something to do with the bank. Withdrawal, deposit, inquiry, about a real account. That's the only thing that's going to tie up a counter clerk, keep your man in there, and not look suspicious.'

Selim seemed to think I was being stupid. 'But what account? We don't have an account with Javert, Valjean. How do we do that?'

It was the first slip he'd made. The right answer, of course, from his point of view, was to have someone go into the bank today with a nominal amount of cash drawn on a credit card to open an account, explaining he'd be back in the morning with a serious bank transfer. Then if he arrived just after us, we'd already be with the manager and he could legitimately be waiting in the banking hall. But that was one little bit of procedure I wasn't giving up. Not now. Because I had an idea which, although it had precious little head on it, gave me some hope.

'This is international banking,' I told him. 'The account doesn't have to be here, it can be another branch of the bank. He could be asking them to telex for instructions or information, or to supply those things. Which would take time. Which would keep him where he was. The point is, though, the details of the account he's seeking access to have to look right. It has to be the right kind of number, and I don't know what this lot's internal systems are like. But we do know someone who has details of a real account at another branch. O'Malley has given us the details of this Irishman's account in Geneva. What we didn't ask him for – we didn't know we'd need them – was the branch codes. If we can get hold of him, we can use those.'

He looked at me for some time before saying, 'It might be worth a try.'

I don't know what I'd planned to do with talking to Myles, what I hoped to make of it. As much as anything I suppose I wanted to hear a friendly voice and make sure the old bastard hadn't given up on me. As it was, I hardly got to talk to him at all. Selim had handsets shifted around so he had an extension in the same room as me. When I got through to IIIB what I got was Stiffy Durrant, sounding embarrassed.

'Johnny! Where are you?'

Selim shot me an, unnecessary, warning glance.

'Never mind, Stiffy. Get me Myles.'

There was a pause at that. 'Erm . . . not quite that simple, old man.'

I lost my temper. I'd been wanting to do it for an age. 'What do you mean it's not that simple? He's supposed to be on permanent call on this line. Where the fuck is he?'

'It wasn't his fault, Johnny. It was Lady Polly. She made him go home. You know what she's like . . .'

Yes, I knew. Not that it mattered in the end, as Stiffy blathered on.

'But it's all right though. We've set up a permanent patch on his cell phone. If you hang on I'll patch you through.'

That made me feel a little better. The old sod hadn't forgotten me entirely. But it didn't encourage Selim at all.

He was keeping an eye on his watch, and time, time in which calls could be traced, was ticking away.

He cut in. 'No. We'll call back in fifteen minutes. Or rather I will. You know he's all right now. Have O'Malley waiting by the phone with all the details of the Irishman's account at Javert, Valjean in Geneva including the branch codes.' Then he hung up, with time to spare.

Fifteen minutes later, all I could do was listen impotently to Selim's half of the conversation as he took down the details, having to repeat everything at least once, the patched in line was so poor, and getting increasingly anxious and tetchy as he did so, worrying always against the clock.

I knew how he felt. All I could do was will Myles, telepathically, to know where I was, to get Rachel's heavy mob, to do something, to get me out of this mess, before I found myself facing five men with machine-guns the following morning.

But that wasn't the way it was going to work.

Nothing was going to work.

I wasn't exactly overjoyed, either, when Selim told me he was leaving me to the others for a couple of hours. 'It's time I got over to La Paitilla,' he told me. 'We're going to need a plane.'

CHAPTER THREE

I think I must have gone a little mad. I know I went into some kind of shouting fit when I finally realised Selim had meant to do the job the following morning.

What I'd been trying to tell him was that he couldn't. That some banks in Panama did open on Saturday mornings, but none of them would tomorrow, not the day after the New Year Bank Holiday. But looking back on it, though I got that message through, whatever came over me wasn't about Saturday trading at all. It was about some kind of panic.

Somewhere along the line it all rolled up and dumped on me. Everything from Miami on – the planning, the Irishman, the job, the loss, the killing of Saul and the taking of me by Mossad, and me and Myles by this lot, the whacking about, the harness, the flying around, the fear – it just came together and hit me, along with the realisation of what I was being set up for. So it wasn't about giving him information, not really. It was panic.

To tell the truth, I don't remember that much about it. I have this picture, like, in my head, of me gasping and shaking and sweating and shouting, or trying to. I think I may have tried to attack them, to shake them and knock some sense into their teacloth heads.

I think they were gentle with me. I don't know how they got me to the ground. I suppose they wrestled me down. But they didn't hurt me. Nothing to compare with what Khalil had done before, and when I start being able to remember it again, I was on my back with Selim kneeling on my shoulders, holding my mouth open with both his hands in my cheeks, like I was having a fit or something. Like I was liable to chomp out my own tongue. He was muttering something to me, trying to calm me down. And, I suppose I better tell you this – you don't know who I really am, you've got no way of holding it against me, and you'd suffer if you ever tried – I think I was doing something I hadn't done since I was a kid. I think I was crying.

I pretty much passed out after that. No use to man or dog. I think I may have had some kind of fever. Hot and cold sweats. But that might just have been the tension working its way out, like when you take some bad knocks in a boxing ring. I don't know.

I do know, a couple of times on the Saturday, it must have been, I came round and Selim and Khalil were feeding me soup. Chicken soup with sweetcorn in it. I remember thinking, leave it out, this is daft. This is like all those Woody Allen movies all the tossers wank about. Never seen it myself. He just doesn't make me laugh.

By sometime on the Sunday, late morning I reckon, I was pretty much OK. Sitting up, able to move around, able to give them a bit of stick. Able to think.

I even managed to give Selim a hard time.

'You haven't got a chance,' I told him. 'They must know you're here by now. We had to log our passports when we checked in. They must have an Interpol report out by now.'

I could tell he'd thought it over. He shrugged, but he didn't quite shrug it off. 'It's possible,' he admitted. 'It's possible. But they haven't come for us yet, which says something. They don't exactly love Interpol, or any interfering white boys, round here. And we have our own connections with the authorities here. A private army has to buy its weapons where it can. But it may be we're walking into a trap. There isn't anything we can do but risk it. We have to have our money. We have to have a try. And we have one advantage over any Panamanians.'

209

'Oh yeah?' I asked him, trying it on. 'And what might that be?'

He smiled a little sad smile and told me, 'It's our money. It's our cause. We have a reason to be ready, ready to die for it, if we have to. They don't. They're just policemen. Why should they try too hard?'

He had a point, at that. It wasn't one I wanted to think too hard about. It wasn't my cause. I didn't want myself getting killed for it, for someone else's problem.

He let me sleep, but after that it was my problem, too. I was going in with them. I was the only one who knew the systems, knew the ropes. They made me talk it through, like some kind of whacko trainer, over and over and again.

I kept angling for some way of going in solo, going in first, some way of tipping the manager off and getting help and getting free. But they weren't having any of it. They knew their man. They were watching me like hawks. In the end, we could only keep it simple, we could only hope to keep it clean, and I could only whisper prayers up to O'Malley, wherever he might be.

Khalil would go in first, ahead of us, to put his enquiry in hand. He'd park right up in front, on the main road. That was our preferred way out, our exit.

Selim and I would follow along after. Selim had already checked there was a side door. We'd park by that, to give us an alternative if we needed it. I'd have given a great deal to know in advance what that door led in to. A storage room, packed with boxes, hard to fight your way out of, and we could be in a world of shit. Funny. Thinking the words made me think of Rachel. So where was she right now, when I really needed her?

We'd park, go in through the front door, ask to see the manager. Meanwhile the two goons would be approaching the bank on foot. That was the tricky part. We just had to trust them. They had to look inconspicuous, not set off the guards at the door, but be close enough to hit them when the balloon went up. Well, at least they were the right sort of colour.

As soon as we brought the manager out of his office, they were to disarm the guards at the front door and bring them in, while Khalil took out any guard in the banking hall itself. I hoped they were good, because they were going in without guns. Selim had one and Khalil had the other. It didn't seem to worry the goons, though. They kept fingering wire garottes. After that, the goons would use the guards' guns to secure the ground floor. Khalil would lead the move down into the vaults, gun up, in case there was a guard left down there. After that it was up to me and Selim to persuade the manager to do his business. I hoped the goonies understood that in the meantime one of their main duties was to find out where that side door was, and how we got to it if we had to. Then La Paitilla, and the plane.

I got sick of going through it.

Actually, I just got sick. I think Selim understood that. He backed off on me at last, backed off enough for me to try to ask one favour. I said to him, and I used his name, 'Selim, there's one thing. I don't know what it's going to be like in there. I don't know how fast we might have to move. Any chance I could have the cock-guillotine off? I can't run in a harness. I might have to. We all might.'

He shook his head. 'No, John. No. I can't do that. It's important. It will remind you of something you need to remember, all the time.'

'Such as?'

He smiled a quick little smile and let me have it. 'I think I like you, Mr Ford . . .' he got formal all over again, 'and who knows, in other circumstances you might have liked me. But that doesn't matter. Not now. Because we cannot trust you. And you shouldn't trust us.'

211

CHAPTER FOUR

5 a.m., Monday January the 4th, Panama City. Guess who hadn't slept a wink.

They, on the other hand, had reduced themselves to two-hour watches keeping an eye on me, one man on, three men off, to make sure they got some. After all, they had a busy day ahead of them.

The sun, as it always does in the tropics, had gone up like a rocket. Scared the living daylights out of me, literally. That was the only whizz-bang I wanted to see today. I got one of the goons to order me some breakfast, just so I'd have something to throw up before we started.

It worked. It always does.

They relented and took the harness off before we left in case I needed room for movement.

Anyway, they had one thing going for them. Javert, Valjean wasn't, as it might have been, on the other side of the city. It was about a mile west of the Continental on Via España. But maybe that wasn't so great after all. It put them on the wrong side of the city for La Paitilla, the little airport. I wondered if they'd thought about roadblocks. I made a mental note to keep my hands up. If the local fuzz and army did get us, I wanted to make sure they asked me questions first and shot the others later. After all, to them I was just another wise-guy.

I think they must have thought about roadblocks, because when we came out of the hotel the surprise that was waiting for me was the cars. They were different from the ones they'd hired at the airport. Those had been American saloons. These were Toyota 4x4s, the trendiest, all-terrain vehicle in Latin America. The Nips flooded the market with all the surplus they weren't allowed to sell in the States. Selim must have traded them round after he'd dealt with the airport.

Selim, Khalil and I took the first one. Selim drove while Khalil sat in the back with his head over my shoulder, Selim's pigskin attaché-case on his lap. That was new as well. I wondered what was in it. I could guess. The other two came up behind in the second Toyota.

A couple of hundred yards from the bank we stopped to let Khalil out to get there under his own steam. The goons behind us idled to dead slow.

It's a low city, Panama. Cities in earthquake zones usually are. Mexico's the exception and, increasingly, Tokyo. Low and spacey, the buildings strung out in what look like rubbish dumps. Lots of air to park between them, between buildings painted pink, or blue or tan against the dust. Selim backed into the big alley just before the bank. When I looked round, the goons' car had dropped back pretty much out of sight. It was just past eight o'clock.

I wondered how Khalil was getting on with his idiot English and the letter of instruction Selim had prepared for him with my help. It was, I suppose, a good job that international banks have English-speaking staff. I wouldn't have fancied his chances trying to make himself understood in wog or dago. Not with his accent.

I'd tried at the last to persuade Selim he should be the first one in and Khalil and I could do the manager, but it hadn't worked. He didn't trust me, and I don't blame him. I'd been half-counting on Khalil not understanding all I was saying to the manager.

We gave him a couple of minutes and went in.

By the time we got there he looked pretty well stuck in, confident enough to give us a friendly little nod, just like any well brought-up boy seeing strangers on a sunny morning. It made my heart skip, but I settled myself with

213

the thought it wouldn't look at all odd to the Latins. I told you, a formal people. You make eye-contact in the street, you say *buenos días*. Any less is rude.

Selim asked for the manager, explained we wanted a safety-deposit box. It took a couple of minutes. I wished I hadn't thrown up. That way I could have shat.

He was a little man, the manager. Swiss. Little, fat and balding. That's what too much time away from the regular exercise of the Swiss Military Reserve will do for you. All resident male Swiss citizens have to do it. Which means there are two things about doing business in Switzerland which can confuse you. The number two at the bank you're dealing with may be his boss's superior officer in the army, which can really confuse the inter-personal relationships. And, all those bloody forced marches together, they all call each other by nicknames and diminutives. Bit hard being surrounded by the Gnomes of Zurich when they're busy calling each other Hansli, Pauli and Steffi. Where's Snow White, you wonder?

Still he seemed quite pleased when I greeted him in German. Selim wasn't taking any chances with a language he didn't know. He cut us back into English as soon as we were in the manager's office.

I had to admire the poise with which he did it. While the manager was still turning round, explaining his name was Hans Gretel or something of the sort, Selim set his case on the desk, flicked the catches, put his right hand in and pulled a gun. Shoved it right in the fat man's face. Then he closed the case with his left hand.

'No fuss. No alarms. No deaths,' he explained quietly. 'All we want is access to the safety deposit vault.'

The fat man tried to bluster. 'But there are armed guards. You . . .'

Selim lifted the gun, just a fraction. 'That's my problem. Now, you're going to need your keys, I expect. Or a coffin.' The fat man began to reach. Selim waved him back with the gun. 'No. Show him.' He indicated me. The fat man pointed listlessly at a drawer on the right side of his desk.

214

There was a bunch of keys in it, and some security cards with magnetic strips in a wallet and, as I had expected, an alarm button. I guessed there was another set in the underside of the desk and one more in the floor. I wondered, for half a beat, what would happen if I pressed one of them, but one look at Selim put me off the idea.

He nodded at me. 'You go first.'

Thanks a fucking bunch, I thought, but I went.

It was a European layout. The manager's door led directly into the public area of the banking hall – double doors, actually – without going through the clerks' desks and the counters in the American fashion. As soon as I came through the door, Khalil took two steps backwards, wheeled and drew a gun from a shoulder holster and jammed it in the face of the guard by the back wall. Then he punched him in the gut and grabbed his machine-gun in his left hand.

The clerks were beginning to stir, and the two guards at the front door turned to see what was going on. That was when the two goons hit them from behind, off the street. Kidney-punches, and they were down, being stripped of their weapons.

These people are good, was what I thought, and somehow it made me feel even more afraid.

Selim turned to the manager again. 'Tell everyone to get on the floor, hands clasped behind their heads. No reason for anyone to get hurt.'

Fat Boy did well. Fat Boy did as he was told, in Spanish, began to repeat it in German. Khalil and the goons hauled the guards into the middle of the hall. Khalil kept them covered with a handgun while the other two, both equipped with machine-guns now, stood over the counters.

Then it all went wrong.

The noise. It must have been the noise.

Something, anyway, brought the vault-guard up and out through the security door at the far side of the hall. He had maybe half a second on us. It was enough. Shielded behind the security door he pulled left first.

215

The burst of three lifted one of the goons, the one whose name I'd never known, right off his feet. His blood hit the counter windows first, then the rest of him. I never did work out when the glass shattered. And then there was the screaming. The women screaming.

Khalil wheeled and raised his gun and hit the vault-guard smack between the eyes. He went down, his legs holding the door open. Khalil nodded to Nayef who headed for the door, swung it open, and went flying backwards, his legs kicking the air in a crazy, drunken can-can in a spray of broken glass and hot metal. He hit the deck with his right shoulder a bloody rose.

Khalil dived across the floor and crashed into the wall beside the security door, now hanging crazily from one hinge, took one breath and dived head first low and fast over the corpse of the guard, down the stairs, his gun held in both hands in front of him, and loosed off most of the magazine. For a second after there was an eery silence, and then an inconsolable wail went up, that turned almost at once into something that bubbled.

Khalil came back through the door, on his feet, took Nayef by the scruff of his collar and helped him kick himself back across to the far wall. Then he put his gun into Nayef's good left hand, smacked in a fresh magazine and turned to reach for a machine-gun.

Which was when the three guards came off the floor and hit us.

Fuck this, I thought, and went down like a stone.

Then Fat Boy was on my back and trying to smash my face against the floor. There were those noises again, those bad noises, machine-gun fire, and then it felt as though someone had dropped a deadweight on my back. Which they had. Nayef took out two of them, left handed. Selim took out the third, who went down onto Fat Boy and to me.

When they got me out from under there, Selim was just standing in the middle of the hall, his gun-hand still extended and a completely vacant look in his face. I think

216

it must have been the first time he'd done it. Khalil stepped over one of the bodies and slapped him hard, just once, back into life. And then he was standing over the room again, machine-gun in hand.

Selim grabbed Fat Boy by the right arm, said, 'Come on,' to me in a funny strangled voice and headed for the security door. I wasn't taking any chances. I grabbed him by the left.

We wrestled him downstairs, picking over the bodies, trying not to slip on fake marble floors slimy with blood.

At the vault door Selim just said, 'Open it.'

Fat Boy wavered, not knowing if he was scared or crazy, mumbling, 'It's over. Can't you . . .'

Selim grabbed him by the tie and jammed the pistol in his mouth, shouting in his face, shouting, 'Open it! There isn't any point in stopping now.' For a second there, I wondered if he meant the job, or killing.

Fat Boy opened it fumbling, out of fear not cunning. It took two of the cards and a combination.

When he swung the door, Selim nodded us both inside and my last remaining half idea – locking him in the vault – went nowhere.

It was a small vault, strong-boxes floor to ceiling on three sides. The big ones were set above waist height. Nice. Made them easier to handle. Fourteen of them, six each along the long walls and two in the short one at the end. Selim stepped out of our reach, palmed a fresh clip into his gun and opened fire at the locks, one after the other. Sparks flew, and smoke, and shrapnel. Something hit Fat Boy in the face and cut his right cheek open. He hardly seemed to notice, pumping on fear and adrenalin. The box doors flew open, one after another and Selim went back down the line pulling the interior boxes to the floor. They clanged down, spilling cash, and securities, jewels and loose gemstones, spilling money, but he wasn't interested in that.

The sixth one was the jackpot. It was two thirds full of IIIB CDs in ten K denominations.

'This is ours,' he said gently. 'Now move.'

We moved. He followed after us, gun in one hand, box swinging by shattered handles in the other.

As we came out through the door, Khalil stooped to help Nayef up. We headed for the main door in a line. Nayef first, then Khalil, then me, then Selim. As a farewell present, he dropped Fat Boy with his gun-butt.

Nayef went first.

Nayef . . .

Well, they hit him with so many machine-guns, they almost tore him limb from limb. His bone fragments cut our hands and faces to pieces.

They took us down as well, and saved our lives.

The Panamanian Army was waiting for us. The shock almost seemed to make Selim himself again. 'Side door,' he hissed. 'Get round to the other car.'

Khalil's English was up to that. He pointed back towards the manager's doors. Yes, I thought. Yes. Connecting door into the clerks' room and probably a pair of security doors out.

We went, kicking the intervening doors open, scattering papers, bills, people. The fire doors were locked. Khalil shot them open. My eyes were watering from blood, sweat and cordite. The next thing I knew, he was behind me, his arm round my throat and a barrel to my head.

We went out first. I suppose I'd always been a hostage.

They held their fire just long enough. I suppose it was my being white that did it. I didn't look like them. I might have been bank staff. Whatever it was, it bought us just enough time. Time to get in the 4x4 and moving, reversing fast up the alley, and then a spin, and careering crazily away with the army on our tail blazing away like something from a Western.

Khalil took us into a corner fast, and cut off the main road, looking for a way round, and as we hung on, Selim smiled at me oddly and said, in his calmest manner, 'Goodbye, Mr Ford,' and hit me full in the face, hard.

The next thing I knew, my back was being burned open

by gravel, and I was curled in the road, trying to protect my guts, my balls, my head as vehicles squealed round me, my back past saving.

Maybe I blacked out. I don't know. I know it went quiet. I know I was aware of a dark shadow beside me. Something solid, stationary. Another fucking 4x4.

A hand reached out of it, down towards me, and a voice said something. Eventually it made sense. Then it made no sense at all.

It was Myles, saying, 'Well, will you get in now, me bucko?'

He didn't get out to help me in. He just grabbed me by the hand and heaved. As I crashed across him, half on to the back seat, half in to the well in front of it, as I wondered faintly just how much more pain this money was going to cost me, I took in the fact that Rachel was at the wheel. And I realised I had absolutely no idea what had been going on any more.

What I did manage to get out, croaking, was, 'La Paitilla . . . Flying . . . out . . .'

Myles looked at Rachel, who raised an eyebrow. He raised the handset of a radio, pushed a fat yellow button and started talking.

'*Senor Coronel, Senor Coronel. El Ingles aquí . . .*'

Something like a smile crossed his face. A great compromiser when he had to be, Myles, and there can't have been any point trying to explain to the Panamanian army what Irish was. The handset crackled.

'*Sí. Que pasa?*'

'*Creemos que la salida están de La Paitilla . . .*'

'*El aeropuerto?*'

'*Cómo no?*'

'*Bueno. Vamos!*'

'Tambièn!'

He switched himself out and looked back at Rachel, who smiled and said, 'The docks?'

Myles nodded in agreement. 'The docks.'

My brain stopped working.

She ground the gears, and we were off, on the long road round and over the Ancon hill and down the other side into

Balboa and the canal quays, the dust of the Tropics spinning out from under our tyres in clouds. Myles was working something out as she drove. 'We're going to have to tell them. How much time do we need?'

She was serious, efficient, skilful. Somehow it made her seem younger. I think I must have been going off my trolley. Banking us into a long bend she answered, 'Not long. Five, six minutes. But we're going in different directions, so half that really. Give them three then tell them we got lost but we think we've sighted them on their way down the Balboa.'

He did as he was told.

We came over the brow of Ancon hill four wheels in the air and yawing and came down with a crunch which left my body squealing, and maybe my mouth as well, because Myles looked round and said, 'Hold on, son. Hold on.' It didn't make me feel a whole lot better.

Down in Balboa, everything changed. American-planned, American-built and mostly American-maintained, it's a small, low, quiet, clean, sterile little town. Just the kind of place I needed, if I hadn't been in the hands of a pair who weren't making any sense.

As the landmarks flipped past – the YMCA, Chase, Citibank, the Masons, all blurred and mixed up with Stevens Circle and the Prado, the hospital and the reflecting pool – till I didn't know which way I was going anymore, and still less why, I kept trying to tell them we should be going to the airport, but either nothing came out or I didn't make sense because they wouldn't listen or didn't hear. I think if I'd been up to it I would have wept. I kept thinking of the money, of the quick flash of the certificates in the vault, and the hell before and after.

Suddenly she shouted, 'There! Ahead!' and pushed the pedal to the metal, trailing a wild cloud of dust. Then I was all over the place, banging around in the back like cabbages, and I knew that they were right and someone up ahead was trying to shake us off.

Next thing I knew, I landed on my neck, shaken across

221

the seat like a rat in a terrier's grip as she put us through a wheelie and the gears unmeshed and she lost it and the engine screamed as she worked it back together and she took us off again, away from the Canal quays this time or at an angle to them with a cry of 'What the . . .?'

Myles understood, or seemed to. 'Fort Amador,' he said. That didn't help the rest of us. 'The Yacht Club,' he explained. 'They're picking up their plane at the Balboa Yacht Club.' I gave up any hope of trying to understand.

But I began to understand about a minute later, once she thwacked us to a halt and Myles wrestled me to my feet, dragging me past the *Entrada Libre* sign and into the cool hall that crossed the clubhouse, leading to the marina and sheltered harbourage.

They were up there ahead of us, their feet smacking irregularly across the ash-white boards of the pontoons. Selim limping and labouring under the weight and the size of the box. They were heading for a small outboard. And they were heading for something else. A Cessna seaplane, single engine, moored just within the harbour-wall.

Khalil half-turned, half-dropping, to one knee, raising his right arm, fore-arm gripped in his left hand, and I went down thinking, not me, not now, not ever. Myles and Rachel went sideways, in opposite directions as the first shot rang out, taking such cover as they could behind mooring posts and cables. I realised I was the only silly bastard left out in the open, and started wriggling and squirming, trying to move, but nothing seemed to work, and the planks in front of me came up in a storm of flakes and splinters and I just managed to shield my eyes.

Then Rachel was up again, grunting encouragement and I heard the slide and croak and whine of a motor cord being pulled and pulled again, and the engine turning over, choking once and firing. As we hit the edge of the wooden dock they were already under way, heading unsteadily for the plane, Khalil hunched and working over the engine, Selim forward of him and unsteady on his feet, while I

222

wondered what to do.

I needn't have bothered. Suddenly, everything seemed to go quiet and calm. Even the popping of the outboard motor seemed distant and unreal. It was her, I realised. For the first time since I had met her, she was at ease, doing what she knew best, doing what she understood. She was taking the same stance Khalil had taken. She was lifting the biggest handgun I had ever seen.

They hadn't bothered mooring. Khalil was already squirming into the plane. Selim was trying to follow him, being pulled badly from foot to foot as the boat shifted beneath him, thrown further off balance by the weight of the strong-box. He looked small, and sad, and painfully frail.

'Don't kill him,' I said.

She wasn't listening. She was taking aim.

I said it again. 'Don't kill him. He didn't kill me. He could have.'

I don't know if she really paused. Time seemed to have no meaning any more. But I remember what she said. She said, 'Who cares?' and squeezed the trigger.

I don't know where she hit him, not that first time. He had just got the strong-box in through the door and was hanging on to it as his hook into the plane.

She hit him somewhere. I saw him crumple, and lose his footing. The boat began to pull away beneath him, opening up water between him and the plane.

I think he gave up hope. He seemed to turn towards us and loosen his hold. There was a blank expression in his eyes but a funny kind of smile in his mouth, the smile of a kid caught out by a grown-up and wondering what happened now.

She fired again, and he died.

She raised her aim a fraction and pulled off two shots in quick succession. Both of them hit the fuel pod on the starboard wing as the propeller began pointlessly to turn. The first shot opened up a gash in the tank. The second did something worse. But not at once. There was a pause, a hesitation, a single lazy flick of flame across the tank, and then the whole wing blew, and then the plane. It looked like rhododendrons made of fire and smoke and oil. Flowers of force that threw me on my back, hacking out my feet like hockey sticks and restoring me to a world of time and noise and pain.

Out behind us, out beyond the club-house, in the lot, army trucks were burning rubber as they clashed and twisted to a halt. Frightened members, tourists, tarts, were running out shouting, screaming, crying, wondering what the hell had happened.

But I didn't register any of that at the time. It only sank in later. What I registered, up there, in a blue sky scuffed by cloud, in amongst the smoke and flame and debris drifting back to earth, were little scraps of paper, still burning, still turning to ash. Fifteen hundred of them. Fifteen million dreams.

What could I do but whimper?

'My money. My money.'

CHAPTER SIX

I came round in the hospital nearly twenty-four hours later. The Gorgas Hospital, and they must have pulled strings for that, because it's usually reserved for Canal staff, but I was well past worrying.

She put me through the business first. The debrief. Four hours of it. I don't want to go over it now. She was a cold, hard bitch. For all I know that did me good – gave me someone to resent, someone to hate. She wanted names, descriptions, locations, the *modus operandi*. I couldn't really see the point. They were all dead, weren't they? That wasn't enough for her. She wanted the details, so she could kill some more. I didn't know if what I was telling her was any help, and I didn't really care.

The vets jammed me full of tranqs and pain-killers once she was done and I went out before I knew it. It was late next morning before I surfaced and Myles told me what had been going on, or tried.

He wasn't exactly generous. 'A lot of strings got pulled for you, me boy, and I had to spend a lot of money.'

I was listless and pretty shagged off. 'So what do you want? A cheque?'

He grinned and said, 'You're covered.'

'I don't know how.'

So he began to lay it out, and he took it easy, because my head was out of working order. 'Once I found out the stuff was in Panama, once I'd told you and them that, I knew they'd have to bring you here. There didn't seem any point in waiting for confirmation or trying anything fancy. Fortunately, Major Stern and the funnies in London could see the point of that. The problem was that bloody phone number I was supposed to be on all the time. String one was organising an international patch off a radio phone into that number. We used the international airline link first. Then a satellite patch once we were here. Not cheap. But more important it takes time to put through, which was why I was supposed to be at home and you ran into delays trying to get through. And here we got lucky.'

I found that hard to credit. 'Lucky?'

'Yes, lucky. There's shit in the air, John, and it made us smell good.' He settled back in his chair and pulled out his cigar-case. Never one to be sympathetic to the limitations of an invalid. His explanation billowed out of smoke.

'The CIA like the Pineapple. He's their kind of guy . . .'

'A son of a bitch,' I interrupted, 'but our son of a bitch.'

'Exactly. They know very well he's shipping cocaine into the States but it's a price they're willing to pay. Unfortunately for them, it's a price their political masters are increasingly unwilling to pay . . .'

I interrupted again. 'Nancy just says No.'

'That's the one. So, in all kinds of ways they are having to go easy, and one of those ways is arms. I think you will find that the price paid for allowing us to operate here with the help of the army is a whole bunch of guns with Israel End-User Certificates actually ending up in Cristobal. Oh, and the Pineapple charged a one. I've paid the mill up front already.'

I didn't want to think about money just then, so I didn't. What I did want to know was why they hadn't pulled me out earlier. 'Myles, our names will have been on the flight manifest. Our passport details were logged at the Continental. Even if they weren't the police could have put out an Advisory – a Brit travelling with an unknown number of Arabs – how many groups like that could there be in Panama? Why didn't you track me down?

Why didn't you come for me? Why did you put me through all that?'

For a moment he looked embarrassed, almost ashamed. 'I'm sorry about that. It was her idea,' he explained, 'she wanted them in the open all along. She wanted them dead. Inside you were in the way. I went along with it. We had very little time to plan, and I didn't call the guns. And I was busy.'

I gave him jip. 'Busy? You were busy? What do you think I was? I could've done with a little help. What the hell were you doing?'

He was matter of fact. 'We were checking plane bookings. We'd worked out they'd had wings before and could have them again. Getting out overland didn't make any sense. Boats are too slow. And a scheduled flight would have been stupid.'

I could see the sense in that. 'They weren't stupid, Myles. He wasn't. You'd have liked him. Hired him.'

It did, it could, not mean anything. They had never met. Myles just ignored it. 'Security at Tocumen's too tight for them to fly from there, so the options were La Paitilla, a private field, or something else. We couldn't be certain which, and a whole lot of planes get hired in Panama every day, John, most of them by people with something to hide. But we guessed, the Major and I. We guessed they were bright. We guessed the seaplane. We guessed they'd head for Golfo Dulce in Costa Rica. The escape routes were just shorter that way. And it was, of course, why they let you live, why they let you go. It made no sense their telling you La Paitilla unless they wanted to head us in the wrong direction. Which was fine by us because we needed the Panamanians but we didn't want them crowding us.'

I could not quite let it pass, not without comment. 'It wasn't the reason they let me go. It wasn't the only reason.'

Myles pursed his lips and said nothing. I knew what he was thinking. He was thinking Stockholm Syndrome.

227

He was thinking proximity had turned me round, to their side, but I knew it hadn't. All I could say was, 'You had to have met him.'

He's a strange man, O'Malley. He has odd sympathies, and he tried. 'I'm sorry, but you have to have known that, after Saul in London, one of the prices that was going to get paid was their lives.'

I suppose I had, at that. I suppose Selim had, too.

He wasn't going to let me brood. 'There were other things that kept me busy, John. I had your interests to protect.'

That was a bad joke if ever I heard one, but I played along. 'What other things?'

He smiled and took a big pull on his stogey, making me wait. 'I'm afraid I told you, and them, one lie . . .'

'Yes . . .?'

He let it fall quietly, as though he had hardly noticed it himself. 'Javert, Valjean played ball.'

It wouldn't sink in. I couldn't work out what he meant. Played ball? 'How?'

He was serious and thoughtful and reflective. He was a banker again, talking policy. 'The Swiss will these days, if the Americans are involved and are prepared to make politics of it. That's what's happening with Aquino. Well, with a little encouragement from the Major, the Americans were prepared to play politics over the PLO. Which is why I had access to that vault the night before you did.'

I was in a world I didn't understand again. 'But . . .'

'Just listen,' he said. 'It helped that I was prepared, provided no one looked too closely at what I did with the contents of the box, to have the value of those contents totalled and to issue an undertaking to indemnify Javert, Valjean for the value of those contents if they ran into any legal problems for the beneficial owners. I'm afraid to cover myself for that I had to arrange a short-term fifteen million drawing-right with IIIB in your name. We've charged you a commitment fee of one per cent. I told you it ran expensive.'

He could have charged me ten per cent for all I cared now. 'It's a jest, Myles. You should have drawn it from the box while you had it in front of you. I don't have anything left.'

And then at long last, O'Malley laughed, choking on his cigar smoke, and told me. 'Oh yes you do. I'm afraid that the other little delay at the London end was getting Bradbury's to print me up fifteen hundred fake ten K CDs. Not very fake. Plenty good enough to pass anything but a thorough checking. As a general rule, the technical copy of our CDs doesn't finish with the words, "And if you believe that you will believe anything."'

I looked at him, stunned, not daring to hope or take it in.

He spelled it out. 'Your CDs are in a safety deposit box in our Panama branch. Those were the fakes that got blown up yesterday. Not that anyone else needs to know that. As far as anyone else is concerned, what I swapped in was a miscellaneous collection of CDs issued by a number of different houses. I took the precaution in London of buying you a hundred K's worth, which are right now lodged in my hotel room rather, though I say it myself, artistically charred and sodden. Which, with a bit of strong-arm work at Lloyd's should be enough to get the underwriters to indemnify BHM for their stolen fifteen mill, which should take the heat off you. The Major wasn't too keen on the deal you struck with her and her bosses and would have loved to stiff you. I thought I should cover your back. I don't think there'll be a problem with the insurers. We can, after all, demonstrate a straight line link between the original fifteen mill and these damaged CDs.'

If I hadn't been so weak I would have laughed myself. Instead, all I could say was, 'You bastard. You cunning, conniving, brilliant bastard. I forgive you the shit, Myles. You saved me all my money.'

It was time for him to wake me up. 'Not all of it, John-boy. I told you we had expenses. They ran pretty steep.

But I think you'll find when I give you your settlement statement in a day or two's time you'll come out of it with thirteen and a half million clear.'

I might have guessed.

I might have guessed O'Malley would work it so it cost me, exactly, the Irishman's share.

CHAPTER SEVEN

It worked out exactly as he had said, and I did exactly
what I had always planned to do, though he made me do
some of it his way.

Once I'd told him my plans he arranged to swap the
London-issued Certificates of Deposit for ones issued by
IIIB's Panamanian operation. He made me hold all but my
immediate requirements, which were one and a half million, in Panama. And he insisted on having discretionary
authority over them. I wasn't too happy about that, but I
could hardly blame him, or Polly, for wanting to make sure
he had access and a say. I had put him through it, I guess,
and he told me very firmly, 'As of now, my boy, I am your
head banker, and no mistaking.'

Well, why not? Thirteen and a half was pretty small beer
by the standards of his treasury operation, but why not let
him look after it? Why not the best?

Once I was well, or well enough to move, once I had paid
off all my bills, I headed north, crossing, gratefully, the
Boredom Border, the threshold of yawn.

I went to Canada.

Canada, you ask? Why Canada?

Several reasons.

They speak English, of a kind, where I was, and I was
too shagged and stupid to set about learning a new language.
They have banks which know and understand about Central
America and the Caribbean, which was useful considering
where my money was. They had banks which understand
about hot money. They had been in the business since the
days of Prohibition in the States, when Canadian breweries

and distilleries ran their product illegally over night into Buffalo, Detroit and Chicago, and Capone and others salted half their loot away up in the ice above the Parallel. They have cities full of good looking, unattached women. They're always heading down south to the sun, which was one of many reasons why a Canadian passport was as good as any in the world to travel on. The other being that no one hated them. What harm have the Canadians ever done?

And they had the most wonderful new immigration law.

They'd set it up after the British government sold the Hong Kong Chinese down the river, changing their nationality status, giving them no right of abode in Britain. Can't have the country swamped by slit-eyes, can we?

It hadn't taken the Canadian government ten minutes to figure out Hong Kong was rotten with rich Chinese who needed a bolthole for their money, and possibly themselves.

Enter the new immigration law. Anyone who showed up at the front door with two hundred and fifty K Canadian to invest in a business proposition got immediate landed immigrant status. Anyone showed up with a million Canadian, not even for direct investment in business, government bonds would do, got citizenship as well. And I had one and a half US. Nearly two Canadian. There was a marginal downside, of course. It isn't much of a currency the Canadian dollar. They'd have been better off sticking to wampum. In relative terms, that million was bound to decline in value against other currencies, but that seemed a small price to pay for a country and a passport. I had more where that came from anyway.

It took a little sorting, but not much. It is true that money talks. The one thing I was glad of was to get through the window of opportunity. The new law couldn't last forever. Too many immigrant Canadians, first, second or third generation, incensed their relatives couldn't get in while anyone with a cheque-book could. A lot of the Chinese weren't even moving over. They sent their children to school in Canada. They bought businesses and

232

houses. But they moved back to Hong Kong themselves to see how the handover to China played before they did a final bunk to a world of snow, Big Macs and round-eyes.

The final thing I had to do, and it took Myles to call in a final favour from Special Branch and Rachel's friends, to confirm me as a hero of the fight against international terror, was to change my name by deed-poll, retroactively, so none of my Canadian records appeared in my old name. And no, the new one isn't John Ford, but that'll do for you.

I spent a good few months, despite that fucking awful winter weather. Bought a condo. Did some chicks. Started looking around for business opportunities. It's funny that the second biggest country in the world should have so few people in it, so that every city is almost like an island, desperate for new faces and new sensations. I went down a storm. I even got grateful for the dullness, the looking over the shoulder at those bastard Yanks, the love-hate affair with New York, the desperate desire to be world class. The way to get Canadians to love you is to tell them that they are. Nothing counts for them unless an outsider tells them that it's good.

I chilled out with the weather. Time came when I felt cool enough to ask Myles to have a sly word with the family to let them know I was all right and that, before too long, I'd find some way to see them. I started to daydream about that a bit. Dream about hearing London voices, talking London things. I'd never have guessed how bad you could miss the Arsenal and the Holloway Road.

I suppose that was my mistake. Dreaming. I got careless. I got stuck into having good times. And I had to wait like everyone else for the news programmes on the 5th of March to learn the Panamanians had closed down all their banks.

I'd kept half an eye on the situation, of course. From what I'd learned from being there my guess was always that the CIA and State Departments would always shaft any attempt by the Justice Department to louse up Noriega. That was pretty much the way it worked, too. What I hadn't counted was on the Americans being so split amongst themselves that part of the administration kept piling on the pressure. A dumb thing to do, unless you're certain there's a major revolution in the offing, because it made a local hero of the bastard Pineapple. The day the Nicaraguans started calling him a Latin hero, I knew they'd cocked it up.

Not that I didn't keep in touch, you understand. I'm not a plonker. Not like that. I stayed in regular touch with O'Malley and my Canadian bank, who were IIIB's correspondent, about the safety of the money.

No one was shifting. Why should they? Noriega was toughing it out and had half the American Establishment on his side. We all left our money in. Where else was there to shift it? It looked as though the Swiss were going off under American pressure. There was Liechtenstein, true, which is your very best and safest, but it takes time to set up a Liechtenstein Anstalt and it can be a bitch to run it. Nassau, all the bankers have prehistoric brains and three rows of teeth. And Grand Cayman's too much like hard work.

No, we looked at the Pineapple, and we looked at George Bush, and we liked what we saw, and we left our money where it was.

So, the one thing I didn't expect to happen, and no one did, was that the banks would be closed down. They were the country's only profit centre. When the Americans started buggering about and seizing US-based Panamanian assets and stopped their own banks shipping dollars down there, the foreign banks were the only access Panama had to its own currency, the Balboa/US Dollar. Except, of course, for the plane-loads the cocaine dealers ferried in. It was bound to drive the country deeper into trafficking and the arms of Cuba, which supplied a good half of the refuelling bases.

They did it anyway. I phoned London.

'O'Malley, get my dosh out.'

'I wish it were that simple, boyo.'

'Make it simple.'

'I can't. They've put the army into the foreign banks. We're already having to pay bribes to stop them looting the security vaults.'

'Well, do something, Myles. I wouldn't like to have to get a job.'

He chuckled. 'I wouldn't worry yourself too much about it. I have been keeping an eye on it and I think there's something we can do. Just give me a couple of days. How are you for the readies?'

'OK. I've got some penny-ante, and I can always borrow against the interest on the mill. If I have to do that you'd better tell me if there's any particular bank I have to use, or do I go on using the present arrangements?'

'Leave that to me.'

I did.

It took him more than a couple of days to sort it out. It took him weeks, and I began to sweat a little. One day in April, though, he phoned again.

'I think it's done,' he said. 'I think I've found a way to sort it out which should satisfy all our customers in your position. But I think you and I need to meet.'

'Fine,' I told him. 'There are half a dozen flights here a day.'

He hesitated. I could understand it. I could understand him wanting to find some neutral territory. I suggested New York. He turned it down.

'No. Somewhere less obvious. I've got it. Two birds with one stone. Polly's been nagging me for an age. Look, I'm going to send someone over to babysit you. Don't worry, you'll recognise them. I'll make all the other arrangements. In the meantime, you buy yourself an open ticket down to Orlando. I'll see you there.'

Orlando?

Florida?

Where did he think we were going?

Disney World?

CHAPTER EIGHT

Disney World was the second surprise. The first was who he sent to babysit me. Rachel arrived at the condo on the Thursday afternoon, the 14th of April, and made it pretty plain she wasn't too pleased to see me. The politest thing I remember her saying was, 'There are better things I could be doing.'

We spent a pretty frosty evening. Twice she insisted in putting through international phone calls. It wasn't until the itemised bill came through at month's end that I was able to confirm they had been to Tel Aviv. By then I hardly needed the confirmation. She spoke in Hebrew throughout. The only English words I recognised were Golden Sunset.

Later, alone in bed, despite everything wishing she had not chosen the spare room, I remembered where I had heard the words before. Rabin, her boss, months before, had said he could be reached through the Golden Sunset War Room. I wondered what they were up to, what it could be that had been so long in the planning. We left too early in the morning for her to be receptive to any enquiry.

We flew into Orlando at lunchtime and hired a car at the airport where she also confirmed the reservations O'Malley had made for us at the Disney desk at the airport. I was beginning to feel embarrassed. I took us out on Route 528, picked up Interstate 4 at the edge of the complex and hooked past the Epcot Center to the main gates and on another four miles to the Transport and Ticketing Center where our five-day passports were validated, where we parked, and where we picked up the monorail to our hotel. Already it was the scale of the place that was beginning to get to me. I had had no idea a kiddie-camp could be so big. And I have to admit the monorail got through. I was beginning to be impressed.

Myles had booked us into a suite at the newest hotel, not that it looked it. The Grand Floridian looks out over something called the Seven Seas Lagoon. The Disney people's brochure says it's an attempt to recapture the nineteenth-century elegance of the old Royal Poinciana in Palm Beach where John D. Rockefeller and Teddy Roosevelt used to winter. To me, it looked like an old-time tart's idea of a palace. You get the picture: turrets, towers, wicker, lattice, ceiling fans, wrought iron, stained glass and chandeliers, and the kind of lobby that makes you wonder if the Edwardians did acid. For all that, it was comfy.

Unlike my companion, who parked me off in a room of my own and got on the phone again. I wondered what was up. I wondered what was making her so tense. I let it go for now, to deal with a more pressing matter.

'When do Myles and Polly get here?'

She was staring at the phone she had just put down with a loathing and ferocity which made me wonder if it had taken on a life of its own, if it had started crooning dirty words in her ear. She sighed, and said, 'They're in Miami already. They should be here tonight. You're on your own till then.'

Well, what do you do when you're somewhere you don't know and didn't want to be in the first place? There was a wet-bar in the suite, so I took in a couple of sharpeners, took a walk on the beach, took a swim in the pool in front of the hotel, realised there was at least one other hotel on the lagoon, realised that almost all the talent was daytripping in from hotels off the site and I've never fancied the young mother alternative, checked out the bars and restaurant, put in a quick half hour in the St John's fitness center, and ended up late in the afternoon watching the orientation video playing in a continuous loop on Channel 5. She spent her time doing slow lazy lap after lap of the pool, coming back up to the suite occasionally to interrupt what I was watching, zapping from channel to channel, looking for Lord knew what. I will say one thing for her, though. In a bikini she was sensational. She could have stunned cattle. She stunned me. One way and another, it was a relief when Myles and Polly arrived, about half past five that evening. It would have been good anyway. I'd begun to miss the old faces. Myles began, as always, with room service, whistling up club sandwiches and extra supplies of beer. It took an hour or two of eating, boozing and joshing before I could get him to tell me what he'd brought me here for. In the meantime, though, I did discover one reason why he'd chosen here.

He hadn't. Polly had.

'Myles is impossible,' she said, looking wonderful in a cream silk Bette Davis blouse and a linen skirt, fixing herself another gin and tonic. 'The only way I can ever get him away on his own is if I tell him I want to check a new place out before taking the children there. But he isn't getting away just with Toytown. After this is over he's taking me up to New York for a couple of days. A girl has to shop.'

O'Malley snorted with outraged disbelief. 'Be off with you, lassie. I spend half my life buying you stockings in Bloomingdales. What more could a woman want?'

She shot him her wicked smile and said, 'I want you to take them off me in the middle of Manhattan . . .'

He kept shtum, but I think he liked the picture, and who was I to blame him?

It was Rachel, prim and tricky as ever, who got him back on the straight and narrow. In the middle of one of his wilder tales of interest rate swaps and drinking she said, 'Don't you have some paperwork to complete?'

He stopped immediately and asked me if I wanted to do this privately. I couldn't see the point. Nor could he.

'Your money, John-boy,' he said, reaching for his document case. Well, I knew it wasn't in there.

'What about it?'

He hauled out a stack of documents, settled them on his lap, and went on. 'The Panama business is a bitch. We're pretty much making arrangements on a client by client basis . . .'

I interrupted him. 'I don't see the problem, Myles. They're your CDs. IIIB three-month paper which, may I remind you, has already fallen due. You know I have the certificates, in one of your branches. Just give me the money and wrap up the paperwork later.'

He shook his head. 'No. I can't. It's bearer stock, John, and right now you don't bear the certificates. We don't know what's going on in Panama and we don't know how long it's going to go on for. Could be three weeks. Could be ten years. In which time the certificates could disappear. There isn't any way my auditors will allow me to reimburse intangible CDs without a 100 per cent reserve for potential dual-claim bad debts. You know as well as I do the funny money market is awash with unofficial paper allocation securities held in Panama at 25 per cent of face value as people try to raise cash. But what happens if there's an ownership dispute after Panama reopens? Who gets hit? We get hit. I won't have it. Until you have that money, I can't give you any.'

He had a point, but it didn't make me happy. I snapped open another Dos Esquisses and asked, 'So what are you proposing?'

He riffled through the papers. 'I want you to confirm what I've already done in your case.'

'Which is?'

He sat back and smiled, pleased with himself. 'You need access to your money. I need to hold paper to justify your drawings and, for practical purposes, the paper in Panama doesn't count. So what I've done and I've back-dated the paperwork, is to generate instructions from Panama to use those CDs, twelve mill, to buy you a basket of zero coupon bonds to be held in one of our nominee accounts in London. I've bought you a basket of bonds totalling 26 million dollars with a variety of redemption dates in 1998 . . .'

I lost my temper. 'What fucking good does that do me, Myles? You've tied up money which is already due to me in one of your accounts for another ten years, and I don't even get to see any interest.' Which is the point of zero coupon bonds. They don't pay any interest. That's why they sometimes call them zero yield. Instead their nominal value, for which they're redeemed at the end of their lives on maturity date, is considerably greater than the price they're issued at. The difference between the two amounts is what you get instead of interest, but you take it all at the end. There can be beneficial tax implications, which isn't much consolation if you've just been left without capital or income.

Myles cut me off. 'It clears the paperwork, John, as you very well know. It gives us ten years if we need it to unlock those certificates from Panama. We won't need that long, I don't think, but it keeps us covered. This is just an internal paper transaction in the bank which won't cause the accountants any trouble. And don't knock it. Twenty-six million for twelve over ten years. It's the equivalent of an annual yield of just over 8 per cent. It's all right. And I haven't finished. The twenty-six million is being used to guarantee a current account in your name, which you can draw against now.'

Polly interrupted us. 'It sounds all right to me. Nice clean paper transaction for the bank and twenty-six million for Johnny.'

Myles smiled. 'Not twenty-six, not right now. There is a technicality. It's an account on which John will be permanently overdrawn until the end of the ten years, so we reduce the potential drawing right to twenty-six by the amount of each drawing and the interest on that drawing calculated out to the end of the ten year period. But because it's you, John-boy, and because we've got the underlying basket of securities, I'm fixing the interest rate on this account at 8½ per cent which, as of close of business

240

yesterday, was only five-eighths over LIBOR.' He was referring to the London Inter-Bank Offered Rate, the rate at which major institutions lend each other short-term money. 'Which is bloody good, considering you're not IBM.'

He was right. I also knew he was doing me a favour, fixing the differential between the yield on my securities and the fixed rate on my overdraft (unusual itself over such a long period) at under a half per cent. I had my calculator out.

'Put it away, John. I can tell you. If you want to, you can draw just under eleven and a half million now and you and I need never see each other again. You get 75 per cent of your money. Now. You know the going rate's half that. I'll clear the paperwork as and when it's necessary and the account will wash its face at ten years' end. But I don't think you should do that.'

I tried to be ironic, but my heart wasn't in it. 'And why not, may I ask?'

To my surprise, Polly answered, as the shadows began to lengthen. Her voice was low as she said, 'Because you're a silly little prick, John.' She settled back in her chair and caught me in her pale clear blue gaze and the dark drift of her voice.

'I've always liked you, John. So has Myles. And he tells me you're very bright. For all I know, he may have a point, but I don't really see it. From where I sit you've always seemed too spoilt and too sorry for yourself to be that. You're a well-balanced boy because you've got chips on both shoulders. You've spent the past few years whining about being undervalued, shoving shit up your nose and yourself up scrubbers, and I think I know what'll happen if you take all the eleven and a half million now. You'll just piss it away.'

There wasn't any point in trying to shut her up. Never was when Polly was in this kind of mood. Even Myles just sat there and let her get on with it.

'I'm not saying you should get a job and pick up the

241

twenty-six in ten years' time. Pointless. But I think it'd be good for you to let some of it build up, and see if you can do something useful with what you do draw. But it's up to you. You can either be stinking rich for five years and in the shit afterwards. Or you can get serious and be comfortable forever. But that's your decision. I couldn't care less one way or another.'

I raised my bottle and gave her a wink. 'Well, thank you, Polly. I'd hate to think you had my best interests at heart.' Then I looked to Myles. 'All right, sunshine. Let's do it your way.'

He smiled and slid the papers over, and his pen, the fat vintage Waterman Polly had given him for his fortieth birthday. I initialled each of the pages, signing the last ones on each document, and passed them to Rachel and Her Ladyship to witness. As I did so Myles added, 'There's another thing, John-boy.'

What now? I wondered.

He told me. 'If we're to look after your interests for the next ten years, I want you to make a will. I want you to make a will right now. I've brought some blank will forms with me. I don't care if you get yourself a brief in a few days' time and redo the whole thing, but I want something in my hands tonight.'

I tried to laugh it off. They made me nervous, though I knew they shouldn't. Everyone should make a will. I hadn't for all the usual reasons. 'I don't see why,' I told him. 'I'm not planning on dying just yet.'

He looked thoughtful. Then he said, 'You may not be, but you ought to know the Irishman resurfaced three weeks ago.'

I could feel my face go red and my hands go white as the blood rushed northwards from my heart. 'Where? How . . .?'

'I had a call from Javert, Valjean. After that business in Panama they had to notify all the strong-box holders. They didn't say so, not as much, but pretty plainly his forwarding address for correspondence from the Panama branch is their head office in Geneva. He resurfaced there and finally got the notification he'd been stung. Made no fuss at all. Which is why they rang me, to tell me there'd been no claim so I could stand down my offer of indemnification as far as they were concerned. He made no fuss to them, John. But he will.'

I understood at last. 'That's why I'm here, isn't it?' I nodded at Rachel. 'Her too. You set me up.'

Polly answered. 'No, Johnny. He didn't. I did.'

I twisted up out of my chair, went to the bar, poured myself a bourbon, drank if off, poured another. I was shaking, and I didn't know if it was because I was angry or afraid. 'You bitch.'

She put one hand out to restrain Myles and said, 'Grow up. I don't know what you've been up to and I don't know how Myles got involved, but I know he is involved, just like the Major. I also know that whatever it is you've been up to got ugly, in London and Panama, and I'm not having it. I'm not having Myles in permanent danger. I happen to love him, and he happens to be a pretty good father to our children. I want him around, and I can't be certain he'll be around unless this Irishman is dealt with.'

I couldn't believe it. 'So you set me up.'

Rachel answered this time. 'No, we set ourselves up. All of us. Mr O'Malley tells me that it's an open secret in the banking world that if anyone would know where you were he would, which means the Irishman will have been watching him, would follow him, to any unusual destination. Which this is. That, in part, is my doing.' I waited for her to explain. 'Mr O'Malley didn't think you'd cross the Atlantic, not just yet. I didn't want this operation happening somewhere like New York. Too many people, too many escape routes. And anyone trying anything violent here will have to be circumspect, which reduces the chances of innocent people being injured. Which is what I want. Because, frankly, I don't think you're worth it. I'm only here because Rabin insisted we had a duty to finish what

243

we started. I told you, there are better things I could be doing.'

I was feeling sorry for myself. 'So what's the deal, then. Twenty-four hour surveillance? SWAT teams dressed as Donald Duck, just waiting for him to show? Hoping he's a Snow White fan? Where are my guard dogs, Rachel? Where are my hundred and one dalmatians?'

She closed her eyes in what looked like contempt. 'All you have is us, for now. He hasn't committed any offence here. I have notified the authorities, though. This is one country where Mossad gets some support. They know what's going on, and will be ready to respond if they have to. The other good thing is that they've cleared us to take any necessary precautions.'

I'd had enough. 'What precautions, Rachel? Two tarts and a paddy against the Invisible Arsehole?'

She looked at Myles. 'Did you go to the outlet I told you about in Miami?'

He nodded. 'It's in our room.'

She went to their door, turned back to me and said with all the impatience of a child-minder, 'Well, come on.'

I followed her.

They were spread out on the bed: six .357s, two .45s, two Uzis and a MAC 10, a pump action magazine-fed shot gun, holsters, ammunitions, some aerosol canisters, and a dozen grenades.

She smiled, and swallowed, and said, 'Choose your weapon, Mr Ford.'

CHAPTER NINE

Later, much later, she came into my room.

I could not sleep, and was sat up in my bed, zapping listlessly from channel to channel, unimpressed by Letterman or Carson, by movie specials, MTV, old football games, by CNN All-News or (surprise, surprise) The Disney Channel.

I knew they had a point. I knew they were right. I had been putting the Irishman out of my mind, but he waited to be dealt with. And from what I had seen of him before, he was not a man to give up easily, to take too kindly to the fact that I had stolen back the money he had successfully ligged off me. He wasn't the kind to laugh it off and chalk it up to experience and hope for better luck next time. However much I wanted to, I couldn't just ignore him, hoping he would drift away, that somehow it would all sort itself out, that it would come out all right on the night. I had to go for a result. But I wished they had talked it over with me. I wished I had had a say. Especially after seeing the kind of armoury Rachel had obviously thought necessary.

And the papers I kept turning over as I tried station after station only made it worse – the will Myles had insisted I draft. Pretty lowering experience at the best of times. Right now, it made me want to chuck.

She came into my room, wearing nothing but a shirt, or not so as I could see. Khaki job. I wondered if it was Army issue.

She stood in the doorway, half in shadow, half illuminated by the flickering lights from the TV screen, and said, 'You took it better than expected.'

I couldn't think of anything smart to say. 'Took what?' I asked instead.

She closed the door behind her and came and sat on the end of the bed. Her hair glowed reddish in the low light and her skin filled out to a tawny brown. She seemed solid, sat there, somehow, her shoulders broad and strong and her breasts full and heavy beneath the shirt. It was reassuring as much as sexy, but it was that as well. 'What Polly had to tell you.'

'Oh. That.'

She looked me in the face, her eyes so dark they were almost black, but shining in the matt of night. 'You should be grateful,' she said.

I couldn't see it myself. 'What for?'

'The fact they care.'

I don't suppose my smile was very convincing. 'She called me a kid. She called me pathetic. He let her get on with it. You joined in. Is that caring?'

She smiled this time. 'They wouldn't want you better, they wouldn't want to improve you, if they didn't.'

Well, it was worth a try. 'You'll be telling me you care next.'

She shook her head, and brushed the heavy coil of hair back away from her right temple. She had strong arms, and the cotton of her shirt slid and sizzled. 'You wouldn't believe me,' she said. She had a point. 'But he, he seems to know what he's doing. And I like her. You may be better than you seem. Only time will tell. So tomorrow we'll go out there and try out the attractions and see if we can't find you time.'

She hauled herself on to the bed, stretching out beside me, face down, her arms crossed in front of her and her head turned away, and said, 'I need a back rub. Flying seizes me up.'

I nearly blew it. Beautiful woman laid out in front of me, and I told her, 'Go ask your friends.'

She looked at me again. 'Don't be stupid. It isn't personal. I just have jobs to do, and I need to be ready.

I need a back-rub. You're to hand. Don't fight it. Don't be a child. We all get used. You should know that better than most. I'd guess you've done your fair share of using. That's how the world is. What matters is how you get used, and how you deal with it.'

I slid out from under the covers. She didn't bat an eyelid, didn't seem to notice I was naked. (What do you sleep in, Johnny? In women.) I straddled across her arse and told her to take her shirt off. She wriggled out of it and lay down again, her big breasts swelling out beneath her, curving out between her sides and arms.

She had a good back – long, lean, not as broad at the top as I'd expected (her breadth was in her shoulders) but tapering down to a waist smaller and tighter than I'd dared hope, before flaring out to strong hips and an arse all muscle.

I knew if I could only be patient, I had it made. My brothers taught me that. Odd, isn't it, what boys get wrong about fucking? I remember them sitting me down when I was barely fourteen and them giving me the business.

'You can have the dosh,' they told me, 'you can have the car, the whistle, the looks, the chat, and none of it will necessarily work. But you stroke a tart's hair a hundred times and you've got it made, sunshine. You just remember that.'

I had, Bros. I had. And developed it, too.

I gave her the business, working the muscles at the side and the back of her neck beneath my fingers. She was tense all right, but I suppose we both had good reason to be. I did her back in long strokes first, long and quite light, from her neck to her crack, then pushing back up with the heels of my hands, working the thick sheets and coils of muscle, taking more time over the shoulder blades and shoulders, working them outwards and in. I did it again and again, alternating with light stroking traces, and random spider's foot patterns.

As she relaxed I started to stroke the insides of her arms and the edges of her breasts. She stirred and shifted and

247

wriggled up the bed a little. I bent over her, and licked her from her crack up to her neck, pausing at the end, to lift her hair and kiss her neck.

She breathed a sigh, a good one, and twisted beneath me, saying, 'My legs. Do my legs.'

Sometimes, I'm not too smart. Not always. I told her, 'I don't take orders.' She half-turned and gave me one of her looks. I did as I was told.

I kneeled beside her, working the big muscles of her thighs and calves, then stroking her all the way back up slowly, toying with the backs of her knees and the deep fold at the bottom of her bum. I chopped her muscles fast, and stroked them slow. Then I took her right foot in my hands and worked the tendon, and turned the whole foot, clockwise and anti, before forcing the ends of my fingers between the bones of her foot from above and then below, spreading her sole and easing the muscles. I took her toes one by one and shook and stretched them and bent them up and bent them down.

'Eat them,' she said, her voice thick and distant. I hesitated. 'Eat them.'

So I took them into my mouth, one at a time, and kissed them, and sucked them, and stroked them with my tongue.

She pulled away from me a little and rolled on to her back, her breasts spilling, lush as uplands, her private hair thick and full almost up to her navel, and said, 'Do it again.'

I did it again, and as I did, she parted her legs a little, and her breathing grew heavier, and I could just begin to smell her as she started to idle with herself, the longest finger of her left hand between her legs.

'The other one,' she murmured.

I had begun to learn my lesson. I did as I was told.

And when I had done, I kissed her arches, and her heels, I kissed her narrow ankles and their jutting little bones. I kissed the insides of her calves and licked the insides of her thighs. She moved her hand, and I knew that I could smell her.

I buried my forehead in her private hair, and licked her twice, and let her spread herself. She opened to my nose.

She was moist already, but she wasn't wet. I liked the smell of her, rich and dark and woody. I liked the taste as well.

I put my hands under her buttocks and spread them a little, and lifted, and licked lazily up and down, opening up her outer lips a little first, all the way down. Then more, and more. And then the inner ones, teasing them with the tips of my teeth.

She had her hands in my hair, and I had my tongue in her. I pulled it out a little, exploring, up and down, from side to side, in circles, till her breathing quickened, and I was there, and took it easy, and slowly, and in my own good time, freeing my right hand to open her up further, and stroke her, and slide my fingers into her.

I moved my hand again, spreading her own smell over her, combing out the big stiff curls of hair, stroking her flanks and the curve of her belly, flirting with her breasts.

She shifted, lifting her hips, and I lost myself in her lower mouth, we lost ourselves in each other. I sensed her breathing quicken another stage. Her belly swelled and her breasts thickened, her nipples coming up stubby, and her skin deepening under a thin haze of sweat. Then her stomach flattened, and she stiffened, all the long strong muscles of her body heaving her upwards, concentrating her and her attention down there, beneath my tongue.

And then she came, in a series of sharp whimpers, plunging her hands into my hair and forcing my face into her, bruising me up against her bone.

I didn't stop, even when she fell back to the bed, and started twisting, her legs beginning to shift and stir, then twitch and thrash. She was saying something, in a language I couldn't understand. Then she was pulling at me, at my hair and shoulders, but I held back, not letting her take control until at last, to her relief, I let her go, and licked up across her, across her hair and stomach, teasing her navel, and up, licking the sides of her breasts, then taking her nipples, still stiff, one after another, softly between my teeth and flicked the very tips of them with my tongue, hardly making contact at all.

I was over her, my weight on my hands and toes, my head bowed over her face, the only touch between us the tip of me nuzzling her, almost trembling where it barely made contact between her legs. I wanted to kiss her. I wanted my tongue in her mouth. But when I tried she shook her head and turned her face away, and in that movement took charge.

She slipped her hand down, and took hold of me, pulling me back till I felt naked and breathless. Then she used me to stroke herself, as though she were wanking us both.

I wanted to be inside her. I wanted to be safe. I wanted to come up to her throat, but she held me back, and slipped her other hand down, cupping my balls and slowly, grindingly began rotating her hips. Then at last she moved her hands, using them to hold me away from her, at the hips, so we still barely touched, and took me just inside her, rocking slowly backwards and forwards and round and round, drawing me in and out, but only just each time, till I felt naked, naked as bone.

She kept her head still turned away, so I kissed her ear, her throat, and drew back to kiss her breasts, and then her hands had moved away, tickling patterns on my arse, and she lifted her legs, bending them and spreading them, her knees almost up to her breasts, and I was right inside her, almost at once, and came and came and came.

I could have wept in disappointment, but she hadn't finished with me. She flexed the muscles of her cunt, the neck narrowing and holding me in her. She set up a steady rhythm, holding me inside her, holding me to her at last, and I joined her, though it hurt a little as I softened. But she kept rippling the muscles inside until I felt myself stiffen again and everything fell silent but for the steady hushing of our breath.

When I was hard again, she pulled herself a little away, putting her hands on my shoulders and pushing me down a couple of inches. It almost took me out of her, just the tip of me inside her lips. And then, very slowly, she began to turn her hips, twisting them and rolling, and I felt absolutely naked as she brushed me in and out and round the very edge of her lower mouth, each little stroking slowly pushing my foreskin back across my cock, her pubic bone. And then we alternated at last, deep strokes and the small light ones barely in her, and she quickened up her pace and I quickened with her, till I could hold back no more and the little strokes disappeared and I was in her as deep as I could manage again and again, almost hurting and no longer caring as I crushed against her cervix.

I kissed her mouth, her nose, her eyes, her ears. I buried my face in the sharp wet smell of her armpit. I had my hand on her left breast more and more firmly, flicking the nipple with my thumb. I had my left hand underneath her, lifting her, stroking a finger into her arse. She reached down herself, between us, with her left hand, tickling herself off, with her right hand holding my balls, and both of us were wet with sweat, and then she came again and so did I in long deep shudders from the base of my spine, from the small of my back, and came some more until I felt that both of us must be drowning, must be melting, till I felt certain she could taste me in her mouth.

When we fell apart at last, almost sobbing with effort, I wanted to take her in my arms and stroke her hair and soft skin, its fine haze of small hairs slick with sweat now. I wanted to feel her breathing against me. I wanted us to settle ourselves together. But I couldn't.

I couldn't because she rolled away, still smiling, and curled herself up, and fell asleep.

She fell asleep.

All that, and all she could do was pass out on me.

I know that this sounds daft – I know it does – but I felt used.

It was well light when I came round in the morning. She was up already, cross-legged on the bed, the TV remote control in her hand, flicking from channel to channel, intent on how they reported the big story of the day. I tuned in to it slowly, my head still thick and throbbing, and wished I hadn't.

You all know about it. It hadn't all come out by then. It took a few days. But the main outlines of the story were clear enough.

Some time after midnight local time, the Israeli Navy had put a twenty man commando ashore in Tunisia about twenty miles north of Sidi Bou Said. Why Sidi Bou Said? Because Abu Jihad lived there, the military commander of the PLO.

Mossad agents were waiting for them, with a Peugeot 305 and two VW vans, and drove them to the door. Meanwhile, more agents sabotaged the local telephone network, and a 707 packed to the gunwales with jamming equipment took up position about a hundred miles outside Tunisian airspace. Close enough. Close enough to jam all electronic communications in the area. And it was the relay station, too, to headquarters in Tel Aviv.

At quarter past one in the morning, twelve of the commando secured the outside of the house. The other eight went in, storming up to the second landing. He was in his study, working, and heard them coming, and picked up his gun, and headed out to meet them. They hit him with more than sixty rounds. Along the way, they killed two guards and a gardener as well, but they left his family alone. Jolly good, eh? They were back on ship by 4 a.m. They got back to Haifa a few days later.

It wasn't my war. It wasn't my problem. I should care less. But I couldn't because the programmes kept talking about him, kept saying his real name. Abu Jihad. Khalil al-Wazir.

Al-Wazir.

Awa's Ear.

All that time I'd spent trying to figure out his name, and I'd still not cracked it. Not till now. Even when she debriefed me, in Panama, she showed no recognition.

Selim Al-Wazir. He had said there were senior military commanders who understood at last that the Uprising was the way forward. Was there any bigger threat than that? He had said he had a powerful distant relative. He . . . He had said a lot of things.

I lay back on the bed, blinking, and said, 'There were better things you could be doing . . .' She made no reply. I tried long again. 'How long had you been planning this? How long had you and Rabin been sitting in . . .' I searched my memory for the words. '. . . the Golden Sunset War Room cooking this one up? Months, wasn't it? As long as I've known you. Longer. And that wasn't enough. You wanted the whole bloody family. That was what all this has been about, as far as you're concerned.'

She shook her head. 'No. Only the active ones. We don't kill civilians.'

My arse. 'He wasn't a soldier. He wanted food and medicine for his people. That's all. And he'd persuaded the old man. I told you that. I didn't know what it meant, but I told you that. You knew. You went after them both because they'd found a way to beat you without any more killing and you didn't want them spoiling your comfy little war.'

She killed the volume with a flick of the remote and told me, 'It isn't that simple. It's the others. We could settle with them. You've never had to plan for the worst. We have to plan for it all the time. Even if we settle with the Palestinians, some of them, there's the rest of the Arab world. And we know what they do when they screw up their own countries. They make war on us. They try to drive us to the sea. They make a habit of it. So we take no chances. We plan for the worst.'

I had had more than I could take. I was sick of it. 'Fuck off. Just fuck off. I told him not to give me any of his shit.

I don't want any of yours either. He did what he did. You do what you do. And it never bloody ends. When's it going to end, Rachel? You tell me that. I liked him. You have your moments. Does it go on until there's no one good left standing? Is that the point? To leave the desert to the shits?'

She shook her head, sadly. 'No. Not that. You don't understand, do you?' No, I did not. I still don't. I don't understand what she told me.

'The world being what it is, it goes on, and on, until it forces us, both sides, to the table.'

CHAPTER TEN

We gathered in the sitting-room, where Myles was already in to his second breakfast. Great man for room service, Myles. Me, I didn't feel up to eating anything – dry toast, sliver of grapefruit, nothing would go down. What I wanted was a drink, but I'd worked out already that wouldn't be too smart a move. I needed my wits about me, and theirs. I steamed in to the black coffee.

Odd how Polly proved to be the practical one, the one who took control. And how completely both she and Rachel ignored the fact that Rachel and I emerged from the same room. Only Myles seemed to take it in and that only with a lazy lift of one eyebrow. I felt like a spare prick at my own wedding.

'Right,' said Polly, dropping a jammy knife into her plate (but it wasn't jam; Coopers Vintage Oxford marmalade; I guess she brought it with her), 'how are we going to do this?'

Rachel stretched out on a sofa, nursing a coffee on her breast. I'd rather she'd been nursing me. Sunlight flared in through the big picture window, so bright it was hard to see her, except as a smear of shade. She, too, was matter-of-fact.

'He has to come to us,' she explained. 'This is a moderately busy season at Disney World. There'll be anything between fifty and seventy thousand people here today. He can't hope to just track us down in the open, out there. Not in those crowds. And even if he did, what could he do? Too many witnesses, too many people in the way. So he has to come for us. He has to come for us here.'

I shuddered a little, feeling suddenly cold, despite the sunshine and the steadily growing Florida heat. In the past few months I'd been beaten up in shuttered rooms and hunted down in the open, and somehow the rooms were worse. It had gone into my nightmares – long corridors, flaring fluorescent lights, and windowless rooms. They always felt underground, even if they weren't or there wasn't any way of knowing. I don't know what it is. Perhaps it's just the sense that in the open you can run. Indoors all you can do is hide, and wait.

Rachel was still being businesslike. 'From what Myles tells me, the one thing we can count on is the fact that there isn't a computer system in the world he can't get into. Which is why I asked for the booking here and Myles and Polly's flights to be booked through a High Street travel agent. If he's as good as you say he is . . .'

I had to speak, if only to prove I still could. 'He is,' I told her.

She looked surprised, and I realised I'd gaffed it. I'd pretty much assumed she'd guessed I knew the Irishman, that I had something to do with half-inching the money in the first place. Or maybe I'd just got careless. I covered it as best I could, shrugging, and saying, 'The man's a legend. One of the best four in the business.'

She let it go. 'Well, then, if, as we must assume, he's been keeping an eye on Myles, he'll have cut into the travel agency computers, and the airline's. He'll know they were coming here. And by now he should know which of the Disney World hotels we're in, and even what suite.'

I was worried enough not to care what I looked and sounded like. It was too late in the game for bullshit. 'Then why don't we just get the local police in. Protect the place. Protect us.'

She had an answer to that. She had an answer to everything. Training I suppose. I suppose she was good at what she did, though it wasn't anything to be proud of being good at. 'Even if we could,' she explained, 'it would be counter-productive. At most, it would scare him off, this time. We'd still have to deal with him, another place, another time, not necessarily of our own choosing.'

'This wasn't my choice.'

She let it pass. 'And in any case, it isn't possible. We have good relations with the CIA and FBI, despite occasional problems . . .' I guess she was referring to the conviction of American spies working in the defence industry for Israel. '. . . and they've got us some purchase on the local police. But he isn't guilty of anything yet in the States and certainly not in this county and I can't blame the locals for not wanting to move yet, not until there is an offence. The last thing they want to do is frighten holidaymakers unnecessarily. This place is the county. It's everybody's living.'

I didn't fancy that. I could have done with a bit more active participation from the local woodentops. Still, I was getting the picture. I knew the business. I knew how to play this game. I'd seen *Alien*. Terrific, isn't it, all those horror thriller movies? Greebo blood-crazed alien death-fiend, out there, trawling the air ducts, snacking on humans. Thing the size of a beer-truck and all the patience and good manners of an SS Strike Commando. What do they do? Evolution's pinnacle? They split it up and take it on one by one. Result? Mincemeat. Oh very good, very intelligent. I'd learned my lesson. I knew what you did in situations like that. You stayed together, in the communications centre, with all the weapons you could lay your hands on. Then you fried the shit out of it when it came to the door. 'So we wait,' I said.

She took me by surprise. 'No. We don't. I do.' I didn't see it. She didn't give me a chance to ask. 'You're at the end of your chain. You're bad now and if you stay cooped up in here you'll only get worse. You'll be no use to anyone, and it may take all four of us. I can secure this room on my own, and I don't think he'll move unless it has you and Mr O'Malley in it. The fewer occasions you're in here, the more control we have over his timing. I don't believe he'll move against you in the open. So we're going to arm you all. And you're going out to have a good time. I'll give you all the direct line number for LaSalle, the local police chief, just in case. And in the meantime I can get some work done, on my own and with LaSalle, setting this whole thing up.'

I didn't fancy it, but Polly made it pretty plain she hadn't come all this way to sit around playing Sweet Fanny Adams. She had her kids to think of. So Myles and I did as we were told, all three of us equipped with shoulder-holsters and snub-nosed .357s, Rachel taking us through the whole business of safety catches, stances and reloading. The bad news was we had to wear jackets over them, despite the Florida heat and humidity.

She saw us off with a wave and a smile and a mocking call of, 'Have a nice day!'

I have to tell you that I loved it.

It took about half an hour to settle down, to settle in, ambling down Main Street USA, a cleaned-up, pepper-pot Victorian fantasy of the perfect town, with courteous shopkeepers, crinolined girls and horse-drawn traps. But then we were in the middle of it, of the Magic Kingdom, at Cinderella's Castle, and we were kids again.

It was one of those days when everything was what it's supposed to be. The sun was the sun, beating down out of a brilliant blue cloudless sky. The kids who surrounded us everywhere were being kids, running around and squealing, in amazement or temporary fright. The Americans were Americans – enthusiastic, happy, open, and dressed in the most appalling clothes. There were enough Bermuda shorts on display to drain the Caribbean. The ice cream was ice cream, tasting as though it had run straight from the udders of some Arctic cow, and the hot dogs were borzois, afghans and Baskerville hounds.

I think the figures must have something to do with it. Everywhere you turn there are life-size Disney characters. I knew damn well they were people in costumes, but the fact is, in a place where you can have your picture taken with Minnie Mouse or ask Donald Duck the time, it's hard to believe the world can be such a terrible place, or disbelieve that everything will be all right. I could see why Polly might want to bring the kids here. Where Goofy walks, a kind of innocence descends, and anything might be said. You could tell your kids you loved them. They might tell you that they care.

We went to Liberty Square and the Hall of Presidents, and laughed and cheered as the computerised figures nodded and swayed and fidgeted as the dummy of Lincoln spoke, and wondered if the Ronald Reagan would simply go to sleep. We went to Fantasyland and spun round and round on the Mad Hatter's Tea Party ride, and did it again till we were almost sick. We passed by *20,000 Leagues Under the Sea*, but they wouldn't let me go down in the Nautilus and do my Captain Nemo routine in the fake fight with the giant squid (James Mason, he's your man) because the queues were so long and Polly's guide book said it wasn't that hot anyway. Myles joined in with the Dapper Dans, the strolling barbershop quartet, and proved to have a wonderful baritone voice, and the kids gathered round and made him do a solo, singing the 'Mountains of Mourne' while the Dans did a sad oom-pah in the background. We went and looked up the skirts of the can-can dancers in the Diamond Horseshoe saloon and, though it was a hell of a way away, we took the monorail over to the Epcot Center and the World Showcase to have lunch in Au Petit Café and a beer in the Rose and Crown. We laughed at the Hollywood London streets and the shrunken Venice, the jungles of the miniature Mexico and the foreshortened Eiffel Tower, and by the time we were done and reeling Myles and I wanted to do it all over again and could hardly wait till the following morning and getting in to the Epcot Center itself and being allowed to play with the Living Seas (Mickey in a diving costume and a ride through a Caribbean coral reef), the electronics and the holograms. We wanted to run back to Tomorrowland when Polly told us about the Space Mountain and the ride through space and shooting stars.

Money? A bundle. But who cares?

It was getting on for six by the time we got back to the hotel and, even in Florida in April, the afternoon was drawing in and darkening. Myles used one of the lobby phones to call up to the room as instructed. Rachel had told us to phone up on our return and, at the door, to have Polly call her name as a second security measure. But we never got that far, because there was no answer. We picked up the spare keys at the desk and raced for the lift.

The suite looked like a war had taken place there – curtains torn down, covers off the beds, the coffee table broken, vases smashed and chairs overturned. Myles checked her room. She hadn't even had a chance to get to the fire-power stored there.

And there was a message for us, in the middle of the carpet, near the door. It read, 'I have her, and I want my money. Wait for my call. Call no one yourselves. I will know.'

What scared me was, if he could take her, who knew what she was doing, what chance did the rest of us have?

Myles went into his room and came out carrying the kind of tape-recorder radio journalists use to send their reports by phone. This one it transpired worked in reverse, too. It could receive as well as transmit. He attached the rubber cup to the mouthpiece of the handset, on its underside, so he could talk over it, snapped a tape into the machine and pressed a couple of buttons. Then he called down to the desk. We could hear him speaking, of course, and the desk-clerk as well, through the tape deck as it recorded. Neat device. A true trader's back-up. These days no real trader makes phone orders without recording, for the back-office, and the insider dealing trial.

'Hello,' he said, his voice its softest brogue, 'I'm calling from Suite 322. We were expecting our friend to be waiting for us. Ms Stern. Can you tell me, did she have any callers today?'

The desk clerk's voice was salt of the earth mid-Western,

exaggerated by the tape-deck. 'Not so far as I know, sir, no. If you'll just hold on there I'll check with my colleagues for you . . . No, sir. No one here recalls a visitor for that suite. She can't have gone very far or she would have left the keys at the desk.'

'Yes. Yes, I see. Well, thank you.'

He hung up, keeping his hand lightly on the handset.

'The service lift,' he said at last, 'he must have used the service lift. But how did he get in?' He thought some more, and then he asked, 'Well, do we call LaSalle?'

I wanted to. I wanted to call LaSalle and get the hell out. Leave it to the authorities. She was a professional herself. She ought to understand that. Before I could say so, the telephone rang, startling us all so that Myles, his hand still on it, lifted it before the first ring was complete, before any of us could think.

The Irishman's voice came through the recorder. 'Well done, O'Malley. I can live with internal calls. Just don't try calling out. I've got her, O'Malley. A tough bitch that one, but the rest of you will be easier. I'm coming for you, one after another, till I get what I want. So maybe you'd better talk it over with your friend, before the wife gets hurt. I'll call you back in an hour.' The line went dead.

I didn't understand it. I didn't understand the mechanics. I understood what he was up to well enough. 'How's he doing it, Myles? This is one extension off a switchboard. How's he cutting into it?'

Myles rubbed his temples with the tips of his fingers, thinking it through. 'One of two ways,' he suggested finally. 'Either a physical tap somewhere between here and the switchboard. Or, more likely, knowing him, he's cut some patch into the computerised switchboard, just for this number, so any calls get routed to a radio phone as well. His.' Suddenly he snapped his fingers. 'Which is the answer. We can't do this on our own, and he's committed a local crime now. I'm going down to one of the payphones off the lobby to call LaSalle. He can't cover

261

those. You two stay here. Don't open up unless you hear two knocks, a pause, and then three more.'

He was gone before we could stop him. Polly headed for the guns.

Twenty minutes later there was still no sign of him and I was getting scared. The phone rang. Polly just stared at it. I picked it up. It was the Irishman again.

His voice seemed louder in the growing gloom. 'He should have listened. You should all have listened. I have him now, too. Put on the wife.'

She took it from me and cradled it to her ear with care, as though she and it might do each other harm. 'Yes,' was all she said.

'Ah, dear lady.' He sounded smug.

'Let me talk to him,' she asked. There was tenderness to it.

'No. Not yet. But you can tell the little English bastard that I win, one way or another. Either he gives me the money, or you do. I know about the insurance, dear lady. I have access to the Lloyd's computers. I know about the kidnap policy you made him take out. I'll take one and a half million from you, and only kill the Englishman. The underwriters will do that, rather than have to pay out all ten. Or I'll take fifteen million from the English, in which case he gets to stay alive. Or I'll get nothing, and kill you all. The kidnap underwriters have a twenty-four hour helpline. The London banks open at four in the morning Florida time and the Swiss ones at five. Make the transfer. The Englishman knows the account details. There'll be a confirmation number, depending on the amount. One of you had better have one of them when I phone at half past five, or this will all start getting serious.'

He hung up.

Polly stood there, still cradling the handset, the tape-spool still turning in the machine. Finally she spoke.

'I'm going to do it, John. I want my husband. The rest is your problem.'

I shook my head. 'I haven't got fifteen million, Polly. You saw me sign the papers. I have not quite eleven and a half.'

'Well, you'd better find the difference, then, or I think you're going to die.'

She started tapping out the number of the underwriters at Lloyd's.

I went through to Rachel's room and picked the shotgun off her bed where Myles had left it. I wondered if I should just lift it to my head, and get it over and done with. I wondered how it had gone so badly wrong.

I went and leaned my forehead against the french windows of her room, cooling my head against the metal frame, looking out over the balcony. It was a corner room, a corner of the building, and looked down across the palms and bougainvillea, the swimming pool and the lake. It looked peaceful, the last latecomers drifting home to shower and change before dinner. It looked as though nothing would ever darken or disturb it, but something already had.

I pulled away and, as I did so, the door clicked open. It was unlocked. And then I guessed.

I looked along the balcony. It wrapped around most of this stretch of the building. And then I knew.

I went back to the bed. I didn't want anything fancy. I suspected the grenades would kill us all. I couldn't make sense of the machine pistols. But I already had one fully loaded .357 and I needed another. I tucked it into my waistband. Then I took the shotgun and a box of cartridges back in to Polly. She was an Irish lady. She would understand about such things.

She had finished her call, but I didn't speak at once. I wanted to think it through one last time.

I couldn't telephone down to the front desk, not safely. I didn't even have a name. But I didn't need to. I knew. Yes, I knew.

I couldn't call for help. He'd know.

I couldn't even walk down the corridor to the lifts, or send Polly. That was how he'd got Myles.

There wasn't another damn thing I could do, not even run away, not now. Except turn my face to the wall and die.

'Polly,' I whispered. Again, a little louder, 'Polly?' She turned to face me, looking at me as if I was shit on her boots or a peasant tenant late with the rent. And then I told her.

'He's next door.'

I stood outside the door of 321, checking the gun in my hand obsessively. Loaded. Safety off. Ready. Loaded. Safety off . . .

Polly was on the balcony with the shot-gun, in case I drove him that way but I hoped to God it wouldn't get that far. I hoped that it would be over fast.

And I had the shakes. I tried to quieten them by thinking it through one last time.

He had known the details of the booking through the travel agency computer. He had simply booked himself in next door, perhaps even in advance. He might already have been in there a couple of days before we arrived. Room service would have kept him out of sight.

From the next room he had been able to put a physical tap on the extension. He had come for Rachel from behind. Along the balcony and through the french windows. He had set Myles up to leave the room, and taken him in the corridor. He had had us at his mercy all the time.

I pulled back the slide. I tried to remember the position Rachel had taught us. Then I fired three times, taking the door right off its hinges in a crash of veneer.

The room beyond was empty, or looked it. I went to one side of the open doorframe, glancing in. Nothing. And to the other side. The same. I went in, almost sniffing for him, wondering where the hell he was. There were side doors to the right. Two of them. I watched them for a second, expecting hell to emerge, but nothing came. On the other wall, the left one, microphones were taped, with trailing wires. The son of a bitch had been bugging us through the walls as well.

I must have covered the room in four, five, big paces, throwing open the french windows but remembering not to go through them in case Polly got trigger happy.

'Get in,' I called to her. 'He's not here.'

She came in low and fast, almost tripping over something on the way into the room, on her way to the side doors. It was a head.

It was Donald Duck's. There was another alongside it. It was Goofy's. There were costumes with them too.

Suddenly it all made sense. How he'd been able to get around without our spotting him, although he was so close. Who looks twice at Goofy in the heart of Disney World? If they're over ten years old, that is?

Polly snapped me out of it. 'The bedrooms,' she said. Her voice was low but urgent. We went through the first door together, caution forgotten. It could have cost us.

It didn't. Myles was on the bed, trussed up like some sex-game. Chains and leather restraints and some kind of weird leather mask that let him breathe but not speak. Polly went over to him straight away and started working on the buckles, putting down the shotgun as she did so.

I hesitated, half between helping her, half leaving her to it and checking the other room. Rachel had to be in there.

That hesitation must have hit my hearing. The next warning I had was Polly looking up and gasping. I half-turned. Mickey Mouse was standing in the door behind me. He was over six feet tall and he was lifting a gun.

Polly shrieked, 'No!' wailing like some banshee and went for the shotgun as he steadied his hand. He was squeezing the trigger. She had the stock in her gut. She pulled, wildly, on the pump action, and the report filled the room. I fell to the floor, blown over by flying shot, but I got a glimpse of him as I went down, his whole left shoulder flaring red as he flew backwards out in the main room.

I staggered to my feet and Polly was back at the bed tearing at Myles's restraints and shouting at me, 'Finish him, you bastard. Finish him now!'

I went out into the main room, looking about me, and he kicked the legs from underneath me.

He was up himself, half up, dragging himself with his right arm, holding the smashed left one to him. Crawling away towards something.

The gun? Where was my gun?

It had fallen away from me. He was crawling towards it. I grabbed him by the legs, or tried to. I only got one of them. It brought him down, but he raised the other one and kicked down hard, into my face, and I rolled back, letting him go, gagging and puking, my nose a mess of snot and blood and my mind not working.

Then he shot me, as I tried to stand, in the hip, and the force of it lifted me clear from the ground and smashed me against the door frame. He was lifting the gun again, taking more careful aim. As I looked up at him everything went slow. Everything became those stupid big ears, that silly black nose. I half jumped, half fell, backwards into the bedroom. Polly was rising again, fear in her mouth and eyes, but I got there first, I got to the shotgun and rolled back towards the door and pulled on the action once.

More thunder and then silence.

I waited, waited just long enough to wonder about shells and looked back towards Polly. 'It's OK,' she was mouthing, 'four more.'

I got myself up, pulling myself up against the wall, smearing a trail of blood against it, and made myself stand, and went back out into the main room. It was empty. He wasn't there.

Rachel! I thought. That door was still closed. Was he in there with her? I leaned against the wall, and fired sideways across the door. It was still enough to blow it open. She was in there, bound and gagged like Myles, but on her own.

The corridor or the balcony? I tried the balcony.

I turned as I went through the french doors, first left, then right. He was on the right, and firing, and I fired in return.

We both went down. It was all pain now, from the chest

down, as though someone had been at me with a bat. And he, he had been blown against the parapet railings, the Mickey Mouse head blown to pieces, shards of it hanging at his neck, the rest of the costume slashed in tatters. There was blood all over him, from the face to his feet.

But he wasn't finished, not yet. He was pushing, with his shattered legs, sending them sliding and bloody across the balcony to jack himself up on the railings. He was still steadying his gun.

I groaned and flung my hand out, pulling back the shotgun, pulling it back towards me, as a mad look built in his bloody eyes, and I had the stock against me, and I aimed it the best I could, and I pulled.

It tore a hole the size of a grapefruit out of him, a clean hole filling with blood and something thicker, and it blew him back across the parapet, but not over it, not quite.

It settled there, his body, swinging like a seesaw, his gunhand thrown outwards, his useless weapon somewhere far below.

I got myself up. I don't know how I did it. My legs were lead. But I got over to him. I wanted to see him for myself. I wanted to see him dead.

He was hanging away from me, his face out of sight. I had to lean out over the parapet to see it. As I did so, a bubble of blood burst at his lips. Then he opened his eyes.

He grabbed me by the shirt and spat out, 'No surrender,' and he launched himself out into the empty sky.

He almost took me with him.

When the others came to get me, I was swinging from the railings by one hand.

267

CHAPTER ELEVEN

LaSalle put us through it for the next few hours, but in the
end, with a little help from Rachel's friends in Washington,
he sorted it all out and squared things up with the Disney
people. The medics came to me and finally agreed once
they'd cleaned out my legs and patched them up and set
them that I'd feel safer and happier with my friends and
heal faster. The hotel even found us another suite.

I wasn't terribly surprised the following morning when
Polly announced that she was taking Myles off for a proper
holiday, somewhere safe and quiet like the streets of New
York City. I was glad that things seemed easier between us.
I think she thought I'd shown some guts at last. She even said
she thought that given time I might just turn out all right.
Myles stood down the panicking underwriters and took my
papers off to safety promising to be in touch in Canada once
things had settled down. And, bless him, he stumped up
the money for me to stay on in Disney World for a few more
days, before travelling back to a doctor of my own. I wasn't
exactly the flavour of the month with the hotel staff at first,
till LaSalle told them some tale about international terrorists
and Rachel let them know how I'd saved her and Myles's
life. I didn't quite see it that way myself, but I wasn't
complaining. And I couldn't help laughing when I heard
she'd told the maids, of the Irishman, that it just went to
show you should never trust a man who tied you to a bed.

She left herself round about lunchtime, and I was still
too mixed up about what I felt about her, and Selim, and
the rest of it, to know if I was sad or not.

Before she went, she gave me a funny kind of warning.

'Be careful,' she said. 'You managed, in the end, but it took a lot of help. Not just me and Polly and Myles, but the Americans and the British too. I'm afraid that none of us are the type to forget our favours. They will be called one day.'

I didn't get it, but I tried to brazen it out. 'Well, if I have to pay it all back some day, how about a final favour?'

'What favour?' she asked, surprised.

'How about a final fuck for a sick man?'

She laughed. It was good to see her laugh. 'No. Remember what I told you about being used. And anyway, I was just curious.'

'What about?'

She almost looked shy for a second. I liked it. 'I'd never had a man with a foreskin before,' she explained.

'What was it like?'

She shrugged, and grinned, and said, 'You all feel the same to me.'

I missed her, for a long time, after that.

Well, my recovery got started, and I retired up here, though I get south to the sunshine when I can.

I haven't decided what to do with all the money yet, but I've begun to see that Polly may have had a point. And I've been thinking a lot about what Rachel told me.

I know now there is a price to be paid for all the help I got, and I'm going to have to pay it. Which is why I decided to write this down and publish it.

You may not know the real names, but they do. And now they know I'm keeping records, and those records will go public if anything ever happens to me. My insurance policy.

And, speaking of insurance, the first favour that got called was Myles's. Bastard got me involved in a reinsurance scam in Bolivia. Or rather, in trying to sort it out.

But that's another story.

THE END

THE DARK APOSTLE
by Denis Kilcommons

The man who called himself Raoul was in Spain and was selling his story for £250,000. He claimed that he set up the assassination of Martin Luther King in April 1968. He also claimed that King organized it.

For Peter Lacey, checking out Raoul is a chance to end months of boredom, a chance to get back into action again. It's a low-priority job but Lacey's recent track record makes him very lucky to get any kind and, Lacey knows, even low-priority jobs can get you killed.

The conspiracy story that Raoul spins involves a potential Presidential candidate who had been one of King's aides, and Lacey's researches at Raoul's villa make him increasingly uneasy. Especially when he encounters Sutherland. For Sutherland is a ruthless killing machine and his brooding and calculating presence threatens Lacey's survival.

THE DARK APOSTLE is a riveting and compelling thriller to rank alongside the best of Ken Follett and Robert Ludlum.

'Lifted well above the run-of-the-mill by the fiendish ingenuity of the plot'
James Melville

0 552 13211 X

CROWS' PARLIAMENT
by Jack Curtis

Simon Guerney plies a lonely trade. He specializes in the rescue of kidnap victims; his unrecognized skills the last resort of the rich and desperate.

At first the disappearance of David Paschini seems a straightforward abduction case and Guerney joins the boy's mother in New York to play out the usual waiting game. Once there he begins to sense inconsistencies in the pattern of events – but it is not until the unknown kidnappers demand that he travel to London that Guerney realizes the game has turned and that suddenly he is the prey not the hunter.

Strikingly original in its combination of power politics, the growing menace of kidnapping and the disturbing but very real world of ESP, *Crows' Parliament* will take its place amongst such classics of the genre as *Rogue Male* and *The Third Man*.

0 552 13081 8

A SELECTED LIST OF FINE TITLES AVAILABLE FROM CORGI BOOKS

☐	13081 8	CROWS' PARLIAMENT	Jack Curtis	£2.95
☐	12550 4	LIE DOWN WITH LIONS	Ken Follett	£3.50
☐	12610 1	ON WINGS OF EAGLES	Ken Follett	£3.50
☐	12180 0	THE MAN FROM ST. PETERSBURG	Ken Follett	£3.99
☐	11810 9	THE KEY TO REBECCA	Ken Follett	£2.99
☐	09121 9	THE DAY OF THE JACKAL	Frederick Forsyth	£2.99
☐	11500 2	THE DEVIL'S ALTERNATIVE	Frederick Forsyth	£3.99
☐	10050 1	THE DOGS OF WAR	Frederick Forsyth	£3.99
☐	12569 5	THE FOURTH PROTOCOL	Frederick Forsyth	£3.95
☐	12140 1	NO COMEBACKS	Frederick Forsyth	£2.99
☐	09436 6	THE ODESSA FILE	Frederick Forsyth	£2.99
☐	10244 X	THE SHEPHERD	Frederick Forsyth	£2.50
☐	13211 X	THE DARK APOSTLE	Denis Kilcommons	£2.95
☐	12541 5	DAI-SHO	Marc Olden	£2.99
☐	12662 4	GAIJIN	Marc Olden	£2.99
☐	12357 9	GIRI	Marc Olden	£2.99
☐	12800 7	ONI	Marc Olden	£3.50
☐	13214 4	TE	Marc Olden	£3.99